Dedication

To Paul – this book wouldn't be half as magical without your encouragement.

Chapter One

To human eyes, she looked like a shadow. Crouched in an unlit corner of the museum chamber, the darkling watched a group of children gather around a glass display case. They poked and prodded at the glass and each other, their whispers rising up to the lofty, domed ceiling. Their teacher read from a leaflet in a monotone voice while her metallic assistant kept watch of the fidgeting children.

"So ferocious was the explosion that destroyed the bank building, very few recognisable remnants survived." She pointed to the display case. "The items recovered in the aftermath of the explosion can be seen in case 44a."

"What happened, miss?" asked one of the boys.

"I've told you before, Ronnie. Criminals set off a bomb in the Central Plaza to cover their tracks after they had robbed the bank. Hundreds of people were hurt."

"Bad people blew up the bank," said the smallest child, a girl with tightly bound braids.

"Criminals," said the teacher.

"Were we alive then?" asked Ronnie.

"Don't be silly," said another child, elbowing him.

"Of course not," said the teacher. "That was almost fifty years ago."

"*You* were alive then, weren't you, miss?" said Ronnie.

"Come along," the teacher snapped as she marched out of the room, the assistant waving its long metallic limbs as it silently herded the children after her.

The darkling watched the class trundle out of the room. She saw something in the children that humans were blind to: each movement trailed a tendril of colour, each word breathed a delicate cloud like wind-blown powder paint, each giggle threw a sunshine glint around their small bodies.

When she could no longer hear their voices, she stood and took solid form as she stalked across the floor. By the time she reached the glass case she looked like a teenage girl, maybe seventeen years old, with cropped dark hair and dressed in t-shirt, jeans, trainers and a hooded jacket. The only details that picked her out as anything other than normal were her eyes, which were immense and indigo blue. That was the one detail of the human form that she could never perfect, no matter how hard she tried.

She kept the doors to the chamber at the edges of her vision, ready to return to shadow if anyone entered. In that form, it would be easy to loiter at the base of the display case or attach herself to a passer-by's shadow.

The glass case held an assortment of mundane finds: a decorative hair comb, loose beads, a tattered wallet. Each item was labelled with a number and a description.

What she was looking for sat at the centre of the display.

The dark metal disc, the perfect size to fit into an average adult palm, was just as she remembered it. A pronounced ridge ran horizontally across the disc, near its top, the section above the ridge divided into three parts: the middle section wider than the others.

The darkling closed the fingers of one hand into a fist, opening them to reveal a keycard in her palm, a card which she had taken from the curator's office earlier that day. She inserted it into a slot on the side of the display case. There was a decisive click and the lid of the case popped up an inch.

This is it, she thought as she opened the cabinet. *I have it at last, my friend. You can rest easy now.*

She picked up the disc between finger and thumb then slipped it into her palm. It was the first time she had ever held the disc and it was lighter than she had expected.

She held her breath, waiting for some kind of response from the object, but the disc sat cold and lifeless in her hand. She frowned and turned it over. The label that ran across the back read, *'Replica'.*

"No." The word caught in her throat. She looked again at the display case. The description for the disc simply read, *'42. Large, metal item, possibly a pendant'.*

"You're not supposed to do that, you know."

She dropped the disc back into its place and leapt away from the man who had silently appeared in one of the two doorways.

"That's museum property," he said, walking towards her. The sleek modern lines of his dark suit looked out of place in the antiquated museum chamber. He carried a small black box in his outstretched hand.

"And?" she snapped.

"Come with me, darkling," he said as he reached for her.

She released a breath and her solid form dwindled as it returned to shadow.

"That won't save you." The man was almost upon her. "I have a shadow-compass," he leered.

She shuddered at the mention of the one thing which never failed to track down her kind, then she heard the footsteps of the other two men. The tall one, his cap perched on his bald head, strode ahead of his shorter, rounder companion who was reaching out with chubby, ring-clad hands towards her.

She dwindled further, evading the grasps of her would-be captors, seeping between their legs as she turned into her shadow-form.

"Don't lose her," yelled the suited man.

She flowed along the floor. The two men stumbled after her, snatching at her shadow. As she reached the doorway, she threw herself into solid form, kicking the men's legs from beneath them. They tumbled to the floor at the feet of the suited man. Before they had the chance to stand, she leapt through the doorway and into the next chamber.

The schoolchildren gasped as she landed beside them. Their teacher shrieked, while the assistant stretched two of its eight silvery arms to encircle the class and pull them away. The chasing men barrelled into the room, skidding on the marble floor. The suited man was a step behind, eyes on the shadow-compass in his hand.

The darkling leapt away from them—one, two, three somersaults across the museum chamber—and then she was out into the rain-filled city air.

Casting about for a place to hide, the darkling felt trapped among the glass-and-steel reflections of the city buildings. Her usual tactic was to hide in a crowd by attaching herself to a human's shadow, but the rain had chased away most of the people that day. Her only options were a young couple, huddled under a hover-brolly, and two street-cleaner robots travelling up and down the granite paving on opposite sides of the square.

She released her solid form into shadow and fled towards a narrow alleyway in the furthest corner of the square, a welcome pool of darkness between a holographic panel that displayed tourist information and a souvenir shop offering holo-crystal snapshots of the city. She waited there as first the suited man, and then his accomplices, ran out of the museum.

"There." The suited man pointed to the alleyway where she hid.

"I see her," said the taller of the two men as she took solid form.

With one last look at them, she darted away round three corners into three more backstreet alleyways: a route spanning the edge of the warehouse sector, past boarded up houses and immense, blank faced buildings. All the time her pursuers kept pace, maintaining the distance between them.

She slipped around a corner and into a dead end. The alleyway was empty, except for a single door to her left. Above it, a peeling, painted sign read, *'Stage Door'*.

The men gasped around the corner behind her, their footsteps clattering to a halt.

"Nowhere to run," said the tall thug, grinning.

She backed away, half-crouched and her arms tense.

"Give it up, darkling." The suited man still held the shadow-compass. "You can't escape us."

She tilted her head, weighing up the chances of diving between them.

"Now, Mr Kendra?" said the shorter man as he reached inside his jacket.

The darkling leapt for the door and yanked it open. Rusted-over hinges screamed as the door slammed shut behind her.

The unlit interior stank of mould and neglect. Seats ripped from the auditorium lay askew in backstage corridors. Shattered scenery panels leant against walls which wept powdery plaster. A decrepit billboard displayed the words *Deepening Theatre*.

The darkling prowled amongst the bones of a theatre long since abandoned in favour of digital entertainment. Her natural instinct was to merge into the shadows but if the one called Kendra could so easily find her with his device, then another tactic was required.

She heard the stage door open, followed by the footsteps of the men and then Kendra's voice.

"Go that way," he said. "And be ready."

The derelict hallways led her through empty wings into the gaping maw of the open stage. Rusting lighting carcasses hung from the riggings above. At each side, ragged curtains strained from their fixings.

She started to move across the stage. The floorboards creaked under her weight, some sinking to the point that she thought they would crack.

"Not so fast, darkling." Kendra stepped out onto the stage before raising his voice to call to his henchmen. "You can come out now."

The doors on either side of the auditorium banged open, and the two henchmen charged into the space, wooden rods clasped in their hands. Each wore a shaded visor across their eyes. They halted at the edge of the stage and looked to the suited man.

"Darkling." Kendra reached inside his jacket and pulled out

two wooden rods, identical to those held by the others. "Do you know what these are?"

"Yes," she growled, spinning around to face each man in turn. "Get them away from me."

"Good. That simplifies things." He withdrew a pair of black-lensed sunglasses from his pocket and put them on. "My supplier informs me that these flares are coated with hairs plucked from the manes of the stallions that draw the sun across the sky. I'm not sure I believe him, but they haven't failed me so far in my darkling hunts."

He nodded to the others, who raised their arms into the air as they turned their heads to the side and slammed their flares together. Each flare leapt into yellow, then white flames so bright that they wiped any colour from sight.

The darkling cried out as the intense light touched her form, weighing her down. She released a ragged breath, trying to force her body to move, but the light froze her in her tracks. She staggered down to her knees.

"My turn." Kendra slapped his flares together, their blazing light joining with that cast by the others.

The darkling screamed. She covered her head with her hands, drawing her body into a shaking ball.

"Now!" Kendra shouted. "While she's down."

The two men climbed onto the stage, the flares held above their heads. Kendra took a step toward her, the boards creaking beneath his feet.

The darkling peered up from her hands as the floorboards began to splinter.

Kendra shrieked as his foot dropped through the surface of the stage. The flares fell from his grasp, their flames guttering out to embers.

"Get me out." He lay with one leg splayed to the side, the other lodged in a hole in the stage. "I'm stuck."

"Yes, Mr Kendra." The shorter man dropped his flares and ran to his boss.

"What about the darkling?" The tall man was still holding his flares.

In the reduced light, she felt her strength return. She took a trembling breath.

"Keep her there," shouted Kendra as the floor beneath his feet gave way even more.

"Yes, sir." The tall man turned back to the darkling. "Where is she?" He lowered the flares and slowly turned around in a circle. "She's gone, Mr Kendra."

High up in the wall, from the darkness of a gash that had once housed a balcony box, the darkling watched the tall man join his companion in attempting to rescue Kendra.

She opened her hand and dropped Kendra's device to the floor then, with a smile, she brought her foot down hard. The shadow-compass splintered like the stage below.

Chapter Two

"You promised."

"I know I did."

"You said I wouldn't have to be a boarder anymore."

"I know."

"If Dad was here—"

"Well, he's not. That's the reason this is happening. I have to find your father so I can tell him that your uncle has died."

Steve glared at the back of his mum's head as she hunched over the steering wheel. She'd said he wouldn't have to put up with the nightmare of boarding anymore. She was going back on her word. *Dad wouldn't go back on his word. This isn't fair.*

"Where is he then?" The front passenger seat, where his dad always sat, was awkwardly empty. Steve slouched in the back of the car, his rucksack grasped on his lap.

"On the Continent," she said. "I think." Her knuckles were white on the steering wheel.

"Why don't you use the automated driving system? You don't

like driving."

"I don't mind," she said.

"Dad said it's safer than a human driver."

"Thanks for the vote of confidence." She glanced at him in the rear-view mirror. "Anyway, we're here now."

The car turned off the road, through the tall, wrought-iron gates of the Alastor Phobus Academy for Boys.

Unlike the glass-and-steel city skyscrapers, the Academy was built from sandstone and was only two floors tall, but it greedily sprawled across the school grounds like the synthetic ivy that covered its walls: all of which was designed to give the impression of old-school tradition. With its beige stone walls, looming doors and crenellated roofline, it reminded Steve of an ancient castle-turned-prison, not a boy's school in the year 2110.

A grey shadow loomed in the corner of Steve's eye as they drove along the sweeping driveway. An old man half-ran, half-staggered alongside the car. He was bone-thin and wore a long, black, expensive coat over an equally expensive and black suit. His hair was iron-grey streaked with white and he moved in a way that suggested he wasn't accustomed to speed. Two guard robots pounded after the old man, using all their eight legs for maximum speed.

"What's that about?"

"What's what about?" asked his mum.

The old man stopped and bent over, his hands on his thighs as he caught his breath. The robots closed in.

"Didn't you see it?" asked Steve as the old man, struggling in the clutches of the robots, disappeared from view behind them. Their car passed through a second set of gates into the central courtyard and pulled up at the official entrance to the school.

10

"Shall I get your suitcase?" His mum watched him in the mirror, her hands still clutching the steering wheel.

"I'll do it," he sighed as he opened the door.

"It won't be for long," she said, following him round to the back of the car. "Just until I find your dad."

"Promise?" He lugged his suitcase out of the car boot and tried to put on his most appealing, big-eyed expression. "Just a couple of weeks, yeah?"

"I don't want to make a promise I can't keep." She smoothed down the front of his hair. "When did you get so tall?"

"I'm twelve years old, Mum." His appealing look clearly hadn't worked. He slung his rucksack over his shoulder. "I've been this tall for ages."

The arched, timber doors of the school banged open to reveal the headmaster's secretary, Miss Scritch, crossing her arms across her scrawny frame as she glared down at them. Steve felt his muscles tense at the sight of her.

"Miss Scritch." Steve's mum took his arm and drew him to the entrance. "How kind of you to greet us yourself."

"You're late." Miss Scritch looked them up and down. Steve could see the security robot stood just behind her, waiting for instructions.

"Last-minute packing, I'm afraid." Steve's mum smiled, but he could see that her mouth was too tense for it to be a heart-felt smile.

"Shall I go round to the dorms?" he said.

"Oh no, there's no space for you in the dormitories," Miss Scritch snapped. "You won't be staying long. Will he, Mrs Haven?"

"Well, I hope not," said his mum. "But—"

"You can have one of the old rooms in the school building," said Miss Scritch. "Here." She thrust a keycard tagged with a packing label at him. "Round the back."

"Can't I come in this way?"

"This is not an entrance for pupils," she sneered. "Staff only. The room number is on the tag. Meet me at the back door and I'll take you to your room."

"Thank you, Miss—" His mum's words were cut off as the doors slammed shut in their faces.

"Round the back," grumbled Steve. "Like I'm a delivery of food or something."

"Well, more like a minor annoyance," said his mum. She smiled and this time it was genuine. "Come on."

*

"There you are." Miss Scritch flung the door of Steve's room open. "It'll do until your mother collects you."

The room was half-filled by a narrow single bed. There was a small window at the other end of the room and a shelf that ran the length of the wall. And that was it.

"You can store your things under the bed," said Miss Scritch.

"Thanks," he said. *For nothing*, he thought as he lugged his suitcase onto the bed. He could see now why Miss Scritch hadn't let his mum into the school building; there would have been an almighty row if she'd seen where he was staying.

"Unpack and report to class." Miss Scritch almost bumped into the security robot that had followed them from the back door. "Immediately," she snapped, batting the robot away.

"Yes, Miss Scritch." *Three bags full, Miss Scritch*, he thought.

She made a sharp "Hm" sound as she nodded her head at him, before marching out of his room and slamming the door shut behind her.

Steve sat down on the bed. It creaked painfully, as if it was complaining at his weight.

Here we go again, he thought, leaning back on his hands. *The joys of imprisonment.*

The sound of the end-of-class bell jolted him out of his thoughts. He grabbed his rucksack and dashed out of the room.

Chapter Three

A deftly aimed elbow jabbed Steve in the ribs. He jolted upright, sending the tablet that his teacher had lent him clattering to the floor.

"You were snoring," whispered his friend, Jon. "Really loud."

The teacher's assistant robot skittered across the tiled floor, travelling on four of its eight limbs to stop at Steve's desk.

"Steve Haven." The teacher at the head of the classroom dropped his hand from the text on the holographic white board to point at Steve. "Were you asleep?"

"No, Mr Oxtoby." Steve opened his eyes wide and sat up straight.

"I suppose you were just resting your eyes."

"Yes, Mr Oxtoby," said Steve. "I mean, no, Mr Oxtoby. I was awake the whole time." Jon sniggered and Steve kicked him under the desk, narrowly missing the robot which was in the process of retrieving the tablet.

"Well, if you were awake," said Mr Oxtoby, "you'll be able to recite the timeline we've been discussing in class."

"Yes, sir." Steve glanced at the white board just as his teacher turned it off.

"Well?" said Mr Oxtoby. "Enlighten us."

"Yes, sir." Steve cleared his throat. "2063," he said. "That was the year of the *Garan Sauer Robotics Directive*."

"It was," said the teacher. "Expand on that point, please."

"The directive ruled that robots should not take the form of human beings in any way." He smiled, pleased with himself.

"Examples?" said Mr Oxtoby.

"Well," said Steve, trying to remember the last lesson and wondering if he could blag his way through this one. "They couldn't walk around on two legs or have a face like ours."

"What was the secondary point of the directive?"

"They can't create works of art," said Steve, "because creativity is seen as a human trait."

"Well remembered," nodded Mr Oxtoby. "And what was the response within the robotics industry?"

"Err." Steve stopped. *I really should pay more attention*, he thought. "Well." He looked at the teacher and shrugged.

"Anyone?" The teacher looked around with a bored expression.

"There were the riots, sir," said a boy at the front of the class. "By the robotics industry workers."

"Very good, Kelly. Continue."

As his classmate gushed on, Steve retrieved his borrowed tablet from the robot and put it back on his desk. He cupped his hand over a yawn, looking out of the window that ran the length of the classroom.

The old man Steve had seen running from the guard robots

was stood alone in the courtyard outside, staring up at the classroom window.

Is he watching me? Steve wondered as their eyes met.

Almost as though he was reading his thoughts, the old man nodded to him and raised a hand in a half-wave, mouthing something that Steve couldn't make out.

He is *watching me.*

The end-of-class bell jolted him back to the room, followed by a rattle of chairs as the boys stood up and gathered their things, blocking Steve's view of the window.

"Steve." Someone tapped him on the shoulder.

"What?" Steve jumped at the touch.

"Sorry," said Jon. "Coming for lunch?"

"Yeah, just a minute. Hang on." Steve fought his way through the other boys to stand at the window.

"What are you looking for?"

"I thought—" Steve scanned the courtyard, but the old man had gone.

"Thought what?"

"Nothing," said Steve, turning to his friend. "Let's eat."

*

The canteen was a low ceilinged, windowless cave of a room filled with row upon row of grey plastic tables and benches. Eight food-dispensing units dominated the end wall. A team of server robots, larger than Mr Oxtoby's assistant robot but of the same basic design, ferried food and empty trays back-and-forth between the dispensing units and the teachers' tables. The smaller, more squat cleaning robots trundled around between spillages and the bins. At that time of day there was a constant chatter as the boys and staff ate their lunch.

Steve pressed his thumb to an identification pad at one of the food stations.

"Steven Haven," said a disembodied, monotone voice. "Recalling individual nutritional profile." There was a bell-like 'ding' and a window flipped open in the food-dispensing unit. Steve reached in and pulled out a sealed tray.

"What delights do they have for us today?" said Jon as a second window opened in response to his own thumbprint.

Steve peeled open the wrapper on his tray. A warm, meaty aroma drifted out. "Not too bad," he said. "Chicken and veg."

"You're lucky," said Jon as he peered at his own opened tray. "I've got salad, again."

They sat at the nearest free table and fully unveiled their lunches.

"Mmm, scrummy synthetic chicken," said Steve, wafting a piece of dripping chicken under his friend's nose.

"Stop it." Jon held a hand to his rumbling stomach.

"Tell you what," said Steve. "If you're a very good boy, I might let you dip your lettuce in my gravy." He grinned around a mouthful of food.

"Shut up." Jon pulled a face at him. "Or I won't share my chocolate with you."

"Ooh, I'm frightened," said Steve. "You must be running low by now. How long is it since the start of term?"

"Ages," said Jon. "Mother sent me a fresh parcel." He stuffed a rolled-up slice of ham into his mouth. "I'm glad you're boarding again, Steve."

"I'm not." Steve stabbed his dinner with his knife. "But Mum needs to find my dad and there's no one else to look after me."

"Sorry to hear about your uncle."

"Don't be," said Steve. "I didn't really know him."

A picture of the last time he had seen his uncle flashed uninvited into his mind. He remembered Uncle Rex, dressed in an expensive suit, arguing with Steve's father at the entrance to their family home as his mum did her best to steer Steve up to bed.

"He's family though," said Jon. "Your dad will be upset."

"Move over." A tall, blond-haired boy elbowed Jon as he shoved his way onto the bench. Two more boys, equally blond, sniggered as they did the same to Steve.

"All right," Jon muttered as he shuffled along.

"What you got there, Shaw?" The boy slid Jon's tray along the table. "More rabbit food?"

"Leave him alone, Curtis," said Steve, catching the tray and passing it back to his friend.

Curtis was a head taller than Steve, who wasn't exactly short, and the blond boy used that to his advantage, every opportunity he got.

"Why should I?" Curtis pointed his knife at Steve. "What are you going to do about it?"

"It's okay, Steve," said Jon. "No harm done."

"See?" Curtis wrapped an arm around Jon's neck, drawing it tight under his chin. "Shaw said it himself. No harm done."

"Let him go." Steve tried to stand but the boy next to him grabbed his arms, pinning him down.

"You be quiet," Curtis snarled, finally releasing the struggling

Jon. "This has nothing to do with you. There you go." He patted Jon on the head.

"I'm fine," said Jon, making a weak attempt at a smile. "It's okay."

"So." Curtis leant towards Steve. "Your uncle."

"What about him?" Steve was in no mood to talk to Curtis, but he couldn't get into trouble on his first day back as a boarder and he didn't want to leave Jon at the mercy of the bullies.

"I hear his fortune passes to your father."

"I suppose so." Steve shrugged.

"He's a professor, isn't he? Your father?" said Curtis.

"He's an archaeologist," said Steve.

"Not the kind of person to run a robotics company," said Curtis. "My father says Thomas Winters should be in charge. He says your father will ruin the company. He says—"

"Steven Haven!" called the headmaster from the other side of the canteen.

Mr Hendrickson was a grey, balding man of indeterminate years. His suits, though expensive, did nothing to disguise his bony frame.

"Here you are," he said as he came to their table. "Why are you so red in the face, Shaw?"

"I was running." Jon rubbed his throat. "To get here."

"Whatever for?" said Mr Hendrickson.

"Did you want me, sir?" said Steve, trying to distract the headmaster from his friend's distress.

"Oh yes, there's been a delivery. Most irregular. It was left on the doorstep. Miss Scritch has placed it on your bed."

Thrown it, more like, thought Steve. "Thank you, sir," he said.

"Curtis," said Mr Hendrickson.

Curtis' shoulders jerked at the sound of his name. "Yes, sir?" His smirk turned into a bright smile as he answered the headmaster.

"How is your father?" Mr Hendrickson's face settled into a worried grimace. "I hear that he's thinking of moving the family to the Continent. I would hate to lose you and your brothers."

"No chance of that, sir." Curtis grinned at Steve. "Mother persuaded him that a move abroad wouldn't be good for the family."

"Good, good." The headmaster's face brightened into a smile before turning back to Steve. "Haven."

"Yes, sir?" said Steve.

"You should take your example from Curtis here. One of our best students."

"Yes, sir." Steve inwardly rolled his eyes.

"Well, go on then."

"Sir?" said Steve, not quite sure what he was meant to 'go on then' to do.

"Go to your room so you can open your parcel. You've eaten enough of that."

"But sir…" Jon tried to stand but Curtis pulled him back down.

"Now," said the headmaster.

"Yes, sir." Steve slung his bag over his shoulder.

"Don't worry about Shaw," said Curtis as Steve walked away. "We'll keep him company."

*

Steve sat cross-legged on his bed, waiting for the bell that would spell the end of lunch break.

The parcel had turned out to be a crumpled, brown paper package with the words *'For the attention of Steve Haven, student'* scrawled on it in dark ink. He had stared for a moment at the strange packaging: paper. It had been a very long time since he'd touched anything so rare and precious. And for it to be used just for wrapping something was beyond odd.

Inside he had found a metal disc, a little bigger than the size of his palm, wrapped up in a sheet of lined writing paper which bore five words, *'Give this to your father'*, scrawled in the same handwriting as the words on the brown wrapping paper. There was nothing else written on there, not even a signature.

A ridge ran horizontally across the disc, near its top. The section above the ridge was divided into three parts, the middle section wider than the others. On either side of the disc were small indentations, while on the back there were two cog-shaped spaces.

He lay back on his bed, one arm behind his head and the other holding the disc in front of his face. What was it? It was obviously incomplete, a part of something else, but Steve had no idea what.

The metal it was formed from was dark grey, worn, and warm to the touch. It was heavy too: it felt far too dense for its size.

He sat up and went to the window at the end of the room, looking out over the roof tiles and the heavy rain that had begun to fall.

He wondered where his mum was. Had she found his dad? More importantly, when could he go home again?

He curled his hand around the disc, his thumb and forefinger instinctively finding the indentations on its sides.

The end-of-lunch bell rang, dragging him from his thoughts. He stuffed the disc deep into his trouser pocket, hoisted his rucksack onto his shoulder, and left for class.

*

"Maths next," said Steve. "Joy."

Steve and Jon trudged along the school corridor from one lesson to the next.

"I don't know why you're complaining," said Jon. "You've got a knack for maths. Not like me."

"You're all right at it."

"I suck at maths and you know it."

"You're good at geography."

"I excel at geography," said Jon, grinning cheekily. "I am the king of geography."

"Watch out!" Curtis and his blonde companions knocked Steve and Jon out of the way. "Clumsy," Curtis chided as Jon bent to retrieve his bag. "You should watch where you're going."

"Sorry," mumbled Jon.

"And?" said Curtis, raising his eyebrows at Steve.

"And?" said Steve.

"Apologise."

"What for?"

"Getting in my way." Curtis pushed him. "Look, you're doing it again." Curtis nodded to his companions who grabbed Steve's arms. "Let's see what you have, shall we?"

"Get off me." Steve pulled one of his arms free as Curtis reached for him, accidentally catching the taller boy across the chin.

"Oi!" Curtis slapped out a hand, knocking Steve off-balance and into the arms of the other blond boys.

There was a *'ding, ding, clatter'* as the disc flew out of Steve's pocket and came to a halt at his feet.

"What's this?" Curtis picked it up. "What've you been hiding?"

"Give it back. That's mine."

"What is it then?" said Curtis. "If it's yours, tell me what it is."

"That's really none of your concern, is it?"

The grin slipped from Curtis' face as he heard Mr Oxtoby's voice.

Where did he come from? thought Steve as Curtis handed the disc to the teacher. He hadn't heard Mr Oxtoby approach, but he had been focused on Curtis after all.

"Looks like junk anyway," muttered Curtis.

"Not one more word," said Mr Oxtoby. "You don't steal other people's possessions."

"I wasn't stealing," said Curtis. "I just wanted to have a look."

"Get to class." The teacher glared at Curtis' companions who still held Steve's arms. "All of you."

"Yes, sir," they said in unison, releasing Steve and moving to stand behind Curtis.

"Here." Mr Oxtoby handed the disc back to Steve, still keeping an eye on the three boys as they slunk off down the corridor. "I suggest you don't carry toys around with you during lesson time."

Steve opened his mouth to tell the teacher that the disc wasn't a toy, then stopped. After all, he had no idea what it actually was. "No, sir," he said, tucking the disc back into his pocket. "Thank you, sir."

"Get along, then." Mr Oxtoby nodded down the corridor. "Maths awaits."

"Yes, sir," said Jon, pulling Steve with him. "Thank you, sir. Come on."

"That was a first," said Steve as they turned the corner. Mr Oxtoby was still watching. "A teacher taking our side over Curtis."

"Enjoy it while it lasts," said Jon. "Curtis never forgets."

"Spoil the mood, why don't you?" Steve elbowed Jon with a grin. "Haven't you heard? Maths awaits."

Chapter Four

It had been easy for the darkling to attach herself to the curator's shadow as he entered the museum that morning. The extra security guard, drafted in after the mysterious incident in the Central Plaza Bank bombing display room, didn't even look at the old man. Both the curator and his shadow passed by without interruption.

The curator made his way to his office, a small room adjoining the vast records hall. The darkling travelled with him, flowing over the polished, wooden floor to settle at the old man's feet.

She left his shadow, gathering in the darkness under the desk, and watched as he removed a keycard from his jacket pocket, the keycard she had earlier stolen from him and then replaced.

"How did that get there?" he said, a frown creasing his already-wrinkled face. With the keycard in his hand, he walked through to the records hall, plodding past shelves of boxes and tiers of filing drawers which all reached up to the domed ceiling.

"Better put this away before I forget." The curator held the keycard out in front of him as he crossed the room to a sleek, metal, wall-fitted storage unit. "Here we are."

He opened one of the small doors in the unit, inserted the keycard into the revealed slot, and closed the door again. The light cast by the scanner ran along the gap at the bottom of the door, there was a blip, and the door locked with the quietest of clicks.

"Done." The curator frowned again, staring blankly into mid-air. "Why that display case?" he whispered.

He went to the neighbouring filing cabinet and yanked open a drawer which squealed in protest. He pulled out a bulging ring binder and carried it to the table. The label on the spine read, 'Central Plaza Bank Bombing Room – Case 44a'. He opened the file and flipped through the clear pocket-pages. Dog-eared photographs sat beside letters, receipts and printed news articles. Each item was to him an historical artefact in itself, however small or seemingly mundane; all were religiously filed away, the idea of abandoning them to the cloud rejected as something close to sacrilege.

He jumped at the sound of his wrap-phone and slapped his wrist to pick up the call.

"Hello?" he said. "Oh, it's you. I told you not to call me at work."

Talking on his phone in a hushed voice, he rushed out of the records hall. The darkling flowed from beneath the desk, taking solid form as she reached the table.

Over the years she had done her best to keep up with this world's rapid technological advances. Still, in an age where most archives were held digitally, it was good to return to information sources that she could touch and hold.

The file had been left open at item thirty-nine: a broken, decorative comb. She turned the pages, glancing at old photographs of the near-demolished bank, until she found what she was looking for.

A photograph of the metal disc from the display case was stapled to a page of printed text. *'The disc was found in the hand of a smashed, clay statue in the ruins of the main hall in the bank,'* it read. *'No information can be found on either the disc or the statue. Strangely, the bank denied having had a statue located in that area.'*

Of course, they denied it, she thought. *He was never meant to be there.*

She pulled out the photograph and turned it over, wondering if it was of the original disc or the replica. A printed label on the back read, *'Replica on display. Original purchased by the Haven Robotics Corporation, care of TW'.*

She heard the curator's voice before he opened the door. By the time he reached the file, she was gone.

*

The Saint Mungo's Sanctuary for the Homeless had originally been set up in an old, corrugated steel shipping container hunkered down between two gleaming skyscrapers. Over the years, the Caercester area council had decided that, while there was a need for such a place, the building itself was too unsightly for its beautiful city. The shipping container had been clad in polished steel to match its neighbours, with the intent that it would, in effect, fade into the background. Open all day, every day, it survived on the guilty conscience of the rich and was only noticed by those who sought it out.

The darkling sat in a corner of the shelter's canteen with her hood pulled up and her darkling eyes hidden behind a pair of mirror-lens sunglasses stolen from a shop display. She clasped a mug of black tea in her hands: her solid form required only a basic level of sustenance but accepting the drink also added to the impression of normality and resuscitated her fingers, which were numb from the city chill.

"Back again?" A young boy with an unkempt mop of dishwater-brown hair perched on the bench, as far away from her as he could get. "I've seen you here a lot lately."

She shrugged. "It gets me out of the cold."

"You need anything?" He nodded to a teenage boy stood nearby. "My brother and me, we're good at finding stuff. Stuff that people need."

"No money," she said, taking in the aura that surrounded the boy and his brother which set them apart from the others in the shelter, even the children.

"Shame," he said. "I'm Michael." He smiled a goodbye. "See you." He returned to his brother, tugging on the older boy's arm. The brother turned and nodded at her before the two of them joined the small crowd gathering around the food shelves where the helpers were handing out sandwiches. The darkling liked that there were no robot assistants there, just people helping people in the best way they knew how.

Taking advantage of the distraction, she went to a door at the back of the canteen, nudged it open and stepped through.

The office was small and sparsely furnished with a desk, a stool and a scratched table attached to a blank glass screen which stretched to the low ceiling.

"Hello?" whispered the darkling as she sat down. The glass screen blinked blue, as it had each time the darkling had used the outdated computer. "Information request."

A face slowly emerged from the surface of the screen—nose, cheeks, chin—until an entire head, neck, and shoulders were visible.

"Good day," said the head, a little more noisily than the darkling would have liked. "How can I help you today?"

"Tell me about the Haven Robotics Corporation," said the darkling. "Who is TW?"

Chapter Five

"So what is it?"

"You mean it isn't obvious?" Steve grinned, then shrugged. "I don't know." He handed the disc to Jon. "The note just says to give it to Dad." *Except I don't know where he is, or when I'll be seeing him next*, he thought.

He sat on the edge of his bed, rubbing his chest where Curtis had pushed him. He'd never admit it of course, but it hurt.

"Mysterious." Jon turned the disc over. "It's obviously part of something larger. See the cog shapes on the back?" Steve's friend leant against the closed door.

"Well obviously I saw that," said Steve. "But what uses cogs these days?"

"And there was no sent address?"

"No. Nothing. Just my name, and the note."

"Someone went to a lot of trouble to get this to you, or your dad."

"What do you mean?" said Steve.

"The way it arrived," said Jon. "Haven't you heard?" He grinned. "Do I know something you don't?"

"It looks that way," said Steve, frowning. "Come on, then. Don't keep me in suspense."

"We had an intruder."

"The old man," said Steve.

"Oh, so you do know." Jon sighed.

"I saw him," said Steve. "I saw someone, anyway. When Mum dropped me off, and then in the courtyard during class."

"Why didn't you say?" grumbled Jon. "Nothing exciting ever happens to me."

"I didn't know it was exciting," said Steve. "Unusual. Odd. But not exciting."

"The alarm was raised because of an intruder. You should have seen Miss Scritch racing to release the guard robots. I don't think I've ever seen her smile. Frightening." He shuddered. "And then later, when it had all died down, and no intruder had been found, a parcel turned up at the school front door." He held out the disc to Steve. "Your parcel."

"But we don't know the two things are connected." Steve took the disc and dropped it onto the bed. "Not really."

"Don't spoil my fun," said Jon. "It might be connected."

"All right," said Steve. "I admit it. It might be connected."

There was a sharp rap at the door and, before Steve could reply, Miss Scritch stormed in, sending Jon tumbling onto the end of the bed.

"Haven," she barked. "You're required in the headmaster's office." She scowled at Jon as he floundered to stand up then returned her attention to Steve. "Straight away."

31

"Yes, miss."

"Chop, chop. The headmaster hasn't got all day." She glared at Jon, then stormed out as abruptly as she had entered.

"That's me told," said Steve, standing up.

"Maybe there's another parcel," said Jon. "Or your mum's here to collect you."

"Or maybe I'm in trouble," said Steve. "Care of Curtis and his cronies."

"My idea was better."

*

"Hello, Steve." The woman smiled as she shook his hand. She looked as old as Miss Scritch: probably in her sixties, Steve thought. But, where the school secretary's clothes hung on her like jumble on a scarecrow, this woman was perfectly styled all the way from her neatly-cropped grey hair to her well-polished shoes. "My name is Eleanor Palmer," she said. "I work—" She paused. "I worked for your Uncle Rex as his personal assistant."

"Hi." Steve allowed his hand to be politely shaken.

"That will be all, Miss Scritch." Mr Hendrickson sat behind his desk, his eyebrows drawn into a frown.

"Are you sure?" Miss Scritch stared at Eleanor Palmer. "I could take notes."

"No need for notes," said Mr Hendrickson.

"Well, if you're certain." Miss Scritch hovered at the side of his desk.

"Quite certain." Mr Hendrickson nodded to the door. "Thank you."

"I see." Miss Scritch sniffed and marched from the room.

"Take a seat, Haven." Mr Hendrickson pointed to a chair.

"Yes, sir." Steve sat. "I haven't done anything wrong, have I, sir?"

"No, of course not," said Eleanor. "What makes you say that?"

"I don't know," Steve shrugged. *Being in the headmaster's office?* he thought.

He was only ever called there when he was in trouble. What made it worse was the knowledge that the headmaster could see every area of the school and its grounds from the wall of screens fitted on one side of the otherwise traditionally-furnished room. The only place the headmaster didn't spy on were the corridors in the main school building that led to his office.

"Steve, I have some sad news for you." Eleanor folded her well-manicured hands on her lap as she sat opposite him. The light from the window picked out the silver in her hair, which was almost the same colour as her trouser suit. "It's about your uncle."

"Rex?" said Steve. *Of* course *Rex*, he thought. *I've only got one uncle. Had one uncle.*

"That's right," she said. "I'm afraid I have to tell you that your uncle died just over a week ago."

"I know," said Steve, wondering why anyone would think that he didn't know. After all, the whole school knew about his uncle's death. "Mum told me. Rex was quite old, wasn't he? A lot older than Dad."

"I see," said Eleanor, frowning. "I didn't think the Corporation had informed your parents. I thought that was why they hadn't been in touch. I've tried contacting them."

"Dad's on the Continent," said Steve. "Mum went looking for him to tell him about Rex."

"Haven is boarding with us," said the headmaster. "Temporarily."

"That would explain things. Did they leave a contact number?" She looked from Steve to the headmaster and back again. "I could ring them."

"I can check the files," said the headmaster.

"They always ring *me*," said Steve. "I mean, if they're away. They travel a lot and sometimes they're in these really remote places with no signal."

"But they must ring from a particular number," said Eleanor.

"No. Sometimes, they'll ring from wherever they're staying. Dad says he doesn't like being tied to a phone."

"That's unfortunate," said Eleanor. "I really needed to speak to them."

"About Rex?" said Steve.

"Amongst other things. The Corporation have arranged his funeral. I did suggest it should be delayed until your parents could be contacted. Rex stipulated in his will that you and your parents should attend. I'm the executor. That's why I wanted to talk to them. Unfortunately, I was overruled."

"You don't want me to go, do you?" said Steve. His stomach clenched up with sudden nerves. Surely he couldn't go to the funeral without his parents. "I wouldn't know anyone."

"If we can track down your parents in time, then you won't be on your own," said Eleanor. "Of course, we don't have very long to find them."

"Why? When is the funeral?" said Steve.

"Tomorrow. At the cathedral."

"Tomorrow? That's too soon. Mum and Dad will never be back in time."

"They could be on their way back now," she said. "Of course, if we could ring them…"

"I don't have a black suit."

"Your uniform is smart. You can wear that," she said. "I tell you what, I'll pick you up from here tomorrow."

"Unless you contact my parents before then, of course," he said, with a hopeful smile.

"Even if we do," she said.

"Well, if that's all arranged," said the headmaster, standing and nodding at Steve for him to do the same.

"Right." Steve stood up. "Tomorrow then."

"Yes. Tomorrow." Eleanor smiled at him. "It's been lovely to meet you, Steve, after all Rex has told me about you."

"Right," said Steve, wondering what his uncle, whom he barely knew, could possibly have told Eleanor about him. "Bye then." He half raised a hand to wave, then decided not to. "Bye."

"Goodbye, Steve."

"Yeah." He walked to the door. "Right," he said, smiling weakly. Then he walked out of the headmaster's office and closed the door firmly behind him.

Chapter Six

The darkling flexed her feet in the boots and socks she had borrowed from the shelter. They felt rough and restrictive against her skin: no good for running, but the longer she remained in solid form, the more she succumbed to her human body. She blew on her hands, which trembled in the cold morning air.

The hooded coat she wore smelt of gravy and laundry detergent: an unappetising mixture but it added a layer of warmth over the clothes she had formed out of her own abilities.

Her online research had provided her with a name to match the 'TW' initials—Thomas Winters—and the address of the Haven Robotics Corporation.

Winters had been easy to pick out as he had arrived at the corporation building that morning before setting off again a few minutes later. Winters's aura seethed like a hungry dog waiting for the command to attack, red tongues of magic lapping around his body.

His route took him from the pristine prosperity of the centre to the only bridge that crossed the river within the city boundaries.

The West Temple Bridge, with its white metal construct, gleamed in the daylight and glowed in the night when the windows of the apartments built into the bridge lit up.

The darkling shuddered as she stepped onto the bridge, avoiding the sight of the grey depths of the river below. If she allowed herself to fall into its grasp, she would lose herself, as any darkling would in water.

Distracted by her dread, she didn't hear the two men approach until it was too late, pulling her hood down over her face at the last minute as they passed her: the two men who had chased the darkling from the museum.

"Stupid place to meet," snarled one.

"Mr Kendra's orders," said the other, rubbing his ring-clad hands against the cold.

They reached Winters, the taller one slapping a hand on the man's shoulder.

"We're here, Jared," he said. "What do you want?"

"Don't call me that." Winters pushed the tall man's hand away. "That isn't my name anymore."

"All right, all right." The tall man's companion spread his hands palms up. "Thew didn't mean any harm, did you?"

"Just being friendly, Obadiah," he smirked. "That's all."

"I don't need friends," snapped Winters. "Here." He shoved a piece of paper at Thew. "That's the address."

"How long?" said Thew.

"The funeral should finish by ten," said Winters. "The car journey to that address is no more than fifteen minutes."

"Right then," said Thew, glancing at the address. "Breakfast on the way, Obadiah?"

"Indeed, Thew," said his companion.

"Just one more thing," said Thew as he pocketed the piece of paper. "We're just to take the boy, right?"

"Take him and keep him somewhere safe," said Winters. "For now."

"So we're not to hurt him then?"

"You're not to kill him," said Winters.

"Oh no, of course not," said Thew. "But if he fights back?"

"Restrain him. In whatever way you see fit."

"Got you," said Thew.

"Crystal clear," said Obadiah, rubbing his hands together.

The two men bounded across the bridge, Obadiah pumping his arms as he lagged behind his leggier companion.

Only the darkling noticed the old man, with his dark suit and iron-grey hair, hurry after the two henchmen.

*

She stood at the entrance to the Haven Robotics Corporation building, watching through the glass doors as Winters crossed the foyer and disappeared behind a pair of sliding metal doors.

Like the majority of the city skyscrapers, the Haven Robotics Corporation building was constructed of glass and steel, but where most of the other buildings spanned one-hundred-storeys high, it towered a further hundred floors above the roofline. It took full advantage of its height and the sky-space to reach a cantilevered top section over the rooftops below, forming an upside-down L-shape that set it apart from the surrounding

38

cityscape.

She walked around the outside of the building until she found a spot that was unobserved by cameras and not visible to the main streets.

The glass was cold on her skin as she placed her hand on the wall of the building. She released a breath. Her shadowed hand hovered above the glass, unable to penetrate it.

"Impossible," she whispered.

She tried again and failed again.

Pushing back her hood, she looked more closely and saw that, although the glass wall should have been solid, there was a tiny movement within it.

Water, she thought. The walls were double layered with water running in between. Clever or a coincidence? How could they know that a darkling couldn't pass through water?

She walked around to the entrance again. If she couldn't pass through the walls, she could just attach herself to the shadow of anyone walking into the building.

The words, *'Haven Robots Corporation'* were etched into the polished granite floor on either side of the closed door, written in letters that curled and flourished to the point that they were barely legible.

What's that? She knelt down to look more closely at the letters and realised that they weren't simply letters. Symbols—a downward pointing triangle to signify water, a circle to symbolise protection, a shield knot and so many more—had all been carefully carved into the letters themselves. The doorway was protected against the entry of any magical creature, including her.

She stepped back, looking up at the building. *If I can't go in, I'll have to wait for him to come out.*

When she had returned to her unseen spot, she began the return to shadow. Her coat fell to the floor, pooling around the borrowed boots and socks. She waited.

Chapter Seven

The bell for the first class rang as Eleanor and Steve walked across the school courtyard to the waiting car.

Its long metallic panels reflected the rain-clad sky. Across its roof, beads of water ran off a series of sleek solar panels. A door slid open, hugging the length of the car.

"Wow," said Steve. His family's car seemed dilapidated and old-fashioned by comparison.

"In you get," said Eleanor, guiding him with a hand on his shoulder.

"Greetings, Master Haven." A deep, smooth, masculine voice spoke as Steve slid along the seat.

"Hello?" Steve looked around. There was no one to be seen.

"Welcome back, Miss Palmer," the voice continued as Eleanor climbed in beside Steve. "Should I shade the window glass for your privacy?"

"Yes please," she said as the door slid closed. "I think we need a little privacy."

"Who's speaking?" Steve whispered. He didn't know why he was whispering but it felt like the right thing to do.

"The Robotic Driving System or RDS," she said, dropping her handbag onto the seat beside her. "Haven't you travelled in an RDS vehicle before? It was one of Rex's earlier inventions."

"Yes, but ours doesn't speak." He leaned forward and peered at the front seats. "Dad had one installed, but Mum doesn't trust it. She does the driving."

"How odd," said Eleanor. "Like all Haven technology, the robotic driving system is linked to the Haven Corporation Interhub. It can be instructed from here, inside the car, or from the Haven offices. Driver, what is the weather like in the city?"

"You can expect light rainfall, Miss Palmer."

"Hopefully, the weather will improve for the funeral," she said as the car moved off with a quiet hum.

"I've never been to a funeral," said Steve, pulling at his collar. Eleanor had 'improved' his tie knot, tightening it way past the casual way he normally wore it. It felt like he imagined a noose would feel.

"That's fortunate," she said. "I've attended far too many over the years; but when you get to my age, it's hardly a surprise, I suppose."

"I don't how to act. What do you do at a funeral?" he said, then realised how young that made him sound.

"You pay your respects," said Eleanor. "Just be yourself, but a well-behaved version of yourself."

"I'm not a kid," he said, feeling just like a kid.

"Of course, you aren't." She looked him up and down. "How old are you?"

"Twelve."

"Well, there you are then. Almost a man." She gave him a brief smile. "Of course, it would have been better if your parents had been available but they're rather elusive."

"Dad says it's the nature of his work," said Steve. "Visiting archaeological sites in the middle of nowhere. Travelling at the last minute. It's always been like that." *Elusive*, he thought. *Got it in one.*

"And what about your mother?"

"She usually goes with him," he said, suddenly feeling very lonely. "They're a team."

"That's nice," said Eleanor.

They travelled on in an awkward silence. Eleanor stared ahead, her hands folded on her lap. Steve sat tense, watching the rain slide down the darkened window.

"You worked for my uncle then," he said, when the awkwardness became too much for him.

"I did. For many years."

"So you know Mum and Dad?"

"We've met a handful of times, years ago. I believe there was a falling out between Rex and your father."

"Yeah," said Steve. "Something like that. As usual they didn't think it was worth telling me. There's a lot they don't tell me," he said, surprising himself with his words.

"Like where they are at the moment?"

"Exactly," he said.

"Well, maybe they think they're protecting you."

"I'm not a baby. I don't need protecting. And from what?" He pulled at his collar. "Do you have children?"

"I do not." An expression flitted across Eleanor's face that

Steve couldn't read. It was somewhere between sadness and steel. "I have dedicated my life to my career, and to Rex."

Steve wanted to say something but the only words that came to him were, 'That's sad', and he was sure she wouldn't want to hear that.

The car slowed to a halt and the Robotic Driving System said, "You have reached your destination. I do hope the journey was acceptable."

"Where are we?" said Steve.

"Cathedral Square," said the driving system as the window glass cleared.

Across the square, Steve could see Caercester Cathedral holding its own amongst the taller, glimmering skyscrapers. It had never looked like a cathedral to Steve. There were no arched stained-glass windows or creamy-white limestone. Instead, the cathedral was constructed of glass wrapped around steel which had been polished to a mirror-like sheen. The box-shaped cathedral looked squat compared to its towering neighbours but was actually the equivalent of eight- or nine-storeys high.

"Your parents may yet turn up," said Eleanor. "Who knows, they may be waiting for you inside the cathedral."

"I suppose."

"Are you ready?"

He shook his head. "Not really."

"Don't worry. I'll steer you through it all." The car door slid open at her touch.

In the square, a horde of photographers and journalists, some human, others robotic, waited behind a holographic barrier on which scrolled the words, 'Press and Media'.

"Come on," she said. "Don't look at them. Keep your eyes

on the cathedral door."

"Right," he said following her out of the car.

"And don't say anything."

"I can do that."

"Good boy." She took his arm. "Here we go."

*

The cathedral pews overflowed with men and women dressed in varying shades of grey. Only Steve in his navy school uniform suit and Eleanor, resplendent in lilac, punctuated the corporate spectrum.

Steve checked the time on his wrap-phone. The minister had been talking about Rex Haven, 'robotics genius and philanthropist', for the past twenty minutes. He wondered how much more there was to say about his uncle.

"Did all these people know Rex?" He and Eleanor sat at one end of the front pew, his parents' absence marked by the empty seats beside them.

"Yes. Most of them worked for him. Rex was very well-respected by his employees." She kept her eyes on the minister. "You must speak to Reverend Vernon at the end of the service. It's only right as Rex's family."

Really? Steve thought. He wanted to say, 'Can't you do it?' but he realised how weak that sounded, so he just nodded his head.

The minister gestured to the holographic image of Rex Haven that hovered beside the coffin: smartly cut grey hair, precisely shaven face, eyes the same pale blue as Steve's own.

The open, dark wood coffin lay on a black granite slab. Six pallbearer robots, each bearing a black band around one of their eight limbs, crouched on either side of the slab.

The minister bade farewell to the deceased, crossed himself and then closed the coffin lid. The resulting snap echoed around the cathedral like a gunshot. He nodded to the organist and in response the ornate organ's heaving music blared out, vibrating the air, the pews and the ground beneath.

The pallbearers rose to their four-foot heights, each securing the coffin in four of their limbs. The remaining limbs acted as legs as they made their slow journey to the door at the head of the cathedral.

People left their seats in near silence. A handful nodded to Eleanor. Fewer still looked at Steve, their blank faces showing no sign of recognition.

The benefits of anonymity, he thought. *At least I don't have to talk to any of them.*

"Come on." Eleanor wrapped her arm through his. "The minister is waiting."

"Can't we just go?" he asked, wondering if his appealing, big-eyed expression would work on Eleanor. "I don't know what to say."

"Miss Palmer?" The minister waited at the end of the pew, hands clasped, lips pressed into a smile. "And Master Haven. Would you like to say one last goodbye to your loved one before the cremation?"

"Not really," said Steve.

"Oh, I see." The minister's shoulders sagged.

"What Steve means," said Eleanor, "is that he would rather remember his uncle as he was, alive and well."

"Quite understandable." The minister nodded. "I do hope you both approved of the service?"

"It was in very good taste." Eleanor stood up, taking Steve with her. "Just what Rex would have wanted."

"That is good to hear." The minister stepped back to let them pass. "If you ever need to talk, Master Haven, about your uncle's death or any other matter, the Church's door is always open."

"Thanks." Steve forced a smile. *Not likely*, he thought.

"Thank you again." Eleanor released Steve and took the minister's outstretched hand. "I hope the donation from the Haven Corporation was sufficient."

"Very generous. Much appreciated in these days of non-conformity."

"Bye then." Steve took a step towards freedom but Eleanor caught him, grasping his arm with hers.

"Respect? Remember?" she whispered. "We walk slowly with heads held high."

"Okay," he whispered back. "Sorry."

"No need for sorry." She gave him a tight smile. "Here we go."

*

The dusty chill of the cathedral led out into the damp chill of the city air. Eleanor manoeuvred Steve past the photographers, her head high and her eyes fixed on the car that waited across the square. Steve walked with his head down, contemplating his shoes.

"Miss Palmer." Eleanor turned as a muscular, heavily set

47

man strode down the cathedral steps. "I missed you at the funeral," he said.

"Steve, this is Thomas Winters," said Eleanor. "Mr Winters is the Chief Financial Officer of the Corporation."

"So you're Steve." Winters gripped Steve's hand. "It's good to meet you at last."

"Mr Winters is overseeing the running of the Corporation during the handover period," said Eleanor.

Winters looked Steve up and down. His grip tightened. "Rex's murder was a shock to us all. Your uncle will be missed."

"What?" Steve looked at Eleanor. "Murder?"

"Didn't you know?" said Winters.

"No." The bones in Steve's hand ground on each other as Winters's grip continued.

"Really?" Winters's smile twitched.

"I'm sorry, Thomas but we need to go," said Eleanor. "Steve needs to get back to school."

"Of course." Winters released Steve's hand and refreshed his smile. "You always know best, Miss Palmer." He stepped back a pace. "Like I said, good to meet you."

"Yeah," said Steve, flexing his hand.

"Goodbye, Steve."

"Come on." Eleanor gently slipped her arm through Steve's as she led him away. "I think we need to talk."

*

The darkling loitered in the shadow of the cathedral as the woman and boy walked away from Winters. She had followed him there from the Haven Corporation building; there was no way she was letting him out of her sight.

The woman was obviously a workaday, the colours that shone brightly around non-magical children now greyed with age. That was always the way with workadays. There was something about grown-up life that bleached out the colours in their auras, almost as if they had forgotten to believe in magic at all.

Winters, by comparison, seethed with the brightest of magic. His aura was tense, like a wolf ready to leap. He so wanted to use his magic but was clearly forcing himself to appear 'normal'.

The boy was different. That was the only word that the darkling could think of to describe what she saw. His aura was empty of colours or magic. It was as if someone had drawn a hard line around his shape to separate him from the natural effects of the world.

She watched him climb into the car with the woman and drive away. The boy was an oddity, something she had never seen before, but he wasn't her target.

Winters shook his shoulders and flexed his neck like a wrestler about to engage, intent on the car as it drove off. The darkling wondered if he would dare to use his magic there, out in the workaday world.

Winters shook his head. His shoulders dropped as he released a long breath and then he turned on his heels and marched in the darkling's direction. As his shoes touched her hiding form, she merged with his shadow and was carried along in his haste.

Chapter Eight

"Murdered?" Steve tugged his school tie loose and pulled it from his collar, crumpling it in his hands. "Why didn't you tell me that my uncle was murdered? Do Mum and Dad know? Why didn't Mum tell me?"

"I'm sure your mother would have been informed, but when I spoke to you and it became apparent that you didn't know about the murder, it all seemed such a lot to pile on your shoulders without your parents here."

He stuffed his tie in his blazer pocket and crossed his arms. "I feel so stupid. Everyone at the funeral knew about my uncle's murder except for me." *Something else for Curtis to goad me about,* he thought.

"Please choose a destination," said the Robotic Driving System's smooth voice.

"The Alastor Phobus Academy for Boys via Capital Square, please," said Eleanor. "Steve, I'm sorry." She sighed. "I'm not used to dealing with children."

I'm not a child, he thought, but he stayed silent as the car moved off with a hushed hum.

"Do they know who killed my uncle?" he said after a while.

"No," she said.

"What happened?"

"Rex was found dead in his office."

"And there are no suspects?"

"Not officially," she said.

"What does that mean?"

"The police are looking for Rex's manservant, Abel. He went missing shortly after Rex's body was discovered." She said the word 'body' uncomfortably. "It does strike me as odd that he should go missing."

"So the police think this Abel is the murderer?" Steve had never heard of Rex having a manservant. It seemed an old-fashioned thing to have when the world was filled with robotic assistants.

"That's one theory. The other is that Abel was killed or taken by the murderer."

"What do you think?" Steve uncrossed his arms and looked at her. "Do you think Abel is the murderer?"

"Abel has been in Rex's employ for as long as I've known them. He always seemed very loyal and, to be honest, Abel is so old that I doubt he could hurt a fly, never mind—" She stopped. "But there's no escaping the fact that he's gone, with no explanation."

"We have reached your destination," said the driving system as the car halted. "I do hope it was a pleasant journey."

The door beside Eleanor slid open and a wind-blown spray of rain touched Steve's face.

"Steve, I'm sorry to have to leave you so soon and with this news," she said as she climbed out of the car, "but I have to track down your parents. If I can just find out where your mother flew to…"

"Okay," he snapped, looking away. "Whatever."

"Okay." She smiled as the door began to close. "I'll be in touch."

Steve wrestled off his school blazer as the door shut. He felt like punching something, or someone.

Who else knew about the murder? The teachers? The other pupils? Why hadn't his mum told him? He had too many questions and not enough people to ask for answers. If ever he needed his parents, it was at that moment.

The car moved off. Steve didn't ask for the window glass to be shaded, instead just settling back into the seat and closing his eyes. He needed to get things straight in his head before he returned to school.

*

"We have arrived at your destination, Master Haven."

Steve opened his eyes. "Where are we?"

From his window, he could see a patched-up street that sliced between two derelict terraces. Broken windows gaped with jagged-glass teeth. Doors tottered on their hinges or were blocked with rusted sheets of corrugated metal.

"We have arrived at your destination. Please vacate the vehicle." The door beside him slid open.

"This isn't school."

"This is your destination."

Two men stepped off the crumbling pavement and walked towards the car. One was tall with a cap perched on his bald head. The other was short and round, his head not reaching the taller man's shoulder.

"Close the door and take me to school." Steve slid along the seat away from the open door. "Now."

"This is your destination. Please vacate the vehicle."

"Listen to me: this is the wrong destination. Close the door."

The men reached the car. The shorter one began to climb inside.

"Go!" Steve braced himself against the closed door at his side. "Go now!"

Gloved hands grasped his shirt front and yanked him across the seat. He spilled out onto the road, his shoes scraping on the torn tarmac.

"Have a nice day, Master Haven. Thank you for using Haven Corporation technology." He heard a soft clunk as the door closed behind him, then tyres squealing and juddering on the broken road as the car drove off.

"You're coming with us, boy." His captor threw him onto the ground, forcing Steve into an instinctive roll that tore his shirt sleeves and scuffed his hands.

"I have credits." Steve struggled to his knees and pulled his wallet from his trousers. "You can have them."

"What makes you think we need your credits?" said the short man as he slapped the wallet from Steve's grasp.

"What do you want then?" said Steve. "My phone?" He unwrapped it from his wrist and waved it at them. "Take it."

The taller of the two men snatched the wrap-phone. "Looks

cheap to me," he sneered, dangling it in front of his face. "Are you trying to insult me?" He threw it to the floor and ground it down with his heel.

"Don't give me any trouble, boy." The shorter man grabbed Steve's arm and pulled him to his feet. "You wouldn't like the result."

Their attention was suddenly wrenched away by something behind Steve. "What are you doing here?" The tall thug snarled. "Don't!"

A striking sheet of blue light wiped the scene from Steve's eyes. He heard footsteps running towards him, then his arm was released and he fell back onto the ground.

He lay there, blinded and listening to the ringing in his ears and the cries of his attackers. He flinched as hands touched his chest.

"You are safe now," said a man's voice. The words were reassuring but the tone of the voice was cold.

"Good," said Steve. "Thanks."

"Did they take it?"

"Take what?"

"The Reactor," said the man. "The parcel for your father."

"The metal disc?" Steve's vision was starting to return but the man was still just a dark outline. "It's in my room."

"Good," said the man. "Good."

"Who are you?"

"No time to explain." Steve felt the man's hand on his forehead. "Sleep."

"Wait," he said. "Wait, I—" Whatever Steve had wanted to say was lost as his eyes closed and his mind slipped away to a place of comforting darkness.

Chapter Nine

The smell of sizzling bacon tugged Steve awake. He opened his eyes to see a spider dangling above his face. He batted it away, flapping his hand back-and-forth until he was sure the spider was gone.

Where am I? He sat up and then winced as a river of pain ran down the back of his head. He gritted his teeth and clutched his hand to his scalp. *What did they do to me?* he thought.

He remembered being pulled from the car and dragged across the ground, the broken-up road surface tearing at his skin and the panic rising in his throat like bile. Then there had been that impossibly bright light and the man's voice. What had he said? Steve tried to remember but it was just a jumble in his head.

I need to get back to school. That was the one sure thing he knew. *I need to get out of here and call the police.*

The room was small and windowless. Rolls of fabric filled one end of the space. Cobwebbed pictures of beach scenes and river-slit valleys hung at random angles on the walls. A worn leather armchair sagged in a corner, draped with his clothes, except for his blazer and tie. The only other piece of furniture in the room was the metal-framed bed he lay in.

He reached under the layers of blankets that covered him. Pants. He wriggled his toes. Socks too. Peeling back the covers, he swung his legs over the side of the bed and stood up. The room lurched into stomach-churning action.

He dropped back down and waited for the dizziness to subside. When the room had stopped spinning, he shuffled along the bed, pushing himself along with his feet and glad of his socks on the bare, stone floor. Leaning across to the armchair, he found his wallet in his trousers pocket. He checked the contents. Everything was there, even the photo of his parents.

Once dressed, he made a second attempt at standing. This time, the room remained in one place. He took two paces to the door and grabbed the worn, wooden knob. It refused to turn. He yanked on it and then cringed as the door juddered open with a rasping scrape. He heard voices off to the right. His stomach rumbled as the smell of bacon returned.

He peered out into a long, cluttered, mismatched room. Overflowing shelves laddered the walls from floor to ceiling. Open crates spilled their contents into view: scarves, shoes, balls, boxes and jars. In the middle of it all sat an immense, dark wooden desk and a faded armchair. Light spilled through an uncurtained shop window at the far end of the room, next to which was a door and, in its lock, sat a key.

Got to get out of here, he thought. He took a step. The floorboard beneath his foot creaked.

"Good morning," a deep voice boomed. "How's your head?" The owner of the voice stood in a doorway at the opposite end of the shop from Steve's escape route, wooden spoon in one hand and a floral apron tied around his middle.

The man was tall and round in stature, with a mane of

chestnut hair that flowed down into an impressively full beard. Steve supposed he was in his fifties, from the lines around his eyes, but it was difficult to tell under so much facial hair.

"Eggs?"

"Sorry?" said Steve.

"Would you like eggs with your bacon?" the man said. "I take it you do eat bacon?"

"Yes," said Steve, wondering how much more bizarre the conversation could become. "I eat bacon."

"Good," said the man. "Come on, come on."

Steve followed his host, or captor, through the door at the back of the shop into a ramshackle kitchen. The man went to a smoking stove that looked as if it hadn't been cleaned in a decade and used his wooden spoon to nudge eggs, bacon, and a number of unidentifiable black lumps around a pair of blackened frying pans.

The kitchen was a pickle of different decades, even centuries. The floor was made from worn, deep red, ceramic tiles that had lost the majority of their polished texture. The walls were a mishmash of different wallpapers, some visible through holes in the top layer, each design clashing with the colour of its neighbour. The furniture was all freestanding. Two tall, badly painted wooden dressers—one deep blue, the other a garish yellow—faced each other from opposing sides of the room. A reasonably modern chest of drawers—it reminded Steve of his bedroom furniture when he was very little—made from plastic but with a faux woodgrain surface sat between a doorway and a staircase that led up and out of sight. Heavy, faded, velvet, full-length curtains hid two further doorways.

Light filtered down from a window in the ceiling, which oddly looked as if a normal window frame had been mistakenly fitted into the roof.

At a large, carved table that dominated the kitchen, a girl around Steve's age leant over a leather-bound book, her pale blonde hair trailing in front of her face and onto the pages.

"Hi." The girl pushed her hair behind her ears, flicked her eyes up to him with a smile, then returned to her book.

"Hi." Steve felt his body relax at the girl's smile. She didn't look like a kidnapper.

"Here we are." The man slapped a fried egg onto a plate, draping it with two crispy rashers of bacon and some of the black lumps. "Sit down, sit down." He put the plate on the table. "Tea? Milk?"

"Okay." Steve sat. He eyed the food which swam happily in a sea of grease. It didn't look very healthy, but the smell of the bacon hovered teasingly in the air.

"Sugar?"

"Erm, no, thanks."

"That's good because we've run out. I have honey."

"No, thanks."

"Just as it comes," said the man.

"I don't mean to sound ungrateful," said Steve as the man began to fill a teapot, "but who are you?"

"Oh, of course. Introductions." The man removed his apron with a flourish and flung it over a hat stand. He wiped his hand on his trousers and offered it to Steve. "My name is Hartley Keg. I am most honoured to make your acquaintance. And what about you? What's your name?"

"I'm Steve." He took Hartley's hand. The man's grasp was crushing but brief. "Haven."

"Glad to meet you, Master Haven."

"Steve is fine."

The girl made a small 'uhuh' sound in her throat, raising her eyebrows at Hartley.

"And this is Blessing," he said. "The bossy one."

"Very funny." She rolled her eyes at him and returned to her book.

"How long was I… You know?" asked Steve.

"You've been out cold for almost a day," said Hartley. "I thought you'd be safe here while you slept off your injuries."

"And where is here?" said Steve.

"Well, we're in the old town," said Hartley as he set a plate of food before the girl. "Darkacre."

"I don't know where that is," said Steve. "Is it outside the city? I've never been outside the city."

"We're still in the city," said Blessing. Her voice was gentle but awkward, as if she was unsure of what words to use. "Kind of." She pushed the plate aside and carried on reading.

"How did I get here?" Steve's stomach rumbled, begging him to eat, but the thought of escape still tugged at his nerves.

"A friend of ours brought you," said Hartley.

"Did you call the police? I was attacked," said Steve. "School will want to know where I am. And Eleanor. What's the name of the man who brought me here?"

"Tuck in." Hartley splashed a mug of tea down in front of Steve. "The police don't come into the old town. Our friend said you had no broken bones. Your attackers ran away. We thought, once you woke up, you'd tell us who to contact." Hartley tapped Blessing on the shoulder. "Why don't you put down the book and eat your food?" he said. "It'll go cold."

"I can't eat that," she said. "It's burnt."

"Only some of it." Hartley went to the stove and piled up a plate of food. "Anyway, my grandmother used to regularly eat coal." He joined them at the table. "It never did her any harm."

"Do people eat coal?" said Blessing.

"Would I lie to you?" Hartley grinned at her. "Now, eat your food."

"Okay." She closed the book and pushed it aside. "But you can have the black bits."

Steve's stomach groaned again. The smell of the food hung above the table, inviting him to indulge.

*

"What is this place?" he asked after a couple of mouthfuls. He had identified the black lumps as having once been mushrooms.

"My shop," said Hartley. "I sell antiques, memorabilia, odds-and-ends. Whatever people want. I like to surround myself with history."

"Like books and stuff?"

"Books?" A drip of egg travelled down Hartley's beard. "Well, I enjoy a good adventure story as much as the next person, but history books are simply someone's opinion of what happened. These things, the paraphernalia of people's lives, *these* are the true history. Take this table, for instance. If you were to sit underneath it, you would see a number of initials rudely carved into the underside. Who knows who made them? A king hiding from an assassin? A family sheltering from a bomb raid? It's things like that, the marks that people leave behind, that

61

interest me. Not the words of some scholar or military dictator."

"My teachers would disagree with you," said Steve, attempting to stab one of the charred mushrooms.

"As I said, scholars," mumbled Hartley. "So now you're awake and fed, who should we contact? What about this Eleanor?"

"It's okay, I'll call her." Steve reached for his wrap-phone but found only his bare wrist. He shook his head. "I forgot."

"Anything important?" said Hartley.

"I lost my phone in the attack. Can I use yours?"

"I would be more than happy to oblige," said Hartley, wiping his plate with a thin slice of bread. "If I had a telephone."

"You don't have a phone? Seriously?" *Who doesn't have a phone?* thought Steve.

"Never felt the need for one. If I want to talk to someone, I pay them a visit."

"How am I supposed to get home?"

"Walk," said Blessing with a grin.

"Is there an underground station near here?" said Steve. "I have a travel pass."

"No," said Hartley. "You'll just have to go by your own steam."

"We can come with you," said Blessing, pushing her empty plate to one side. "I wouldn't mind."

"I would," said Hartley. "You have school."

"School is dull." She pushed back her chair and carried her plate to the sink. "I never get to go anywhere."

"There's a reason for that," said Hartley. "Fear not, Steve. I'll take you back." Hartley licked his fingers, wiped his hands on the tablecloth, and grabbed a faded tweed jacket from the hat stand. "It's the least I can do after subjecting you to my cooking."

Chapter Ten

"Why aren't we going out the front door?"

Steve stood beside Hartley in front of a curtained-off section of the kitchen. In place of his blazer he was wearing a long woollen cardigan that Hartley had lent him. After relaxing over breakfast, he was starting to get suspicious again.

"Because that way won't take us where we want to go," said Hartley. "This one will." He pulled back the curtain to reveal a tall, battered, rusting iron door. "See?"

No, thought Steve. *I don't see.* "That looks like it hasn't been opened in years."

"Admittedly, it's been a while." Hartley rubbed his chin through his beard. "Now then." He touched a hand to the door frame. "If I can just remember how to do this."

Open a door? thought Steve. *He obviously doesn't get out much.*

"Ah, yes." Hartley grabbed the door handle and pulled. The door squealed open, raising a draught as it slammed back against the wall. "Here we are," said Hartley, indicating the open door with his hands spread in a 'ta da' gesture.

Steve peered through the doorway into a large, bustling department store. Robot retail assistants sped around the store, carrying merchandise back-and-forth between customers. Steve looked back into the kitchen behind him. *How?* he thought.

"Welcome to Sebastian Green and Sons," said Hartley, pulling him into the store. "The gentlemen's attire department, to be exact." He closed the door behind them. "Do you know it?"

"This store is in the city centre, isn't it?" Steve watched the customers bustle around the clothing displays. "I thought your shop was in the old town." *Wherever that is.*

"Really?" said Hartley. "Well, it's quite simple. My shop backs onto this place. I don't use the back door very often, but I must admit that it's a very useful short-cut. Now, if I recall correctly, the main exit is in this direction. Shall we?"

Steve followed Hartley as he sped off, dodging between the displays and customers.

"Almost there," called Hartley as the space opened out into a polished foyer and the pillared entrance of the store. "Here we are." The automated doors slid aside for Hartley. "Not far now."

Steve shivered as he stepped out into the morning cool of the city air. Crowds of smartly-dressed pedestrians passed around the two of them as Hartley, an unkempt, mis-matched vision in tweed by comparison, looked up and down the street. Steve stuffed his hands into the pockets of the cardigan and tried not to catch anyone's eye.

"This way," said Hartley. "If I can get you to the City Centre Plaza, you'll be able to use a public phone there."

In what century? thought Steve. "I don't think there'll be one of those. Everyone has wrap-phones these days." He rubbed his bare wrist. "Unless you lose it, of course."

"And what do you do in that case?" said Hartley. "If you lose your phone?"

Steve had to think hard about that one. He wanted to say 'buy a new one' but that obviously wasn't an option at that moment. Then, he remembered.

"You can use a police communications unit," he said. "They're dotted around the city on street corners."

"Ah, the police," said Hartley, eyes widening. "Well, I don't think we need to involve them."

"Mind yourself." Steve pulled Hartley aside as a small robot struggled down the centre of the pavement, pulled equally ahead and back by the four dogs it held the leads to.

"Is that normal?" said Hartley.

"Of course. That's the kind of job robots do. Walk the dog. Serve in a shop. Clean up."

"So what do people do?"

"Everything else, I suppose," said Steve. "Or nothing."

"Sounds peculiar to me," said Hartley, still watching the robot as it untangled one of its limbs from the dogs' leads. "Where's the fun in having a dog and not walking it?"

"I don't know," said Steve. "I've never had a dog, or a pet. Mum and Dad said it would be unkind because they're away so much."

"And why are they away so much?" said Hartley. "Adventures? Holidays?"

"Just work," said Steve.

"Ah," said Hartley. "That."

The retail and eateries district that the department store sat in was a grid of mismatched shop fronts. The stores were split into three main types.

There were the older stores, like Sebastian Green and Sons with their faux-old pillars and marble-floored entrances, that attempted to mimic old world prestige. They sold the type of item that needed to be seen before purchase. It was also the kind of item that only the richest could afford, from rhodium jewellery to the latest solar sports car and the rarest of plants.

Dotted in between the shop fronts were the pick-up pods that varied in size depending on exactly what you were collecting. The largest pick-up pod that Steve had ever seen was one that supplied cars. Scan your identity from your wrap-phone, the door opens, and away you go.

"Surely that isn't edible?" Hartley pressed his face against the window of an eatery, the third type of store in the district.

A conveyor belt of food-filled glass plates travelled around the eatery counter. At one end of the belt, waiter robots recovered the plates to serve to the waiting customers. At the other, the nozzles of the 3D food printer moved speedily around each plate, forming the pre-ordered food.

"That's the advantage of synthetic food," said Steve. "You can form it into any shape you want, and it's fast."

"Ludicrous," said Hartley, shaking his head as he stepped back from the window. "There's not enough on one of those plates to touch the sides."

"So, have you lived in Darkacre a long time?" Steve asked as they walked on.

"Sometimes it seems like forever," said Hartley, "but there were other lifetimes before that, in other places. Still, Darkacre suits me fine for now."

"And Blessing is your granddaughter?"

"No, no, no," said Hartley.

"Daughter?" said Steve.

"No," said Hartley. "She's an, err...err..." He paused, frowning. "Orphan? Blessing had no family, so I took her in."

"That was good of you." To Steve, Hartley had the look of a friendly, if disorganised, uncle. Taking in an orphan seemed like the kind of thing a friendly uncle would do.

"So who is this Eleanor you spoke of?" said Hartley. "Not your mother?"

"She's my uncle's PA," said Steve. "I mean, she was his PA, before he died."

"I'm so sorry to hear that," said Hartley. "How did your parents take it?"

"No idea," said Steve. "They're away." He wanted to say *missing* but 'away' felt better.

"Did you get on with your uncle?"

"I didn't really know him," said Steve. "I think we met when I was little." He shrugged. "Or maybe Mum just told me that."

"When did he die?" said Hartley as they turned a corner.

"Last week," said Steve. "I didn't want to go to the funeral." *Massive understatement,* he thought.

"But you went anyway, as a sign of respect."

"I'm not sure respect came into it. Eleanor made me go even though Mum and Dad weren't there."

"I see," said Hartley. "How was it?"

"Big. Expensive. Filled with people who worked for Rex." *People I didn't know,* he thought.

"Rex Haven?" Hartley stopped. "Why is that name familiar? Hmm." He shook his head. "It'll come to me, I'm sure."

Wow, thought Steve. *Someone who doesn't know who my uncle is. That's a new one.*

"And your parents are away on holiday?" said Hartley.

"Dad's working on the Continent. Mum went looking for him."

"It's a shame they missed the funeral."

"I'm not sure Dad would agree with you. He and Rex didn't get on."

"That's unfortunate," said Hartley. "I always think that family should mean something, but look at me. Still a bachelor. Still on my own."

"Except for Blessing," said Steve.

"Oh yes, except for Blessing." Hartley stopped as the paving of the walkway met the polished granite of the City Centre Plaza. Even on a dull day like that, the Plaza gleamed with its sleek metal edges and quartz flecked stone. "Here we are."

"Hartley—"

"Look, there's the sign for the underground train station."

"Hartley, my uncle was murdered," said Steve.

"I see," said Hartley after a moment.

"I found out at the funeral. I don't think I was meant to know. I can't reach Mum and Dad. They've dumped me at school again." The words flooded from his mouth, all at once, unstoppable. "I've been attacked by two men who seemed intent on hurting me. Eleanor is well-meaning but a stranger. I'll have to explain to Miss Scritch why I've been away from school. I'm bound to get detention. It's all a mess." He stopped, drawing in a sudden breath.

It began to rain, a light refreshing spray that coated Steve's eyelashes.

"A mess is as good a place as any to start," said Hartley. "It can only get tidier from there." He graced Steve with a grin. "Perhaps we could inquire about the whereabouts of the nearest police comm thingy. There are plenty of people about."

"No, I can get the underground from here," said Steve. "It'll be easier than explaining to Miss Scritch over the phone."

"The underground." Hartley grinned. "Do you mind if I tag along? I haven't been on a train in ages." Hartley patted his pockets, reached inside his jacket and pulled out a pile of ragged paper slips. "I have a pass somewhere."

"Never mind." A rivulet of rain ran down the back of Steve's neck. "I'll pay."

*

"You know, I can't recall the last time I travelled on the underground." Hartley sat across two train seats with his hands folded over his belly. "I'd forgotten the excitement."

The woman who sat in the neighbouring seat attempted to ignore him as she dictated to her secretary robot. Every time Hartley spoke, she made a sharp intake of breath through her nose and moved a little further away as if Hartley's very existence was a bad smell.

"Excitement?" Steve looked up and down the carriage. None of the passengers met his gaze. All of them concentrated on their wrap-phones or were lost in their own thoughts. "Really?"

"There's something very companionable about a carriage full of passengers," Hartley continued. "Sharing the adventure, together. I daresay many an interesting conversation arises out of such an intimate environment." He leaned towards his neighbour and glanced over her shoulder. "Am I right?"

"Actually." Steve leant forward and lowered his voice. "Passengers on the underground don't normally talk to each other. It's probably best if we keep ourselves to ourselves."

"Oh. That's a shame." Hartley looked a little deflated, eyebrows knitting into a frown. "I hope I haven't broken any rules."

The train shushed to a halt. The windows slid from dark mirrors into a grey panorama of hurrying passengers and robot train workers. The station walls flickered between animated advertisements.

The woman and her robot departed without a backward glance, the woman still dictating to the robot which scurried after her like a pet.

"She was pleasant," said Hartley, waving through the window at the woman.

"Really?" said Steve. *Even though she was doing her best to ignore you?* he thought. *You've either got a very thick skin or you have a subtle way with sarcasm.*

The train moved off again and Steve sank back into his seat. His reflection, tattered and miserable, glowered at him from the dark glass.

*

Steve stared at his feet as he climbed the stone steps up to street level. Hartley walked beside him, his shoulder bumping Steve's arm occasionally as the crowd climbed with them. He was still talking, still cheerful, and still enjoying his adventure.

"I don't often get the chance to visit the city," he said. "Always seems so busy. Everyone rushing around with their eyes on the

71

ground."

"Well, here we are." Steve forced a smile as he stepped out onto the pavement. The crowd from the underground station dispersed around them in all directions. "My school isn't far. Thanks for getting me back safely."

"I can't just leave you here," said Hartley. "Who knows what might happen to a boy out in the city on his own? Now, where are we going?"

"Over there." Steve pointed to the gates of the Alastor Phobus Academy for Boys, across the road from where they stood. "Like I said, not far."

Hartley let out a slow whistle and raced across the road, narrowly missing a solar taxi. "That is—what's the word?—prestigious," he said as Steve caught up with him.

"I suppose it is."

"Would it be at all inappropriate of me to comment that it reminds me of a prison, though?" said Hartley.

"Not at all," said Steve, smiling. "It reminds me of a prison too. Feels like one."

"And this Miss Scritch is the prison warden?"

"She's the headmaster's secretary," said Steve. "Although 'prison warden' would be a better fit. I don't think she likes children very much." Steve brushed his hair off his face and straightened his collar. "I'd best go in. Hartley—"

"Don't worry about me, Steve." He felt Hartley's hand on his shoulder. "I'll find my own way. Now, you have to find yours and people like me can be easy to forget."

Steve took a deep breath, readying himself to step through the gates, but instead he turned to the shopkeeper. "Hartley, can you come in with me?" he asked. "I think I might need some help explaining."

But Hartley had gone.

Chapter Eleven

"This is unacceptable."

The two guard robots who had escorted Steve from the school gates waited on either side of him as he stood before the headmaster's desk. Each robot stood upright on four of their eight limbs, easily a foot taller than Steve. One of them scanned his body with a small device that looked like an illuminated hairdryer and which blipped at the end of each sweep. Steve wasn't entirely sure what it was looking for.

"Absent from school overnight," said Mr Hendrickson.

"Without permission," piped up Miss Scritch who glowered at him from her seat beside the headmaster.

"Without permission," said the headmaster. "What have you got to say for yourself, Haven?"

"It's not my fault," said Steve. "I was attacked."

"Attacked?" said Mr Hendrickson. "What do you mean 'attacked'?"

"After the funeral, the car didn't bring me back to school. It took me somewhere else and I was attacked." He waited for the headmaster's face to show some sign of concern. "There were two of them, two men. They—"

"You're lying," said Miss Scritch. "The car brought you back to the school gates and then you ran off."

"I'm not lying," said Steve, looking to Mr Hendrickson for help. "Sir, I'm telling you the truth."

"We checked with the Haven Corporation. The car returned you to the school gates," said Mr Hendrickson. "What was the name of the person you spoke to, Miss Scritch?"

"Winters," she said. "He was very worried about Haven's absence."

"That isn't what happened," said Steve. "Why would the car drop me off at the gates and not return me to the school building? That doesn't make sense."

"Well, I don't know." The headmaster's angry face slipped for the first time since Steve had entered his office. "Do we know why that was, Miss Scritch?"

"No, but surely that doesn't matter," she spluttered. "Haven ran away from school."

"I did not run away from school." Steve tried to stop himself from shouting. "I was attacked. They beat me and threatened me. I thought I was going to die."

"Yesterday?" said Miss Scritch.

"Yes," snapped Steve.

"Then where are your injuries?" She crossed the room and grabbed his arm, pulling back the sleeve of his cardigan. "I don't see any scratches." She grabbed his chin, digging her fingers into his skin. "Your face is fine."

"It can't be." Steve pulled away from her. "I hurt my hands." He held them out. His palms were smooth and unharmed. "I don't understand. I was bleeding." He unfastened the buttons on his cuff and rolled up his sleeve. There should have been bruises and scrapes, but the skin was perfectly intact.

"And where is your blazer?" said Mr Hendrickson. "And your tie? How do you expect to represent the school in such shabby attire?"

"He leant this to me."

"Who?" said Mr Hendrickson. "Your supposed attackers?"

"No, the man who looked after me. He gave me breakfast." He remembered the smell of bacon and touched a hand to the back of his head where it had hurt when he'd woken up. "He brought me back here."

"Who is this man?" said the headmaster. "Tell me his name."

"He's called…" Steve stopped. *What was his name?* "I can't remember."

"Insolence," said Miss Scritch, pointing a finger at him. "That's what this is, Mr Hendrickson. Plain out-and-out insolence."

"I can see that for myself, Miss Scritch," said the headmaster.

"Of course, you can, Mr Hendrickson," she said, returning to her chair, then, "He'll have to be punished."

"I honestly can't remember," said Steve, feeling his face redden. He knew that tears were on the way and he desperately wanted to leave the room before anyone saw him cry. "I'm not lying."

"Detention," said the headmaster. "You'll spend all of your spare time in detention until you tell me the truth. Is that understood?"

"Yes, sir." Steve bowed his head and nodded.

"Now, go clean yourself up and get to afternoon classes."

"Yes, sir."

"But not in that atrocity." The headmaster pointed to the cardigan. "Miss Scritch will find you a replacement blazer for the time being."

"Yes, sir." Steve wanted the headmaster's tirade to be over so he could go to his room and scream. Of course, he wouldn't scream but slamming his door at least would help.

"And there'll be no lunch for you today, Haven. You can eat in your room after classes are finished for the day."

"Yes, sir."

"Now, get out of my sight."

"Yes, sir."

Steve left the room with the guard robots on either side of him. Jon stood a couple of doors down. He raised a hand and smiled as Steve walked past him. Steve shook his head at his friend and rushed by, eyes fixed on his shoes.

Behind him, he heard the headmaster's office door slam shut and Miss Scritch's voice. "Haven't you got a class to go to, Shaw?"

Prison again, he thought. *I wish I'd never come back.*

*

The blazer that Miss Scritch found for Steve smelt of mould and didn't button up. He decided that it was best if he didn't put his hands in the pockets.

It's not so bad, he thought, trying to keep calm. *I can take it off in class and Mum and Dad can buy me a new one when they come home.*

77

Then it hit him. He had no idea when his parents would come home. A voice niggled at the back of his mind. *If they come home,* it said.

He sat down on his bed and wiped his eyes. Once the guard robots had gone, the tears had come. He'd cried into his pillow so no one could hear him. The last thing he wanted was Curtis or one of his cronies having a go about him being a cry-baby.

The heel of his shoe tapped on something metallic. Half-hidden under his bed was the metal disc that had been left at the school for his dad.

He retrieved it and held it up to the light.

Something tugged at his memory. The disc had a name, but he couldn't remember what it was.

There was a polite tap on his door.

Steve tucked the disc under his bed covers. "Come in."

"Hi." Jon opened the door a little and peered through the gap. "Can I come in?"

"Sure." Steve tried to smile at his friend. "Sorry about before. I couldn't really talk."

"That's okay." Jon stepped inside and closed the door behind him. "Are you all right?"

"I'm fine," said Steve, except he didn't feel anywhere near fine. "You?"

"I was worried." Jon shrugged. "When you didn't come back from the funeral, I thought you'd gone home with your Mum and Dad and then, after tea, Miss Scritch went round asking everyone if they'd seen you."

"I suppose they called the police." The thought popped into Steve's brain that he'd have to go through the same interrogation with the police. Maybe they'd go easier on him than Miss

Scritch.

"No police," said Jon.

"They lose a pupil and they don't call the police?" said Steve. "I feel so loved."

"You know what the headmaster is like. Anything to preserve the school's reputation."

"Well, that's all right then," said Steve. "As long as the school's reputation is unharmed."

"So, where were you?"

"It's complicated," said Steve. *Except it isn't,* he thought. *My stupid brain just won't let me remember, that's all.*

"Complicated, how?"

"I was attacked. After the funeral."

"Who attacked you?" Jon sat on the bed beside Steve. "Are you injured? Should we call a doctor?"

"No, I'm fine," said Steve, looking at his palms. "Except—" He stopped.

"Except what?"

"Except." *Here goes,* thought Steve. "Except I can't remember anything that happened after that, until I walked back into school."

"Really?" said Jon. "Are you sure?"

"I shouldn't have said anything." Steve crossed his arms, then uncrossed them as the stitching on the back of the blazer complained. "Nobody believes me."

"It's not that," said Jon. "It's just odd, don't you think? Not remembering."

"'Odd' doesn't cover it."

"Maybe you're concussed," said Jon. "You said you were

attacked. Did you get hit on the head?"

"Maybe," said Steve.

"That must be it," said Jon. "Do you have a headache?"

"No." He touched the back of his head. "I think I did when I woke up though."

"I thought you didn't remember anything."

"There are bits," said Steve. "I remember eating bacon and eggs and burnt mushrooms. There was a girl."

"Was she pretty?"

"I don't remember. It's all really fuzzy," said Steve, rubbing his head.

"Do you want to see a medic robot?" said Jon, standing up. "We have time before next class."

"No, I feel fine," said Steve. "I just want to get back to normal."

"Fair enough," said Jon. "The head has banned you from lunch."

"News travels fast in school," said Steve, wondering what else the school knew about his disappearance.

"I heard Miss Scritch telling one of the teachers, so I brought you something." He pulled a chocolate bar and a packet of crisps from his blazer pocket. "I know it's not nutritionally correct, but it'll keep you going until tea."

"You're a star," said Steve. "Anything happened while I've been away, other than me riling the head?"

"No, you were the sole entertainment."

The end-of-lunch bell rang. Steve tucked the crisps and the chocolate under his pillow. Grabbing his bag, he followed his friend out of the room.

Chapter Twelve

The Artisan District was arranged throughout a globe shaped, multi-floored building that surrounded an inner courtyard, designed visually and acoustically to suit musical performances. The lack of visible steel in the construct of the building, the intricate lighting system, and the glass walls meant that the district was constantly bathed in light, whether natural or man-made.

There were relatively few robots in the Artisan District. A handful kept the building clean and secure, but this was a place to exhibit human creativity at its best.

For those with the necessary wealth, the district could provide art pieces, clothing and furniture with the guarantee that they were not only handcrafted by a human but also unique, one-off items.

The darkling had always avoided the place and its constant light. There was too much empty space and too few unlit areas to allow her to prowl safely. She was forced to take her solid shape as she followed Winters through the glittering hallways to the central courtyard.

That day the courtyard was empty of performers, the music replaced by the sound of a stylised waterfall which flowed from an upper balcony to disappear into the floor below.

Winters waited on the edge of the courtyard in the shelter of a doorway, his hands shoved into the pockets of his expensive coat. He stared at the ground, jerking his head up every time someone entered the space, then dropping his eyes when he didn't recognise them. The pace of his tapping foot increased as time passed.

A bejewelled vendor, hair bound into blonde dreadlocks, offered him an arm of beaded necklaces. Winters shook his head and the vendor moved on.

Winters drew back his sleeve to look at his wrap-phone, cursed, and then slunk away to join the anonymous crowds in the hallways. The darkling followed, keeping him in sight the whole time.

As Winters reached the exit, a gloved hand tapped him on the shoulder.

"No need to panic," said Kendra as Winters turned to him with a snarl.

The darkling recoiled as she recognised the suited man from the museum. She had destroyed his device, but it might not have been the only one he had. What if he had tracked her again?

"Where have you been?" Winters snapped. "You're late."

"Making sure you weren't followed," said Kendra. "Shall we take a stroll?"

"So?" asked Winters as they walked. "Is it done?"

"Done," said Kendra, "is such a vague term."

"Answer the question."

"The boy was delivered to us, as planned," said Kendra, stopping at the window of a ceramics sculptor. "There were, however, complications. Someone interfered."

"Who?"

"An associate of yours," said Kendra. "The old man's servant rescued the boy."

"Abel?" Winters snapped. "You couldn't handle one old man?"

"He's not just an old man."

"I gave you a simple job. Kidnap a spoilt brat—"

"Keep your voice down."

"Kidnap a spoilt brat," Winters hissed, "and bring him to me. Two thugs against a schoolboy and an old man. What could be simpler?"

"If we'd known of the possible involvement of this Abel—"

"You'll have to try again," said Winters. "Where is the boy now?"

"He returned to school," said Kendra. "Eventually. I do have a morsel of good news, however. When my men were accosted by Abel—"

"You mean, when they were running away."

"When they were accosted," Kendra continued, "they overheard Abel's exchange with the boy. It appears that the Reactor is at the school. We may be able to kill two birds with the one stone."

"So get on with it."

"It's already in hand," said Kendra. "We'll have them both very soon."

"I won't tolerate a second failure."

"Don't threaten me, Winters. It isn't polite and it's hardly good for business."

"You work for me."

"For now," said Kendra. "While this arrangement suits me."

"*I'll* say when this arrangement comes to an end." Winters stepped closer to Kendra and stabbed a finger at the suited man's chest. "Not you."

"I could finish you in an instant," said Kendra, batting Winters's hand away. "You know what I can do."

"Likewise," said Winters. "You may scare all the little magicals who work for you, but you don't scare me."

The darkling watched as the auras of the two men rose and spread, engulfing the oblivious people around them. The red of Winters's aura and the emerald black of Kendra's snapped at each other like jackals ready to strike.

"I have work to do." Kendra's aura dissipated as he stepped back. "I've no time for this posturing. I'll be in touch."

"You'd better." Winters called after him as Kendra walked away. "Do you hear me?"

With a last glance at the simmering Winters, the darkling flowed away in pursuit of Kendra.

Chapter Thirteen

Steve sat in the middle of the empty canteen, cradling a mug of hot chocolate in his hands. With nobody around he hadn't bothered to get dressed, wearing just his pyjamas and slippers.

Saturday had taken an eternity to arrive, or so it had seemed to Steve. His evening meal had been spent in his room. A guard robot had escorted him to all his lessons and back again, standing guard at the door to his room. Even Jon had been prevented from visiting him.

When he dared to open his door that morning, the school building was quiet and the robot was gone. He supposed he was already 'old news'.

He watched a janitorial robot as it busied itself with cleaning the tabletops. The canteen robots had been his only company so far that day.

He finished his drink, returned the mug to the serving hatch it had come from, and then perched himself on the edge of the counter.

What now? Get my story straight about why I didn't come

straight back to school?

The problem was that the more he tried to remember it all, the more blurred his memories became and the less he understood. It was like someone had messed with his memory. Why had the car taken him to the wrong place? Why had he been attacked? Who had rescued him?

What a mess, he thought.

A mess is as good a place to start as any. It can only get tidier from there.

"Well, here you are." Eleanor marched across the canteen, her high heels tap-tapping on the hard floor. "This place is like a wasteland. Where are the staff?"

"It's the weekend," said Steve. "They're either at home or in the dorm wing. It's good to see you."

"Is it? That's nice." She forced a smile for a second, then frowned. "Sorry I haven't been in touch since the funeral. I've been desperately trying to track down your parents. No luck so far though."

"So, you don't know."

"Know what? Have you heard from them?"

"No, not that. I mean you don't know that I was missing."

"Missing what?"

"Me," he said. "I was missing."

"I don't understand."

"After the funeral, after you left me, the car didn't bring me back to school."

"Yes, it did," she said. "I checked the records to make sure you'd got back safely."

"The records are wrong. The car took me to some backstreet

86

somewhere. I don't know where. I was attacked."

"Look, Steve. I appreciate that this is a difficult situation for you, what with Rex's death and your parents' absence, but there's no need to act up."

"I'm not acting up," he snapped. "I'm trying to tell you what happened."

"Not in that tone of voice, you're not."

"Sorry," he said quietly. "I just thought you might believe me. Nobody else does."

"You're seriously saying you were attacked?" She raised an eyebrow. "You're not lying to me?"

"Honestly, I'm not."

"But you look fine." She looked him up and down. "I can't see any bruises."

"There aren't any," he admitted. "I don't know how but I healed. While I was away."

"Away where?" She placed her handbag on the nearest table and sat down.

"Here we go." He sighed and sat down opposite her. "I can't remember."

"What do you mean you can't remember?"

"I can remember bits, but—" He stopped, realising how unlikely his story seemed, even to him.

"Start at the beginning. The car took you somewhere other than school."

"Yes, to some derelict street. The car said I had reached my destination and opened the door. I told it that it was wrong, but it just kept saying I should get out."

"And the attack?"

"I'm coming to that," he said. "There were two men: one tall, one short. They dragged me out of the car."

"For what reason?"

"I don't know." Steve ran a hand through his hair and shook his head. "They didn't say. They just hurt me. Then there was this bright light."

"What kind of light?"

"Just a light." He tried to keep his voice calm, but he could feel his stomach and his jaw tensing up. "It blinded me, for a minute, then a man said I was safe."

"He rescued you."

"I suppose so. My eyes weren't working properly after the light so I couldn't see him. I'd know his voice again if I heard it."

"What did he say, this man?" Eleanor still looked suspicious of Steve's story but at least she was listening. Nobody else had listened.

"He asked if I had something. I can't remember what he called it. There's a lot I can't remember."

"You're not making sense, Steve."

"It arrived the same day as I came back to school. There was a note with it saying that it was for Dad. I can show you." Steve stood up, realising he could at least prove that part of his story. "It's in my room. Come on."

Chapter Fourteen

"It's a metal disc." Steve marched ahead of Eleanor. "The size of one of those old fob watches."

"Steve, will you please slow down." Eleanor hurried along behind him. "I can't walk fast in these heels."

They turned a corner as the sound of a slamming door echoed along the hallway. At the end of the corridor, the old man Steve had seen in the school courtyard held a door shut with one hand. His other hand was pressed to the door's keycard panel and, if Steve's eyes weren't mistaken, there was black smoke coming from the old man's hands.

"That's my room," said Steve.

"Run!" the old man shouted.

"Abel, what are you doing here?" said Eleanor. "Where have you been?"

"Run!" Abel shouted again, launching himself towards them in a shambolic, staggering gait. "That won't hold them for long."

Steve felt Eleanor grab his arm, pulling him as she shouted his name. *Slow motion*, he thought. *So this is what it feels like.*

As the old man reached them, the door to Steve's room slammed open. The two men who had attacked him only a couple of days before burst from his room.

"No." Steve stumbled back. "Not again."

The shorter one glared at Steve, eyes widening. He pointed a ring-clad hand and shouted, "That's the boy."

"Come on, come on." Abel grabbed Steve, pushing him on. "No time for gawping."

"But those men—"

"Later." The old man flipped Steve around, pushing him and Eleanor down the corridor.

"Abel." Eleanor called back at him as she ran. "Where have you been?"

"Not now. Down here." He dragged the two of them round a corner. "This way."

"Abel, I demand to know where you're taking us," Eleanor snapped.

"I don't know," he wheezed. "We need somewhere secure."

"There's the headmaster's office," said Steve. "It has a lock."

"Good, good. Lead on." Abel pushed them ahead of him.

"We have to go up," said Steve as they reached the entrance hall.

"Hang on." Eleanor slipped off her shoes. "That's better."

"There they are." The two men skidded into the entrance hall as Steve and the others dashed up the winding wooden staircase.

"We need to call the police!" Without her shoes on, Eleanor could run surprisingly fast, reaching the headmaster's office before the others. "It's locked," she squealed, pushing on the closed door.

"No problem," said Steve, jabbing numbers into the keypad. "I know the code. Not supposed to but I seem to be in here a lot."

The door sprang open and Abel pushed them all inside, slamming it behind them. There was the sound of a heavy lock clunking into place.

"That should keep them out," he said, backing away from the door.

Almost immediately, the door shook and buckled with a resounding crack as the two attackers collided with the other side of it. Steve heard them curse, then they began to hammer on the door.

"You think?" gasped Steve.

"Give it up, old man," one of the men shouted from the other side of the door. "That's all we want."

"Yeah," shouted the other. "Give us the Reactor and we'll let you all go. Honest."

"You don't believe them, do you?" said Steve.

"Of course not." Abel pulled a lamp table across the door. "I'm not stupid."

"Abel, who are those men?" Eleanor demanded.

"They're the ones who attacked me," said Steve.

"They are?" said Eleanor. "That *actually* happened?"

"They are. It did," said Abel. "I have the Reactor." He pulled the disc from his pocket. "It's safe. Just need to keep us safe too."

"See," said Steve, scowling at Eleanor. "Why does nobody ever believe kids?"

"Well." Eleanor gawped at him, then collected herself. "We should call the police."

"No time," said Abel, pocketing the Reactor as the door splintered and buckled under another blow from the men outside.

"We have to get out of this room," said Steve.

"Working on it." Abel reached into the other pocket of his coat and pulled out a piece of purple chalk.

"What are you going to do with that?" said Steve. "Doodle them to death?"

"Ah, sarcasm," said Abel as he ran to an open door in the corner of the room. "Just like Rex."

"That's a cupboard," said Steve.

"It'll do," said Abel as he closed the door on the headmaster's stationery stock.

He drew a line of chalk up one side of the door frame, across the top, and down the other side.

"What are you doing?" shrieked Eleanor as the door buckled again.

"Not long now. Here." He threw the chalk to Steve. "You might need this." He pressed an ear to the door.

With a splintering wrench, the door to the headmaster's office flung open, sending the lamp table scuttling to the floor. The taller of the two attackers fell through, landing on his knees. His companion stood on the other side of the door, wheezing.

"We have you now," said the taller one as he climbed to his feet.

Eleanor grabbed one of the headmaster's prized porcelain figurines from a shelf. "Get out of here before I call the police. I'm not scared to use this," she said, shaking the figurine at him.

"Please be in," said Abel as he knocked on the cupboard door.

"Get away from there," said the shorter attacker. "I'm warning you."

Abel grabbed Steve's arm and pushed him towards the cupboard as its door opened. The smell of burnt bacon and strong coffee caught in Steve's nostrils as he was dragged into the cupboard.

Through the open door, he watched the attackers grab Abel while Eleanor swiped at them with the figurine and her handbag, shrieking like a banshee. Then the door slammed shut.

Chapter Fifteen

Steve stood in the middle of Hartley Keg's kitchen.

"How?"

"I can explain," said Hartley. "Abel—"

"Eleanor." Steve span around and almost collided with the old rusty door that he had left Hartley's shop through a few days before. He grabbed the door handle and pulled. "The men who attacked me. They'll hurt Eleanor."

"Don't worry. Abel will see them off."

"Why won't this open?" Steve tugged on the handle, but the door remained decidedly shut. "Is there a key?"

"Steve."

"Unlock it."

"Steve."

"I need to save her."

"Steve, listen to me." Hartley grabbed Steve's wrists and pulled him away from the door. "Abel will save her. Just like he saved you."

"What?" Steve snatched his wrists free and pushed Hartley away. "Open the door."

"I can't. The travelling chalk spell only works one way, and I've no idea where you came from. If I haven't been to a place before, I won't be able to travel you there anyway."

"What are you talking about?"

"I'm a traveller."

"Like a gipsy?"

"Look." Hartley ran a hand along one side of the door frame. "Maybe this will help you to understand." He opened the door.

"No," said Steve. "I just came through there." He ran his hands over the brick wall that now blocked the doorway. "This is impossible."

"No, it's not," said Hartley. "It's magic. Travelling magic, to be precise."

"There's no such thing as magic."

"And yet here you are, standing in my shop, after you stepped through that doorway from wherever you came from."

"School," said Steve. "I was at school."

"Exactly." Hartley closed the door. "I'm sorry about Eleanor but she's in good hands. Abel is a magical, just like me. Well, not exactly like me. That would be impossible. The light you saw when you were attacked? That was a magic spell. Abel cast it to incapacitate your attackers so that he could save you."

"That's impossible. Magic doesn't exist."

"Yes, it does," said a familiar voice.

"Where did you come from?" said Steve.

Blessing was sat at the kitchen table with a glass of water in her hand. "I was here all along."

"No, you weren't. There was just Hartley," said Steve. "I'm sure of it."

"Blessing, you shouldn't spy on people," said Hartley. "It really isn't polite."

"Well, it's difficult to ignore the two of you shouting at each other like that."

"I need to go back," said Steve. "Make sure Eleanor is okay."

"Abel has strong magic," said Blessing. "He—"

"There's no such thing as magic," Steve shouted.

"Yes, there is," said Hartley.

"No, there isn't. You're trying to trick me. Both of you are."

"Hartley?" She tilted her head at him.

"Oh, go on then," said Hartley, crossing his arms. "If that's the only way."

"Watch this." Blessing smiled and made a circle with her thumb and finger. She blew through the circle, cupping her hand around the breath. "If there's no such thing as magic, Steve Haven, then how do you explain this?"

When she opened her hand, a small, glowing orb the size of the circle she had formed with her thumb and finger floated up into the air.

"Well, that's... that's..." stuttered Steve as the orb floated towards him. "That's amazing."

"That's magic," she said. "As real as you or me."

"Sit down, Steve." Hartley pulled out a chair at the table. "Please."

"Abel was at my school," said Steve. "The day Mum dropped me off there."

"Yes, he was," said Hartley. "He wanted to make sure you

were safe and leave a parcel with you to give to your father."

"And the attack. Abel was there."

"That was pure luck," said Hartley. "If Abel hadn't found out about the kidnap plan, you would have been on your own."

"That's reassuring," said Steve. "Hang on. If Abel knew who I was, then you've known all along too."

"Well, yes." Hartley ran a hand across his beard. "I did know."

"So all that rubbish about who I should call and introductions, all that was…?"

"Rubbish," said Blessing, grinning.

"Abel thought it best that you be kept out of the loop."

"What loop?"

"This loop," said Hartley. "Darkacre. Magic."

"Chalk that opens doors," said Steve.

"Exactly."

"Whoa." Steve leaned on the table as the room suddenly spun around him. "Headrush."

"It's the travelling chalk. It takes a bit of getting used to. You'll be fine in a moment."

"No, I won't," said Steve, slumping into a chair at the table. "I won't ever be fine again. My parents are missing. I've been attacked, twice, in a matter of days. Eleanor is in danger. And now I find out that magic exists."

"Admittedly, you've had rather a full and eventful week," said Hartley.

"Full?" said Steve. "Eventful?"

"What we really need is information," said Hartley.

"What we need is to find Abel and Eleanor, and go to the

police," said Steve.

"Clearly, it isn't safe for you to go back to school, and the police can't help with this," said Hartley. "Not straightaway. Let's find out what we can first."

"And how are we going to do that?" said Steve.

"What are you wearing?" said Hartley.

"Pyjamas." Steve crossed his legs. "It's Saturday."

"Perfectly understandable and more than suitable for a weekend," said Hartley. "But a tad conspicuous for what I have in mind. I'll find you something better."

"Better for what?" said Steve as Hartley charged out of the room. "Hartley? Better for what?"

Chapter Sixteen

It had been easy for the darkling to travel through the underground tunnels of Kendra's world. The strange, green lighting cast by wall-mounted jars left a pattern of shadows that allowed her to visit every room and corridor.

Only one unopened door remained. It looked identical to every other door except for the mouse hole at its bottom edge. It would be simple to seep through that hole, but she held back.

It was Kendra's room, the place the fair ones called the dust room. She knew he was in there, hopefully alone.

He had tracked her once. He had almost caught her once. He knew of her weakness. She had to be careful around that man.

She left the safety of the shadows and flowed through the mouse hole, coming to an abrupt stop on the other side.

"Just one more," said Kendra.

He stood at a polished wooden cabinet which stretched from the tiled floor to the stone ceiling above. It held many small drawers—some closed, others open—and shelves housing bottles and boxes that had been lined up painstakingly straight, like a row of soldiers. He had his back to her, but she could see that he held a large jar balanced in one hand.

She readied herself to flee, if need be, out through the mouse hole and back into the safety of the tunnel shadows.

"I do like my collection."

He put the jar down on a shelf and reached for a half-open drawer, still with his back to the darkling.

He doesn't know I'm here, she thought, relaxing. *He's just talking to himself.* She flowed a little closer.

"I'm so glad I bought a large stock of these. You never know when you might need one."

He spun around and finally she could see what he was holding. He turned his face away as he clashed the two rods together, the same kind of rods he had used in the theatre.

She recoiled as the light dashed towards her. Where it touched her shadow, she was wrenched into solid form, screaming at the sudden, involuntary change.

He stormed towards her, holding the rods above her as she curled her body into a knot.

"Think you're clever coming here? Think you can spy on me?"

She lashed out but, blinded by the intense light, her blows met with nothing. She felt his hand around her wrist.

"I've got the perfect jar for you," he said. "Welcome to my collection."

*

The shop sat snug in a row of almost touching, mismatched stores. It wasn't just that the materials the shops were built from were different—dusty red brick, grey stone, cobbles and flint—but the roofs had each settled to their own individual level too.

'Keg's Emporium – Whatnots and Assortments'. Steve read the ornate signage that hung precariously over the front door of Hartley's shop. "Doesn't give a lot away, does it?"

He checked his reflection in the shop window. With his unbrushed hair and dressed in clothes from Hartley's stock—a black shirt that had lost its cuff buttons, purple V-neck jumper, too-big faded jeans hoisted up with a belt, mismatched socks and trainers that had seen better days—Steve hardly recognised himself.

"Is it meant to?" said Hartley as he pulled the door to, a tweed duffle coat under his arm. "Here. It's a tad chilly."

"Thanks." Steve took the coat but held it at arm's length. It smelt of dust and tobacco.

"Put it on then."

"Is this yours?"

"Oh no," said Hartley. "It's from my stock. I'm sure it will be a good fit."

"Really?" Steve pulled it on. The sleeves of the coat almost reached to the ends of his fingers. "Where are we going?"

"Well, I thought I should introduce you to Darkacre," said Hartley, "before we attend the Gathering tonight?"

"What's the Gathering?" said Steve, following Hartley as he set off at speed.

"Generally, it's simply a chance for the community to come together, but today is a bit special."

"That sounds ominous."

"No, not ominous," said Hartley. "Well, not *very* ominous. The Council have an announcement to make, which is unusual I grant you. I'm sure it's nothing to worry about. It'll be fun."

"Fun?" said Steve.

"Yes, fun," said Hartley. "You'll see, tonight."

"Okay," said Steve, wondering just how safe this 'fun' would be.

"For now, I want you to meet a few people. Get the measure of us as a community."

"Why?" Steve stopped. "Surely we don't have time for this. What about Eleanor?"

"Do you have any idea where she is?" said Hartley.

"No," Steve admitted.

"Neither do I," said Hartley. "What we need is information from people in-the-know."

"And we'll find this information here?"

"At the Gathering, yes," said Hartley. "People travel in from outside Darkacre to attend. Some of those people live in your city. They may well know what's going on."

"But—"

"Do you have a better idea?" said Hartley, knitting his generous eyebrows into a mass of curls.

"No," said Steve. *Annoyingly*, he thought.

"Come along then." Hartley set off again. "No time like the now."

*

102

'Gargoyle' was the word that sprang into Steve's mind before he could stop it. Frobisher sat in a deckchair beside an archway that stretched between two red-brick terrace houses. His hair was patchy and his baldness, plus his frown, emphasised the generous size of his nose, which jutted out like it wanted something to be hung on it.

"Who's this?" said Frobisher, standing up and nodding his head sideways towards Steve. His voice grated on Steve's ears with its whining tones. It almost sounded like Frobisher was screwing up in his nose in distaste. "He's not a local."

"This is Steve," said Hartley. "He's here for the Gathering."

"I see." Frobisher narrowed his eyes to examine Steve more closely.

"Pleased to meet you." Steve offered a hand to Frobisher.

"I suppose." Frobisher crossed his arms. "I don't remember you coming through the gate."

"You must have missed him in the crowd," said Hartley. "I daresay a lot of people are in town for the Gathering. I'm just showing Steve around. Filling him in on the way we do things in Darkacre."

"I see," said Frobisher, returning to his deckchair.

"Steve, Frobisher is our gatekeeper," said Hartley. "He lives next door to the archway."

"I'm *the* gatekeeper," said Frobisher. "Nobody gets in or out without my say-so."

"Why don't you give Steve the full story?" said Hartley. "You're much better at explaining these things than I am." He winked at Steve.

"That's because I tell it how it is." Frobisher sighed. "The gateway was left as a final link to the outside world when our community was placed in protection. Those in-the-know use the gateway to travel back-and-forth."

"Between the city and here?" said Steve.

"Precisely," he said. "I control it."

"Frobisher has a way with the stone," said Hartley. "It's his gift."

"Anyone who wants in or out comes through me," said Frobisher. "It's the only way to access Darkacre."

"But what about Hartley?" said Steve.

"What about him?" said Frobisher.

"Oh, nothing, nothing." Hartley elbowed Steve. "As Frobisher said, he is the gatekeeper for our community."

"But I thought—"

"Any travellers today, Frobisher?" said Hartley.

"Plenty," said Frobisher.

"Anyone I know? James and his brother perhaps?"

"Aye, them," said Frobisher. "Must be an improvement on that old theatre they squat in. What's it called? The Deepening. That's it."

"Good, good," said Hartley.

"Is it?" said Frobisher. He picked up a book from the ground and pulled a pair of cracked spectacles from his shirt pocket.

"Well, we'll leave you to it," said Hartley, pulling Steve away. "I can see that you're very busy."

"Does he know?" asked Steve when they were out of earshot. "About the door in your shop that leads to the city?"

"He most certainly does not," said Hartley. "And I'd rather keep it that way. I'd never hear the last of it if he found out, and what good is a traveller who isn't allowed to travel?"

*

At first glance, Darkacre's red-brick terrace houses all looked the same, but the longer that Steve walked along the streets with Hartley, the more he noticed the subtle differences.

One house's window-boxes and roof sprouted colourful plants which waved gaping flower-mouths to the sky. The front wall of another house was braced with strips of metal as if it needed reinforcement against some force from within. A third house, when Steve leant against it to tie his shoelaces, was hot to the touch.

"Here we are," said Hartley as they arrived at a small square. In its centre stood a grey brick building with arched stained-glass windows and a steeple that shot up above the surrounding roofscape.

"A church?" said Steve.

"It was," said Hartley. "In decades past. Now it serves as our school. It's directly in the middle of our community. Want to see inside?"

Not really, Steve thought, but he nodded to be polite. "Okay."

Stepping through the arched wooden door, Steve didn't know what he'd expected to find, but what he was faced with certainly wasn't it. The old church interior, with its vaulted ceiling, pillars and pews, had been divided into classrooms by wooden walls.

"Miss Bagshaw won't like it if we disturb classes." Hartley peered through a window in one of the walls. "But she won't mind if we just look."

Inside the classroom, a bone-thin woman with a tightly tied hair-bun on the top of her head read from a book to a class

105

of children who ranged from around seven years old to Steve's own age. Apart from the lack of technology—there was no holographic white board, no tablets and the children didn't have wrap-phones—the Darkacre class wasn't so different to Steve's own.

"This is where our children learn the three Rs: reading, writing and 'rithmetic."

"That's only one 'R'," said Steve, "with a 'W' and an 'A'."

"Ooh, we've been seen." Hartley dipped down below the window. "Probably best if we leave."

"I thought you said the teacher wouldn't mind us having a look," said Steve as Hartley dragged him outside.

"I'm sure she wouldn't," said Hartley, "but best to stay out of her way. We don't exactly see eye-to-eye on education. She likes her books while I prefer a more practical and experimental manner of learning."

"You'd get on with my chemistry teacher," said Steve. "He's never happier than when he's blowing things up."

"Interesting," said Hartley. "I'll bear that approach in mind."

*

"Well, thank you, Billy." Hartley stuffed the lettuce in his jacket pocket. "And I'll have those clothes round to your house as soon as I can."

Billy, a skinny, young man dressed in dungarees and oversized wellies, returned to his digging.

"So this is like a community garden?" said Steve, following Hartley along a muddy path between flower beds.

"It's not *like* a community garden," said Hartley. "It *is* our community garden. This is where most of our food comes from."

The garden was a patchwork of fenced-off, dug-over soil beds filled with row upon row of vegetables and flowers. Steve hadn't seen so many real-life green plants in one place... well... ever.

"This is all for Darkacre?"

"Well, yes. We're not exactly a small community," said Hartley. "Of course, the Earth-smiths tend to most of it."

"What's an Earth-smith?"

They had reached a row of ramshackle sheds, some missing doors, all fronted by some form of seat.

"Earth-smith is a term for those whose magic is connected to the earth and plants. They're gardeners, to put it simply, but so much more really."

"So, are there other magicals here who deal with the other elements, like fire? Elementals?" he asked.

"Elementals." Hartley rubbed his beard for a moment. "I like that. It's catchy. All of our communities have a mixture of 'elementals', as you put it, to maintain a balance. We have an entire family of Pyro's."

"Fire," said Steve.

"And a smattering of Wind-whisperers."

"What about water?" said Steve.

"We are incredibly lucky to have the very last of those living here in Darkacre. Lovely man called Dylan. He'll be at the Gathering tonight. Speaking of which." Hartley pulled a matchbox out of his pocket and poked it open with a finger.

"What's that?" Steve leaned closer to see.

"Just as I thought." Hartley snapped it shut. "Time to get back to the shop."

"Aren't you going to tell me what's in that matchbox?" said Steve as Hartley sped off back the way they'd come.

"Where's the fun in that?" Hartley called back. "Come on."

Chapter Seventeen

It was dark when Steve followed Hartley out of his shop a few hours later. The sky above was inky black, with no moon or stars. *Must be cloudy,* he thought.

"Shouldn't you close that?" said Steve as Hartley left the front door ajar.

"Why?" said Hartley. "The shop can look after itself."

"Okay then," said Steve. *Not at all mad,* he thought.

"Come along then," said Hartley, knotting his scarf under his overflowing beard. "Blessing."

"Here," she said from right behind Steve, causing him to jump a little. "Sorry," she said, smiling at his discomfort. "I'll be noisier from now on."

"Blessing, behave." Hartley wagged a finger at her, albeit with a grin. "Steve isn't used to you, yet."

"I said I was sorry." She took Hartley's arm. Her hair was tied back from her face in a haphazard fashion with blue and green ribbons. "Do you like my hair?" She tucked a loose strand of hair behind her ear.

"It's very pretty," said Steve.

"Pretty," she said. "Hartley? 'Pretty': is that good?"

"Better than good," he said, patting her hand.

"So where are we going?" asked Steve as they set off along the cobbled street.

"We told you. To the Gathering," said Blessing. "You'll like it."

"Will I?" he asked, looking at Hartley.

"Everyone likes the Gathering." Hartley winked at him.

"Where is the Gathering held?" said Steve. "Community hall? Church?"

"You'll see," said Hartley.

Almost every door they passed was open and the further Steve walked, the more people spilled from their houses and jostled along the cobbled streets, all heading in the same direction.

The lampposts were painted a deep blue, and within each flickered a yellow flame.

"Are those gas-lights?" said Steve. "I thought the use of fossil fuels was illegal."

"Don't ask me," said Hartley. "I don't do science."

"Me neither," said Blessing. "Hartley, what's science?"

"Funny," said Steve. *They have to be joking, right?* he thought to himself.

"The Gathering is an excellent way for you to learn about Darkacre," said Hartley. "And if we're lucky, the information we need will be there too."

Lucky, thought Steve. *That's encouraging.*

"Oi! Mind yourself."

"Sorry." Steve backed off from Frobisher, who had barged into him.

"Hello Frobisher," said Hartley. "On your way to the Gathering?"

"Obviously," said Frobisher. "The Hidden are watching the gate while I'm away."

"Care to accompany us?" said Hartley.

"I have plans," said Frobisher. "I've been appointed to greet the Council member."

"Oh, well, we wouldn't want to keep you from your plans," said Hartley. "And you don't want to keep Naomi waiting."

"Miss Onai just appreciates punctuality," said Frobisher. "Nothing wrong with that."

"Not at all," said Blessing, elbowing Hartley.

As the gatekeeper marched away, Steve could see that Frobisher's white hair, which had looked sparse from the front, fell down his back in a long, lustrous plait, tied at the end with a red ribbon.

"He's pleasant," said Steve.

"I think so, too," said Blessing.

"I was being sarcastic," said Steve.

"Oh." Blessing frowned. "I haven't mastered that yet."

"Frobisher is a good man," said Hartley. "Grumpy. Rude. Intrusive."

"You're painting a wonderful picture," said Steve.

"You didn't let me get to the 'but'," said Hartley.

"What's the 'but'?"

"He's also loyal. He watches out for us all."

"If you say so," mumbled Steve. "How much further to this Gathering?"

"It's in there." Blessing pointed to an ornate wrought-iron gateway that rose above the cobbles at the end of the street.

The gate stood alone. No fences or walls ran from its two stone posts but, beyond it, the cobbles gave way to grass and interlocking trees. In pairs and groups, the residents of Darkacre streamed through the gate into the woodland beyond.

"Hartley, may I?" said Blessing.

"Oh, go on, then," said Hartley as she ran to the gate.

"What's that about?" said Steve as he watched her pick up a small lantern from the foot of one of the stone gateposts.

"We need light to guide us through the trees," said Hartley. "Blessing is doing the honours."

"Watch this." She blew a light orb into her palm as Steve had seen her do in the shop, then opened the lantern and dropped the orb inside. "See?" She held up the glowing lantern. "Impressive, isn't it?"

"It's just an illumination orb," said Hartley. "A simple enough spell. It's one of the first things our children learn."

"It's not that simple," said Blessing. "You couldn't do it."

"Could too," said Hartley. "I just like to give you the practice." He winked at her. "Lead on then. You know the way."

With Blessing walking a few paces ahead, the three of them set off through the trees.

Chapter Eighteen

Hundreds of light orbs bobbed among the leaves of the trees that surrounded the forest clearing. As they entered, Steve had tried to count the orbs but given up as the numbers continued to grow with each person who had arrived.

Blessing opened her lantern and her orb floated up to join the others.

The clearing was vast, so long, that Steve could barely see the other end.

"This is the Gathering," said Hartley as he guided Steve through the crowds of people. "A safe place for all the residents of Darkacre to come together and be themselves. I suppose you could say that it's 'our' haven."

The clearing was filled with people: dancing people, laughing people, buying and selling, embracing and remembering. All of them acted with a relaxed freedom and an easy joy that spoke of acceptance and trust. Steve found himself smiling.

"Can you smell that?" Hartley drew Steve towards the market stalls that lined one side of the clearing. "I'd know that aroma anywhere." He took a deep sniff. "Fish stew. Zachary!" He embraced the stall holder: a bone-thin, elderly, dark-skinned man dressed in a suit that had seen better days. "How are you, my old friend?"

"Good, good," said Zachary. "I hoped I'd see you. I have a surprise." He reached beneath the stall and drew out a limp, paper-wrapped parcel.

"It isn't." said Hartley, taking the parcel.

"Have a look."

"Trout," gasped Hartley as he opened the wrapper. "Oh, my friend, you have surpassed yourself. How can I repay you?"

"Well, my knee has been troubling me again," said Zachary. "If Blessing could have a look, that would be payment enough."

"Of course," she said as she took his hand in her own.

"I'd go to the doctor in the city, but I can't afford it. How could I pay those prices?"

"Come on." Hartley, with the trout in his pocket, moved Steve along, leaving Blessing and Zachary to talk.

"She's a bit young to be a nurse, isn't she?" asked Steve.

"Blessing is a healer," said Hartley. "It's one of her magical skills. She healed you when you first came to us."

"That's why I didn't have any injuries on me when I went back to school," said Steve.

"Exactly. She's still learning of course, but the more she heals people, the better her skills become. She's an absolute wonder. Now, then." Hartley stretched up on his toes to look over the heads of a row of people. "Do you dance?"

"Sometimes," said Steve, hoping that Hartley wasn't going to ask him to dance.

"You'll like this then," said Hartley. "Come along."

Hartley led Steve through the layers of people who stood around a roped-off circle in the clearing. Inside the circle, dancers, all couples, flung their partners around the space, twirling and smiling. There were only a few collisions, each leading to a ripple of laughter.

On the opposite side of the dance space bobbed a band of musicians. There was a violinist, a saxophonist, a drummer and a woman with long, ginger curls who played an ornately-shaped harp. The violinist, a tall angle-limbed man, wore an emerald-green waistcoat.

"That's Frank on the violin," said Hartley. "Came to us from the city. No magic about him. The lady on the harp is Frank's wife, Rachel. She's a magical. She has the most moving of singing voices, quite literally."

"They're good." Steve's foot involuntarily tapped to the beat. "Do they play in the city?"

"Just here at the Gatherings." Hartley clapped along to the music. "It's their way of giving back to our community."

"Nobody in the city does anything for free," said Steve.

"Oh, it isn't free," said Hartley. "The music is payment for the protection Darkacre grants to its inhabitants. It's all part of the barter system we use."

"Like the trout for Blessing's healing?" said Steve.

"That's right."

The music slowed to a final chord. The dancers parted and left the dance floor. With swift, sweeping moves, Rachel drew her fingers across the strings of her harp. Some members of the audience sat down on cushions or chairs. Others stood arm-in-arm. All of them watched.

Rachel's music moved slowly at first, its pure notes carrying into the empty space. It gathered speed, weaving itself into a cloak of music that enveloped them all. When it stopped, the audience released a held breath.

The laughter of tiny bells replaced the music of the strings. From a darkness that Steve had not noticed, a dancer stepped forward.

She was tall, taller than most of the men in the audience. The light of the orbs played on the many layers of her dress. Tiny bells ran along the edges of her skirt. The coils of her hair were dark, yet vibrant as if backlit. Her hands fluttered as she moved on bare feet into the centre of the dance floor.

She danced, her movements accompanied only by the music of the bells on her skirt. Every eye was upon her. Nobody spoke; hardly a breath was drawn or exhaled, it seemed.

Steve wasn't sure at what point it started, but he suddenly became aware of a number of things. He couldn't move, except for his eyes. The hair on his head and his arms had lifted as if charged with static electricity, and his mouth was spread into a wide, toothy grin.

He glanced around at the other watchers. Everyone bore the same smile and stood completely still.

The dancer moved around the cleared space in a series of leaps, long steps, and sweeping turns. With each move, her limbs blurred as if they were moving faster than could be seen and yet the rhythm of her dance was languid and slow.

Steve felt as if he should be scared: he was in a strange place, surrounded by faces he didn't know, and he couldn't move his body. He wasn't scared though. There was a rising tide of joy in him as the dancer performed. All he wanted to do was watch.

She danced nearer to him, her hands sweeping so close that,

if he had been able to move, he could have reached out and touched them. From the ends of her fingers, a thousand silver sparks sprang and exploded. For a second, she looked straight at him, and then she was on the other side of the dance floor.

She spun, twisted, leapt, and finally sank to the floor, her face hidden by her hair.

"Wow." Steve found his voice and joined the applause that erupted from the crowd.

"Quite something, isn't she?" said Hartley. "Mariana never disappoints."

"Mariana?" asked Steve. "*The* Mariana? The famous dancer that's dating the Prime Minister's brother?"

"Oh, they're not dating," said Hartley, "but she basks in the media speculation. You'll always find her dancing at our Gatherings. She is one of us after all."

"Really?" Steve craned to look back at the dancer, now taking a bow, as Hartley led him away. "She uses magic?"

"Glamour mostly," said Hartley. "She has always been a great influencer in the workaday world. She dances her magic. Of course, she only uses it here. Her other dancing outside Darkacre is simply that: dancing. And as for the glamour, it's too tied in with her personality to attract any undue attention. Mariana is an enchantress."

"An enchantress?" said Steve. "Is that why…?"

"You couldn't move?" said Hartley. "All part of the show."

"So how do you learn all of this stuff?" said Steve. "Do you have a magic school in Darkacre?"

"A magic school?" Hartley grunted a laugh. "No. Children learn their magic at home with their families. Most kinds of magic are inherited but skills vary from person to person."

"So where does the magic come from?" said Steve. "Why don't people know about it?"

"You mean why don't workadays know about it," said Hartley.

"Workadays?"

"Non-magical humans. Like yourself, and Frank over there." Hartley nodded to the violinist. "Do you think workadays could cope with the truth?"

"I don't know." Steve pictured the headmaster shaking his head and mouthing the word 'unacceptable'. "Maybe not."

"Anyway, it's not up to us," said Hartley. "It's just the rule."

"*You* obeying rules?" said Steve. "That doesn't sound right."

"I obey some rules," said Hartley, breaking out into the broadest of grins. "On occasion."

"So is there a magical source that powers you all? Like a generator?"

"You really are very scientific," said Hartley. "Generator." He shook his head. "Our magic is part of our—what do you call it?—our genes. The only limitation we have is our own physical form and stamina. Using magic has a cost. It weighs on us in the same way that physical exertion does. We need to rest in between."

"So it's more like super-hero powers than wands and spells then?"

"Super-hero. I like that," said Hartley. "It's actually a little of each. We have inherent skills, but it is possible to learn spells: like the travelling chalk that Abel gave you. That was my invention. I believe people your age in the workaday world would call it 'awesome'."

"Well." Steve had to admit, to himself at least, that yes, the chalk which had saved him was indeed awesome. "I suppose," he said.

"We use wands, on occasion, but they're more for effect and focus really."

"And what about Blessing?"

"Blessing is..." Hartley frowned. "Blessing is complicated. I've never met a magical who is so multi-skilled or who has the potential for such power."

"Isn't that good?" said Steve.

"Perhaps," mused Hartley. "Perhaps."

"And what about you?"

"Me?" Hartley grinned. "I am a completely different kettle of trout."

*

The tree that stood in the middle of the huge clearing was enormous, dark branches twisting and entangling into the night sky. Within its grasp, light orbs nestled like shining blossoms. Attached to the branches and at the base of the tree there were hundreds of framed photographs and portraits, each tied with a ribbon.

"I've never seen a tree before." Steve rested a hand on the rough bark of the tree's trunk. "Not a real one." He turned around. "I had no idea there could be so many of them together in one place."

"Are there no trees in the city? In people's gardens?" said Hartley.

"No. No trees. No gardens. It's all steel, glass and concrete.

We have a playing field at school, but even that is synthetic grass."

"How depressing," said Hartley.

"I've seen a hologram of a tree."

"And how does the real thing compare?"

"They're wonderful," said Steve. "They even have a smell."

"Where I come from," said Hartley. "I mean, where I came from, there are many forests like this one. So many that we take them for granted. Which is a shame because, as you say, they are wonderful."

"But this one is special, yes?" Steve knelt down to take a closer look at the images at the base of the tree.

"This is our Tree of Remembrance. It's where we come to remember those no longer with us," said Hartley. "When we lose someone, we leave a picture of them here for the tree to watch over." He patted the tree trunk.

"There are so many," said Steve.

"So many people gone, but we remember them all," said Hartley. "Here, I have something for you." He pulled a photograph from his pocket. There was a hole punched through the top of the photograph and a slim blue ribbon threaded through. "Your turn to add to the tree."

"Uncle Rex," said Steve as Hartley handed it to him. "But he's not from Darkacre."

"No, but many of us knew him," said Hartley. "I'm sure nobody would mind if you placed his memory here."

"Okay." Steve reached up to a branch, tied the ribbon around it and stepped back. "Something else I didn't know," he said. "Any more surprises, Hartley?"

"You know me."

Not really, thought Steve. *I don't think I know anything anymore.*

Chapter Nineteen

"Let's have a bit of hush for the Council." Frobisher stood on the lowest of a series of wooden steps that led up to a raised wooden platform. He held an old-fashioned megaphone to his mouth and waved his long arms around to get people's attention. "Come on now: Miss Onai wishes to speak."

Naomi Onai, Council member and representative, stood in the centre of the platform like a queen resplendent on her throne. She was a petite, older woman, with a gaze that held your attention when it swept past you. Her black braids were coiled into an ornate arrangement that held a silver tiara and she wore a long, cobalt blue gown that pooled around her feet.

"Thank you, Frobisher." Her gaze remained on the gathered crowd as she spoke.

Lowering the megaphone, Frobisher bowed so deeply that Steve wondered if the old gatekeeper would be able to stand again.

"Thank you, people of Darkacre," Naomi Onai continued, "for gracing me with your presence. It warms my heart to know that the Council still holds a place in your esteem."

I don't know about that, thought Steve, looking round. Most of the crowd looked like they just wanted an excuse to party.

"Pay attention," Hartley whispered to Steve. "You may learn something to your advantage. The Council don't visit without good reason."

"I have unfortunate news, I'm afraid." Naomi Onai sighed. "Your sister community of Myrkhof has been sealed. We had no choice," she continued as a buzz of alarm began to build in the crowd. "It was our only option, the only way to avoid the community being revealed to the world. Please, please." She raised her hands in an appeal for calm as the buzz grew and individual heckles could be heard. "We didn't take this decision lightly. We couldn't risk another Xav Mallorick event."

At the mention of that name, the crowd fell silent.

"Who's Xav Mallorick?" Steve whispered to Hartley.

"Shush." A man at his shoulder glowered at him. Hartley shook his head at Steve and mouthed, 'Not now'.

"I know we have workadays amongst us," Naomi Onai continued. "I also know that there is regular traffic between our communities and theirs. Some of you have friends out there. Yes?" There was a general agreement from the crowd. "But they, the workadays, they can't be trusted with what we have. Some of them—not all, but some—would seek to use us. For the sake of our families and our culture, even for the sake of the workadays themselves, we must keep the existence of magic a secret from them."

"Come on." Hartley drew Steve away as Naomi Onai carried on with her speech. "I think you've heard enough."

Steve waited until they had cleared the crowd before asking the questions that had been bouncing round his head.

"So Darkacre isn't the only place like this?" That was the first one.

"No, we are one of several protected magical communities attached to this world," said Hartley.

"And the Council are in charge?"

"They like to think so."

"And who is Xav Mallorick?"

"Someone you hopefully will never need to worry about," said Hartley, speeding off. "No more dawdling. Come along."

"Oi!" said Steve as he dashed after the shopkeeper. "You can't drop that kind of thing on me and not expect me to have questions. I'm an ignorant workaday, you know."

"Curiosity and cats," Hartley called back to him. "That's all I'm saying."

*

With Naomi Onai's speech still continuing, the stalls at the Gathering were quiet and without customers, other than Hartley and Steve.

There was an old lady selling potted plants, which wouldn't have been out of the ordinary if it hadn't been for the flowering vine that slinked around the legs of the stall, singing to the passers-by.

The stall next to that carried rolls of cloth and silken scarves. The two young women who worked there flipped and unrolled the fabric and, with each pass of their slim hands, the cloth changed colour.

Another stall carried water-filled jars of what looked, at first glance, like fish but, on closer examination, turned out to be tiny silver birds.

Finally, two young men were engaged in a light-hearted battle. One, slight and golden-haired wielded a shield of what looked like water to Steve, using it to extinguish the balls of fire that the other man, heavier and dark haired, bowled at him.

When Steve caught up with Hartley, the shopkeeper stood at an empty stall between a tattoo artist and a cobbler.

"That's unfortunate," said Hartley.

"What is?"

"I had hoped Abel's cousin would be here. He sells crystals at the Gatherings. Occasionally demons."

"Demons?"

"Oh, nothing dangerous," said Hartley. "Fire imps, gremlins and the such-like. Gremlins have exceptional mechanical skills, you know. And fire imps, if you can keep them contained, are excellent for finding people."

"Did I hear you say 'Abel'?" The tattoo artist wandered over to them. He was dressed in black from head to foot. Even his hair and eyes were black. "I hear that old fool's got himself into trouble in the city. Got certain parties looking for him." He tutted and shook his head. "But that's what happens when you trust workadays. It's one thing dealing with the safe ones like Frank on home ground but taking your business out there is just asking for trouble, if you ask me." He spread out his hands. The ends of his fingers were stained black. The same black coloured the veins in his hands.

"Abel is a good man, Doyle." said Hartley. "He's helped your family more than once, as he has us all. You should show more respect."

"I was just saying." Doyle's shoulders twitched. "Just expressing my opinion." He returned to his stall, head down, hands stuffed into his pockets.

"And here I was thinking everyone in Darkacre was one big happy family," said Steve.

"There are always some," said Hartley. "Come on. We don't want to be overheard."

"Why? What are we going to do?"

"There's someone here that might be able to help," said Hartley. "Someone who spends most of their time in the city."

Chapter Twenty

"Now before I introduce you," said Hartley as they walked through the stalls, "I should probably give you a little warning about the boys."

"What kind of warning?" said Steve.

"James and Michael are lovely lads, but they can be a tad standoffish, especially the younger brother. Best not to vex them."

"Why? What are they going to do? Zap me with their magic powers?" said Steve.

"They probably won't," said Hartley, smiling broadly.

"Hang on," said Steve. "I was joking. You're not serious, are you?"

"They probably won't," Hartley repeated. "But it's always good to be forewarned. Here we are."

They stopped at a stall that hugged the edge of the clearing. The bare wooden tabletop held an array of stock: packets of biscuits, ladies' hats, toys, jewellery and a pile of newspapers tied together with string. A rusting bicycle leant against one end of the stall.

At the other end stood a tall, gangly teenager. His blonde hair dangled around his face and his dark sunglasses. His hands were shoved into the pockets of an oversized hoodie. At his feet, a younger boy sat cross-legged, a line of lightning sizzling between his outheld forefingers.

"Hello, James." Hartley offered a hand to the teenager.

"Hartley." James shook his hand and nodded to Steve. "Who's this?"

"A friend," said Hartley. "Steve is lodging with me at the moment."

"Not one of us then?" said James.

"I'm not a magical," said Steve, "if that's what you mean."

"Thought so," said James, looking Steve up and down.

"Now then, gentlemen," said Hartley. "Let's keep things friendly."

"You know me, Hartley," said James. "I'm always friendly. Aren't I, Glitch?" He nudged the seated boy with his foot.

"I've told you before," snapped the boy. "My name is Michael. Not Glitch."

"Touchy." James ruffled his brother's hair. "So," he said, "what can I do you for? Biscuits? Teabags?"

"Information," said Hartley. "From the city."

"It'll cost you." James crossed his arms. "What will you give me?"

"What do you want?" said Hartley. "Clothes?"

"Nah, I can steal those out there," said James. "What else?"

"How about a bath and a meal?" said Steve.

"You what, mate?" said James. "What are you implying?"

"What do you need, James?" Hartley stepped in between the two teenagers.

"Money. Credits." said James. "Life out there is costly."

"That's the one thing I can't give you," said Hartley. "You know how things work here."

"James." Blessing did her usual appearing act, suddenly at Steve's shoulder. "Don't be mean. It's us, not some strangers."

"Hmm." James frowned, rubbing his chin, then grinned. "Well, seeing as you put it like that. Come here." He spread his arms wide and Blessing rushed into them, almost bowling him over. "You're getting tall," he said as he released her.

"No taller than before," she said. "Maybe *you're* getting short."

"Cheeky."

"Hi Michael," she said, waving at the boy.

"See, *she* knows my name," he said, losing his frown for a moment to smile at her.

"Sure, Glitch," said his brother.

"That's not my name. I'll zap you," said Michael, jumping to his feet.

"All right, all right. I'm only kidding." James held out his hands in surrender. "Tidy away the stall, mate. We need to be off soon."

"Why me?" Michael kicked at the floor. "Why don't you do it?"

"Because I'm your big brother." James ruffled the boy's hair. "I'm in charge, remember?"

"So you say." Michael pulled out a box from under the stall. "Bossy."

"I'll help," said Blessing.

"You, I like," said Michael, smiling up at her.

"Information," said James, drawing Steve and Hartley away from the stall. "What kind of information?"

"We're looking for Abel," said Hartley. "We fear he's in danger, but we don't know what from or where he might be. We need to speak to him."

"And he has something of mine," said Steve. "Well, my dad's."

"Something a little bit special," said Hartley.

"By special, I take it you mean magical," said James. "Sorry. I haven't seen him but you're not the only ones on the search. Braeden Kendra has been asking after him."

"Who's Braeden Kendra?" said Steve.

"The worst kind of magical," said James. "He calls himself an antiques dealer, but he's got his fingers in all the worst pies. If Braeden Kendra is looking for you, you're in big trouble." He glanced back at his stall. "Looks like we've got a customer." Doyle, the tattoo artist, watched them as he picked through the packets of biscuits. "If I know Abel, he's holed up somewhere safe. You know what he's like. Always planning for something."

"Thank you, James." Hartley shook the teenager's hand. "And if you or your brother ever do want a hot meal."

"I'll remember you offered." James backed away. "And perhaps a bath too?" He winked at Steve, nodded to Hartley, and then returned to his stall.

"They're friendly," said Steve as he watched James join Blessing and Michael at the stall. "Blessing and James."

"Blessing has known the boys all her life. They were the first people she met in Darkacre."

"So she's not dating James, then?"

"Does it matter?" said Hartley, raising an eyebrow.

"I'm just asking," said Steve.

"Of course, you are," said Hartley, repressing a smile.

"What's that place?" said Steve.

He nodded towards a gap in the trees and a broken-down house, its pale bricks illuminated in the orb light.

"I suppose you could say it was a shrine. Or a museum," said Hartley.

"Well, which is it?"

"Both. I'll tell you about it when the times are more conducive to sight-seeing. Come on."

"What about Blessing?"

"She'll find us when she's ready," said Hartley, taking Steve's elbow and guiding him onwards. "Besides, it's been a while since James and Michael were in Darkacre. They'll want to catch up."

"Right." Steve looked back at Blessing and the boys as he was pulled away. In the shadow of the trees, the tattoo artist watched them all.

"Don't worry about Doyle," said Hartley. "James can handle himself."

"It's not James, I'm worried about."

"Feeling protective towards Blessing already? That's nice."

"No." Steve shrugged. "It's just that she doesn't seem very street-wise. That's all."

"She'll be fine. She's with the boys and Doyle knows better than to start something at the Gathering."

"If you're sure." Steve tried to keep sight of Doyle as Hartley tugged him away.

"Do you like mead?"

"I don't know," said Steve. "What is it?"

"Oh, you're in for a treat," said Hartley. "Elsie brews the best mead ever. Come along."

*

"Blackberry, lavender or cinnamon?" Elsie was a tall, stooped, bootlace of a woman with a lilting accent. "Take your pick."

"Steve?"

"I don't know," said Steve, still unsure what mead was or whether he should be agreeing to it. "Blackberry?"

"Good choice." Elsie poured a pale liquid from a jug into an earthenware mug. "Sweet sup for a sweet boy." She winked as she handed him the drink.

"Thanks." He gave it a sniff. It smelt of the blackberry he expected, and something else sweet and familiar. He took a sip and recognised the taste of honey which slowly spread through his mouth, coating his tongue and warming his throat. He coughed.

"Steady, Steve." Hartley patted him on the back. "Let the mead do its work."

"Do its work?" A wave of mellow heat spread through Steve's face. "Oh. I see what you mean."

"And I know what you want, Hartley Keg," said Elsie, pouring another drink. "Lavender mead."

"You know me too well, Elsie, my dear." Hartley took the mug, glugged a huge sip, and belched. "Excuse me."

"Granted. Will you take a cask?"

"And what would you want in exchange?"

"Feathers," she said.

"Feathers?" coughed Steve.

"My pillow's sprung a leak," she said. "Darned cat, sharpening its claws on my bed."

"Deal," said Hartley, taking her hand and kissing it.

"I'll drop off the cask in the week," she said.

"And I'll get you those feathers."

"I like mead," said Steve. He took another sip and grinned.

"A little too much by the look of you," said Hartley.

"And I like you." Steve patted Hartley on the shoulder. "And I like Blessing."

"And that's the mead talking." Hartley tried to take Steve's drink away.

"But I really like mead." Steve drained his mug and slapped it down on the stall counter.

"More?" said Elsie.

"Yes, please," said Steve.

"No, thank you." Hartley pushed the empty mug away from Steve's grasp.

"Aww," said Steve, staggering a little.

"Enough mead for you." Hartley drained his own mug and handed it back to Elsie. "We have plans to make."

"About Abel," said Steve, grinning at Elsie whose edges now appeared to be the tiniest bit blurred.

"About finding Abel," said Hartley. "If only we had an item that he'd touched, we could search for him."

"If that's all you need." Steve dug his hand into his trousers

133

pocket and pulled out a piece of purple chalk.

"Chalk?" said Hartley, frowning. "Of course. The travelling chalk Abel used."

"Exactly. Shhh!" Steve pressed a finger to Hartley's lips. "Don't tell anyone. It's secret."

"The mead was a bad idea," said Hartley, taking the chalk from him.

"I like mead," said Steve.

"I know."

"I like you," said Steve.

"I know that too."

"But I really like mead."

Chapter Twenty-One

Steve sat at Hartley's kitchen table with a mug of black coffee nestled in his hands. He had woken that morning with a head that felt like it wanted to vomit out his brain, which in turn wanted to climb up the walls. Mead, he decided, was never going to pass his lips again.

Blessing stood in the corner of the kitchen with her arms firmly crossed.

"There's nothing to be afraid of." Hartley rested his hand on a cloth covered glass dome.

"I'm not afraid," said Blessing. "I just don't trust those things."

"It can't get out," said Hartley.

"What is it?" said Steve as a rhythmic *tap-tap-tap* began on the glass.

"I'm going to remove the cloth," said Hartley.

"Slowly," said Blessing.

"I'm going to remove the cloth, slowly," said Hartley, nodding to her. "Try not to frighten it."

Hartley pulled the cloth away and Steve jumped to his feet, sloshing his coffee over his arm.

"What's that?" he spluttered.

"I told you not to frighten it," said Hartley.

"Frighten it?" said Steve. "What the hell *is* that thing?"

"It's just a fire imp," said Hartley. "I thought we could use it to search for Abel."

The fire imp scrabbled at the sides of the glass dome, its tiny face scrunched into a snarl. It was the size of a squirrel, but that was where the similarity ended. The imp's orange fur sparked and smoked as it attacked the glass.

"Calm down in there." Hartley tapped on the glass. "You know what'll happen if you don't behave."

The fire imp muttered something and blew a raspberry at Hartley, then threw itself down on the floor of the dome.

"There is no need for language like that," said Hartley. "Right, are you listening to me?"

The fire imp muttered something under its breath and made one curt nod of its smoking head.

"We're looking for a friend." Hartley produced the chalk Steve had given him the night before. "This is his. I want you to find him. Can you do that?"

"Aye," snarled the imp.

"Good." Hartley removed a plug at the top of the dome. "I'm watching you," he said as he dropped the chalk into the dome. "Be a good imp and behave." He replaced the plug and stepped back.

The imp picked up the chalk, sniffed its length, then licked it. "Him." It pointed at Steve.

"And Abel," said Steve.

"Me know." The imp sniffed at the chalk again. "Me show."

"Don't let it out," said Blessing. "It'll burn the place down."

"I'm not a complete fool," said Hartley.

"Not complete," said the imp. "Fool." It sniggered.

"Just ask it questions," said Blessing.

"All right, oh sensible one." Hartley rubbed a hand across his beard. "Is he in the city?"

"Aye."

"Is he in the city centre?"

"Nay."

"That leaves an awfully big area," said Hartley.

"Me show," said the imp. "Me good."

"Don't," said Blessing.

"Don't what?" said Steve. The sight of the fire imp had scared off his hangover and he felt in dire need of a weapon to defend himself.

"It would speed things up," said Hartley.

"You're going to let that thing out, aren't you?" said Steve.

"Not 'ting'," muttered the imp, pointing a tiny, sparking claw at Steve.

"Sorry." Steve circled around the table to stand beside Blessing.

"Now, if I let you out?" said Hartley. "If?"

"Aye."

"Then you'll behave."

"Aye."

"No starting fires."

"Nay."

"No burning people."

"Nay."

"You show me where my friend is on the map, and then you go back in the dome. Understand?"

"Aye."

"Right then." Hartley unfastened the base of the dome. "I'm trusting you."

When Hartley lifted the dome, the fire imp took a deep sniff. Its fur changed to a brighter shade of orange and it grew slightly in height.

"Here." Hartley tapped his finger on a framed map of the city that hung on the kitchen wall. "Show me where Abel is."

The imp shook itself and two wings sprouted from its shoulders. It leered at Steve, pointing a claw, then it jumped up into the air and flapped across the room, alighting on Hartley's outheld arm.

"I'm warning you," said Hartley as he walked over to the map. "Stay put or else."

"Else, else, else," sniggered the fire imp. "Stay put."

"That's right," said Hartley.

"In big city," the fire imp muttered, tilting its head to stare at the map. "Not here." It took a couple of steps along Hartley's arm. "Not here."

"I don't think it knows where he is," said Blessing. "Put it back in the dome."

"Know," spat the imp. "Here." It tapped a claw on the map.

"Abel."

"I see," said Hartley. "That would make sense. There's a hideout there."

"Put it away now," said Blessing. "It's served its purpose."

"Nay!"

As Hartley swiped at the fire imp, it flapped into the air with a spray of sparks.

"I told you this would happen." Blessing unfolded her arms and rushed towards the imp, which had pounced onto a shelf of battered books. "Get down from there."

"Nay!" It touched a claw to one of the books which sparked into flame. The imp cackled, launched itself into the air and headed towards Steve.

Steve grabbed the nearest thing to hand, swiping at the imp with a loosely-bound broom, and sending the creature flying across the room like a tiny flaming missile.

"Good work, Steve," said Hartley, grabbing a pan of water from the stove.

"Boy!" shrieked the imp as it hit the floor. "Burn boy."

"Not today." Hartley doused the imp with the pan of water and picked it up by its dripping fur, which had now turned grey. "Back you go," he said as he slipped it back into the dome.

"Steve, you need to put that out," said Blessing.

"Oh right." Steve dunked the flaming broom into the grey water in the sink. "Thanks."

"Well, that was a success," said Hartley, stamping the burning book under his foot.

"Really?" said Steve.

"Not much damage done," said Hartley, pulling a second

burning book off the shelf. "And we know where Abel is." He dropped the book onto the floor and stamped out the flames.

"Excuse me," said Steve, feeling his stomach lurch. "I think I'm going to be—"

"I'm not cleaning that up," said Blessing as Steve dashed out of the kitchen. "Here." She grabbed the mop from the sink and pushed it into Hartley's hands.

Chapter Twenty-Two

"I still don't see why I can't come." Blessing sat at the table, one hand propping up her chin, the other tapping on the glass dome that imprisoned the still-dripping imp.

"We have talked about this, Blessing." Hartley pulled on his jacket. "It isn't safe for you to leave Darkacre. Not yet anyway." He smiled at her. "It isn't far. We'll be back in no time at all."

"Look after him," she told Steve. "He's not as young as he thinks he is." She pushed back her chair and stomped up the stairs out of sight.

"It appears that you have been assigned with the task of protecting me," said Hartley. "Feeling brave?"

"Not really."

"That's the spirit. I've oiled the door since we last used it. Should be less noisy this time." The door juddered open with only the barest of squeaks. "After you."

"Hang on." Steve poked his head through the doorway as a chill blast of air smacked his face. The department store was gone. In its place, a rundown street of derelict houses hunkered down under a grey sky. "This isn't the department store." He looked back at Hartley. "More magic?"

"What did you expect?" said Hartley. "I'm a traveller. Only one of my kind. I use doors to move to other unattached doors."

"So your shop never backed onto the department store?"

"No."

"Are we even in the city?"

"In a way," said Hartley. "We're removed but still attached."

"So somewhere in the city, there's a gaping hole where Darkacre used to be?"

"No, no, nothing like that," said Hartley. "Well, yes, like that; but it's hidden by glamour. People just walk by without noticing."

"One day you need to explain all this to me," said Steve. He stepped through the doorway. "Promise?"

"You have my word." Hartley closed the door behind them. "If we survive."

"Are we safe here?" asked Steve as he found himself in the middle of an old-style concrete road. The houses on either side of the street looked around the same age as those in Darkacre: much older than anything in the pristine city but, while the magical community maintained their homes, these buildings were cracked and pocked with neglect.

"Depends what you mean by 'safe'," said Hartley. "From the authorities, yes. They gave up on this neighbourhood a long time ago. The locals sometimes get a little stirred-up towards outsiders though."

"How stirred-up?"

"I wouldn't worry about it. We're here now." Hartley stopped outside a terraced house that looked no different to its neighbours. The paintwork on the door was peeling, the handle was so rusted that no metal could be seen, and the letterbox was nailed shut.

"This is one of a number of hideouts that Abel frequents in the city," said Hartley. "Let's hope that the fire imp was telling the truth."

"It doesn't look like anyone lives here."

"That's rather the point of a hideout. Now, shall we?"

"Shouldn't we knock?"

"Abel wouldn't answer if we did."

As Hartley's hand closed on the door handle, Steve saw a snake of smoke slither through a gap in the battered door frame.

"Hartley, stop!" He grabbed his friend's arm as the handle dipped. The door flew open and an explosion of fire and smoke threw them both backwards.

*

Hartley and Steve lay in a pile on the opposite side of the street. Steve disentangled himself, rolling Hartley onto his back. Hartley's beard sparked and glowed like expectant kindling.

"Are you all right?" He patted out the glowing strands of Hartley's beard. "Hartley, speak to me."

The shopkeeper blinked, coughed and sat up. He wiggled his nose, sniffed and coughed again. "Well," he said, climbing to his feet, "that was unexpected."

"We should call the fire service."

"They wouldn't come." Hartley brushed himself down. "Not here."

"What do we do?"

Hartley shrugged. "Needs must."

"You're not thinking of going in there?" said Steve as Hartley strode towards the flaming doorway. "Anyone in that house is dead by now."

"The hideout is in the cellar. If Abel's in there, he'll probably be safe."

"If he hasn't been suffocated by the smoke."

"Are you coming?" Hartley beckoned. "I may need help carrying him out."

"The house is still blazing." Steve crossed the street to him. "We'd be burnt alive in seconds." He pulled at Hartley's sleeve. "We'd be mad to even try."

"'Try' is such an over-used term." Hartley grabbed Steve's arm with his free hand. "'Do' is so much more hopeful." Before Steve could react, Hartley ran the two of them into the burning house.

*

Steve raised his arm in front of his face. There was a moment of intense heat, then his feet slapped down on wooden steps.

He opened his eyes. There was no fire. He took a deep breath and coughed as a fierce chemical scent filled his lungs.

"Are you all right?" Hartley still held onto him.

"You could have warned me that you were going to travel us between doors." Steve yanked his arm free. "I thought we were actually running into a burning building."

"There wasn't time." Hartley trotted down the steps into the cellar below.

"What's that smell?" Steve followed, bracing himself with a hand against the wall.

"The aroma of experimentation," said Hartley. "Abel and his potions."

The cellar was dimly lit by a series of wall-mounted candles. Bubbling glass containers sat beside fist-sized crystals. One wall was filled with ramshackle shelves of books and boxes. At the other end of the room, a table and chair sat beside a dirty kitchenette.

"And I thought your place was eccentric," said Steve.

Hartley pulled back a curtain to reveal a sink and toilet. Something black and long-legged scrambled out and disappeared under the table.

"What was that?" squeaked Steve.

"Dust imp, most likely." Hartley closed the curtain again. "Abel isn't here."

"Obviously." Steve kept an eye on the darkness under the table. "It's not like there's anywhere in here that he could hide." He looked back up the steps and sniffed. "Why isn't this place filled with smoke?"

"Protection seal," said Hartley. "It keeps most things out."

"Even fire? The place is burning down."

"No need to worry. The seal will hold for as long as the cellar door is intact. Now then, what was he doing in here?" He picked up a jar from the table and shook its contents.

"Do you recognise any of this?"

"No." Hartley replaced the jar. "I've never been one for technical magic, but it's Abel's forté."

"Whereas you just magic-up doorways," said Steve.

"Beautifully put." Hartley opened one of the boxes on the shelves and began to pull out a long chain. "My magic is intuitive. While Abel has his own innate magical skills, much of what he casts is learned. I don't know his heritage, but he has a knack for applying magic to devices. My will and my body are the devices I use." He came to the end of the chain and pulled out an animal's paw. "Ah," he said, "that's disappointing."

"I don't think I can stand this smell much longer. I'm getting dizzy." Steve looked back at the cellar door. Faint tendrils of smoke reached around the edges. "We need to get out of here."

"Steve? Is that you?" called a voice.

"Did you hear that?" He looked around but he could only see Hartley. "I thought I heard a woman's voice. Maybe these chemicals are making me hallucinate."

"If they are, they're affecting me too," said Hartley. "Hello?"

"I'm down here." The voice was accompanied by a rapid knocking. "Under the floor."

"Over here, Steve." Hartley was on his knees, pulling on a handle embedded in the wooden floorboards. "Give me a hand."

Steve knelt down, grasped the handle and pulled. A pungent stink of damp poured up as the trapdoor squealed open.

"Steve, thank goodness!" Eleanor climbed out and wrapped her arms around him. "I thought I'd be stuck down there forever."

"Where is Abel, dear lady?" asked Hartley.

"They took him."

"Who?"

"The two men who attacked us at Steve's school. He hid me down in that wretched pit before they forced their way in here."

Hartley slipped off his jacket and draped it around her. "Let's get you out of here."

"Thank you." She pulled the jacket around her. "I'm Eleanor."

"This is Hartley," said Steve. "He's been looking after me."

"I was so worried when you disappeared," she said.

"I'm fine, Eleanor."

"I saw you hide in the cupboard, but when Abel had sent those men packing and I opened the door to let you out, you were nowhere to be seen. I asked Abel where you were but all he would say is that you were safe."

"Come on." Steve pulled Eleanor to her feet. "We need to get out of here."

"Is it safe?" she asked. "They might still be in the house."

"I doubt it," said Steve. "The place is burning down."

"What?"

"It might be best if we hurry," said Hartley. "While the cellar door is still in one piece."

"How do we get out?" said Eleanor. "Is there a secret tunnel?"

"I can do better than that, dear lady," said Hartley. He spat into both hands and rubbed them together.

"You're going to love this, Eleanor," said Steve as they followed Hartley up the stairs. "I think."

Chapter Twenty-Three

"Are you sure about this, Eleanor?" said Steve.

"Of course," she said. "We need him on our side. As you both said, it's probably not safe for me to return home with those two thugs on the loose, and I can't begin to imagine how I would explain it all to the police. This is our best chance."

With her make-up removed, her hair still wet from being washed, and dressed in a change of clothes from Hartley's stock, Eleanor looked like a smaller, frailer version of herself: but still as indomitable as ever.

"Who exactly is this 'Winters' character?" Hartley strode along with them, arms swinging as he attempted to keep up with Eleanor.

"He's the Chief Financial Officer of the Haven Corporation. Basically, Rex's stand-in and in charge until Steve's father takes over."

"I can't see Dad wanting to take over," said Steve. "He's an archaeologist, not…" He paused, lost for the right word. "I don't think he'd want to run a robotics corporation."

"Whatever," said Eleanor. "That isn't important right now."

"And you think Winters will listen?" said Hartley. "That he'll help?"

"I'm sure he will. He knows me, and Abel."

Steve kept his head down as they walked through the streets of the city centre. There were so many people, both friend and foe, who could recognise him. His main fear was running into his attackers. They'd followed him to school. They could be anywhere.

And what if people from school saw him? How would he explain his absence—his second absence—and the people he was with?

"All right?" Hartley nudged him. "You look worried."

"Worried?" *Understatement of the century,* Steve thought. "Just a bit."

"With Eleanor in charge?" Hartley whispered. "What could possibly go wrong?"

"Good." Eleanor stopped abruptly. "We're here." She tucked damp strands of hair behind her ears and straightened the collar of the oversized jacket Hartley had provided.

"This place?" said Hartley, staring up the reaching walls of the city skyscraper. "This is impressive." He cupped his hands around his face as he pressed it to the glass.

"You're not supposed to do that." Steve pulled him away. "It isn't normal."

"Or appropriate," said Eleanor.

The glass face of the building mirrored the twilight sky, grey stretching up into descending darkness. Through the glass front, they could see a security guard robot crouched in front of the reception desk within.

"Are you sure Winters lives here?" asked Hartley. "It doesn't look very homely."

"These are residential quarters for Haven employees. Winters has the penthouse apartment," she said. "If we can just get up there, I'm sure he'll help us."

"What if he won't see us?" said Steve. "What do we do then?"

"Stand back." Hartley flexed his fingers. "I think I can get us through this door and into the lift in there. Shouldn't be a problem." He frowned. "Unless of course there's someone already in the lift."

"You can't use magic here," said Eleanor, stepping between him and the door. "What if someone sees?"

"Good point." Hartley pushed his hands into his pockets. "What do you suggest in that case?"

"You're a Haven employee, Eleanor," said Steve. "Can't you get us in? Look." He opened a flap on a panel beside the door. "Biometric identification."

"Bio what?" said Hartley.

"You use your fingerprint instead of a key," said Steve.

"Not this one," said Eleanor. "It's a retinal scanner. Hartley, that means you use your eye for identification."

"I don't think I like the idea of that. Are there needles involved?" Hartley began to blink.

"What about the security guard, though?" she said. "Won't it want to know who we are?"

"Maybe it'll think we're residents." Steve shrugged. "It's worth a go."

"And if it doesn't?" she said.

"Don't worry. We'll deal with it," said Hartley. "One robot

against the three of us. It doesn't stand a chance."

Steve wanted to say something sarcastic: looking at the three of them, he doubted very much that they could contain a security robot. He decided to keep his mouth shut.

"How do I look?" said Eleanor. "Am I presentable?"

"Beautiful," said Hartley.

"You're just saying that." She sighed and opened the flap on the biometric panel. "Here goes." She looked into the biometric scanner and the doors slid open.

*

Hartley straightened his jacket collar and admired his reflection in the mirrored walls of the lift. His stomach was pulled in and his face a little red from the effort.

"Not bad, not bad." He breathed out and his stomach returned to its normal location. "So how many floors up is this penthouse?"

"Twenty-four," said Eleanor.

"Twenty-four? That's a tad excessive, isn't it?"

Steve shrugged. "It's normal for a city skyscraper. They all have at least twenty or thirty floors. Some have over fifty." It felt good to explain his kind of 'normal' to Hartley, rather than the other way round.

"I like to keep my feet on, or at least near, the ground." Hartley looked at his boots and jumped, slamming his feet down on the tiled floor. "How strong are these lifts?"

"Let's not find out." Eleanor wrapped her arm through his. "I'd rather get there in one piece."

151

Steve watched the floor buttons light up in turn: nineteen, twenty, twenty-one, twenty-two, twenty-three.

"Ready?" said Hartley.

"No," said Steve.

'Ding'. The final button illuminated, and the lift doors opened.

*

"Eleanor, what are you doing here?" The apartment was dimly lit by a handful of lamps scattered throughout the immense room. Steve strained to see who had spoken.

"Thomas?" Eleanor took a couple of steps into the room. "Is that you?"

"Who else were you expecting? Lights up." The lights slowly illuminated until the room was fully lit and Steve could see Thomas Winters standing a few paces away. He was still dressed for work in an expensive suit. Steve wondered if Winters ever switched off his corporate persona.

"Thomas, we need your help." Eleanor stepped towards him. "Steve and I were attacked."

"I had no idea." Winters remained where he was, looking from Eleanor to Steve, and then to Hartley. "Who's this?"

"A friend," said Eleanor. "This is Hartley. He and Abel saved me."

"Abel?" said Winters. "You know where he is?"

"Not exactly."

"We came to tell you the truth," said Steve. "About my uncle's death."

"We knew we could trust you, Thomas," said Eleanor. "That's why we came here instead of going to the police."

"I see." Winters looked them all up and down. "You'd better come in then."

*

They sat at a marble-topped table that wouldn't have been out of place in a conference room: Winters on one side, the three of them on the other.

"Now, I know that some of what I'm about to say might seem unlikely." Eleanor fiddled with her hair as she spoke. "But please bear with me."

"I can do that," said Winters. "Go on."

"A lot has happened since you last saw me," she said. "That's why I'm dressed like this." She touched the sleeve of her jacket, then went back to smoothing her hair. "I went to see Steve at school, and we were attacked." She stopped, her hands clenching into fists. "But that isn't the place to start."

"It started with the deliveries," said Steve. "Didn't it, Eleanor? That's what you told us."

"It did. Thank you, Steve." Eleanor took a deep breath, laying her hands flat on the tabletop. "Abel noticed a number of deliveries being made to the basement of the Haven Corporation building."

"The basement?" said Winters. "But there's nothing down there. It isn't even used for storage."

"Exactly why Abel thought it was odd," said Eleanor.

"Did he mention it to Rex?" Winters spoke to Eleanor, but his eyes kept finding Hartley. "The old man had a habit of keeping his projects secret."

"He did," said Eleanor, "and Rex knew nothing about it."

"Curious," said Winters. ". But I'm still not sure how this has anything to do with Rex's death."

"Murder," said Steve.

"Murder," said Winters, his mouth twitching. "Sorry."

"I'm getting to that," said Eleanor. "Rex told Abel that he would look into it. Errors do happen, from time to time."

"True," said Winters, his eyes flicking to Hartley again.

"Still, it didn't sit well with Abel so, when the deliveries continued, he decided to investigate."

"And what did he find?"

"A laboratory," said Eleanor. "In the basement."

"What was in the laboratory?"

"Somebody was creating, trying to create, a new kind of robot," she said. "Abel disabled the process."

"Disabled?" said Winters.

"He removed a component and took it with him. A metal disc, I believe."

"We need to speak to him," said Winters. "If any hidden experimentation has been taking place, we need the full details. Do we know where this component is?"

"That isn't important right now."

"There will have to be an investigation," said Winters. "This is unacceptable."

"Abel found Rex's body in there."

"That isn't possible." Winters's eyes narrowed. "Rex's body was found in his office."

"Somebody must have moved him," she said. "He was murdered in the laboratory."

"I see." Winters sat back in his chair. "When Abel disappeared, I suspected he had harmed Rex but now it all makes sense."

"Thank you, Thomas." Eleanor took a deep breath and slowly released it. "You don't know what a relief it is to know you believe us. When we speak to the police—"

"In the morning," said Winters. "When you've had a decent rest. You look like you need a good night's sleep, and a clean change of clothes."

"I suppose I do look a state." Eleanor touched her hair. "But I think it's important we speak to the police as soon as possible."

"Tomorrow, when you've rested," said Winters. "In the meantime, I can arrange a car to take you home. Steve, you too. Do you want to go back to school?"

"I think we should stick together," said Steve.

"I tell you what," said Winters. "Why don't I arrange a car for you all and you can decide where you want to go. How would that suit?"

Before any of them had a chance to answer, he stood and left the room. Steve heard Winters talking on the phone as the door closed behind him.

"You trust this man?" said Hartley.

"Of course," said Eleanor. "I've known him for years."

"I say we all go straight to the police," said Steve. "Before anything else bad can happen."

"You can drop me off on the way," said Hartley. "You don't need me there."

"You're a witness," said Steve, surprised at his reluctance to let Hartley go. He'd grown attached to the shopkeeper. "And we

155

need to get our story straight."

"We just tell them the truth," said Eleanor.

"And what about the you-know-what?" said Steve.

"What are you talking about?"

"The travelling through doors?"

"And this is exactly why I don't involve myself with the police," said Hartley.

"We'll figure it out," said Eleanor. "We'll gloss over bits. I was overcome with fright and smoke when you rescued me. I'll say that."

Their conversation halted as the door opened. "It's arranged," said Winters, as he walked into the room. "There's a car downstairs ready to take you wherever you want to go."

"Oh, that is reassuring," said Eleanor. "We've decided to go straight to the police. The sooner this is over and done with the better."

"As you wish," said Winters. "You know best, Eleanor. I won't see you down." He walked across to the lift and touched the call button. The doors slid open. "It's been a rather disturbing evening and I have calls to make. I'm sure you understand."

"Of course, Thomas, and thank you. Your support means a lot."

"I'm sure it does," he said, smiling with his mouth but not his eyes.

"We'll get out of your hair," said Eleanor. "Come along, boys."

"Thanks." Steve nodded as he and Hartley followed Eleanor into the lift.

"Goodbye Steve," said Winters, losing his smile. "Pleasant

journey."

Chapter Twenty-Four

Last time I travelled in one of these, things didn't end well, Steve thought as he and the others climbed into the car they found waiting outside.

"This is plush." Hartley bounced on the seat. "Very nice."

"He didn't seem very alarmed," said Steve, as the car pulled away. "Winters."

"It's late," said Eleanor. "He was tired. It's a lot to take in. I'm still processing it myself."

"It all seemed too easy." Steve looked to Hartley for support. "Don't you think?"

"So this vehicle is driverless?" Hartley peered into the front of the car.

"It has RDS." She paused. "It's driven by a robot," she finished.

"And you don't find that at all worrying?"

"It's perfectly safe," she said. "We're completely in control. I'll show you." She learned forward. "Driver, please state our destination."

The driving system remained silent.

"It isn't talking to you," said Hartley.

"Driver," Eleanor repeated. "Where are you taking us?"

There was still no reply.

"That's odd," she said. "Winters must have told it where to go."

"I thought he said we could decide," said Steve.

"Driver, take us to the nearest police station," said Eleanor.

"Is it time to get worried yet?" said Hartley.

"I don't understand," said Eleanor. "Driver——"

There was a squealing of breaks from the surrounding traffic as the car sped through a red light, diving over a cross-junction. Steve and the others were tossed around the interior like ragdolls in a shaken toybox.

"Driver, where are you taking us?" Eleanor demanded, her arms wrapped around the seat in front.

"I recognise this road," said Steve. "I think I know where we're going."

"Not the police station, I take it?" Hartley had braced his feet against the backs of the front seats. "Or your school?"

"We're heading towards the West Temple Bridge. Once the car drives over that, it's on the road out of the city."

"Well, the police station isn't in that direction, and neither is my apartment," said Eleanor. "Where else would Winters have told the car to take us?"

"The river?" said Steve. "I mean, into the river."

"Hold on," said Hartley as the car lurched forward, speeding up even more to overtake a line of parked cars, and clipping each one as it slid by. "Bumpy ride."

"Don't you dare say this is exciting, Hartley!" squealed Eleanor as she was thrown around. "Don't you dare."

"Can you travel us out of here?" said Steve.

"Only if you can open one of the doors."

"Driver, stop and open the door," Eleanor demanded. "Open the door!"

The doors remained firmly shut as the car dodged between oncoming traffic.

It's happening again, Steve thought. *Why did I agree to get in another Haven Corporation car? I must be mad.*

He braced himself against the window as the car's careening threw him onto the glass. He felt Hartley bash into him, mumbling something about rollercoasters. Eleanor was still shouting at the RDS to open the doors.

Something like this has happened before, he thought, staring at his fingers splayed on the glass. He remembered his mother's face close to the outside of a car window, her hand pressed to the glass as his was now. *Where did that memory come from?* he thought. *Why am I remembering it now?*

"I might have something that will help." Hartley rummaged about in his pockets, as much as he could as the car tossed him around. "Maybe—" He pulled out a piece of string and a white chocolate mouse. "Oh."

"Got it." Steve slammed the side of his fist on a small boxed-off section of the door beside him. "Come on, come on," he said as he punched it again.

"What are you doing?" said Eleanor.

"Getting the door open," he said. "I need something heavy and pointy."

"Like Eleanor's shoe?" said Hartley.

"But these are vintage Jimmy Choo."

"Eleanor!" said Steve.

"Well, if you think it'll help." She slipped off a shoe and handed it to him. "Just try not to damage it."

"No promises," he said, and stabbed the heel of the shoe into the door panel. There was a decisive click and a small square section fell to the floor. "Yes."

"No," said Eleanor quietly as he handed her back the shoe with its heel hanging off.

"How do you know what you're doing?" said Hartley.

"When I was little, our driverless car malfunctioned. I was stuck inside it on my own for a couple of hours." Steve felt around inside the door. "After that, Dad showed me how to do this. If I can just—" There was a quiet clunk and the door opened a fraction. "It worked. Hartley, can you travel us out now?"

"It would be my pleasure. Out of the way."

Steve scrambled around his friend and took Eleanor's hand. "It'll be okay," he told her.

Hartley slid the door aside and ran his hands around the door frame. "This is a new one," he said. "How exciting."

"I told you not to say that," said Eleanor.

"Hold on to me," he said, grinning at Steve. "This could get a bit rough."

Eleanor wrapped her arms around Hartley's neck and squeezed her eyes shut. Steve grabbed onto Hartley's jacket with both hands.

"Here we go!" Hartley launched himself out of the door of

the speeding car, pulling the others with him.

One second, Steve could hear squealing breaks and smell the dry air of the city. The next, he and the others tumbled onto the floor of Hartley's kitchen.

Chapter Twenty-Five

"Blessing, can I help at all?" Eleanor sat at the kitchen table across from Steve, an empty mug in her hand. Her shoes, one with a broken heel, sat on the table in front of her. On her feet, she wore a pair of black lace-ups from Hartley's stock.

Steve chewed a biscuit. It was hard and dry, but it had been all he could find to eat in the kitchen that morning that didn't need cooking, other than a pot of burnt porridge.

"No, you're a guest." Blessing picked up a tea towel and set about drying a pile of dripping, mismatched crockery. "Do you want some breakfast? We have eggs."

"No, thank you, Blessing." Eleanor tapped her fingernails on the side of the mug.

"It's really no trouble." Blessing picked up the pot of coffee from the stove. "I could top up your drink."

"Where's Hartley?" said Steve.

"Still asleep," said Blessing, replacing the pot on the stove. "He'd never admit it, but travelling magic really takes it out of him, especially from a moving car."

"I don't know how he can sleep at a time like this," said Eleanor.

"He says it recharges his brain cells," said Blessing. "Gives him answers to his problems."

"I think I will have another coffee." Eleanor went to the stove and filled her mug with the thick, dark, grainy liquid. "Steve?"

"Not for me."

"I need to do something," said Eleanor, pacing up and down. "All this sitting around is making me nervous."

"That and the six cups of coffee," said Steve.

There was a bang, a thump, and a strangled cry. The curtain that separated Hartley's bedroom from the kitchen yanked open. He staggered out, his shirt untucked from the back of his trousers.

"What are we going to do?" Eleanor was still pacing. "This is a disaster."

"Oh, it's too early in the morning for that word." Hartley shook himself like a bear and yawned.

"I think Eleanor's right," said Blessing. "What are we going to do?"

"Who is this 'we'?" said Hartley. "I know you want to help, Blessing, but—"

"I'm not a child," she said. "You let Steve help. Why not me?"

"There is one way you could help that would be invaluable," said Hartley.

"Yes?" said Blessing.

"You can look after the shop while I'm out."

"Aww, why?" said Blessing. "It's not like you have any

customers."

"I might. I've had them before. On occasion." Hartley tucked in his shirt and shouldered the braces that held up his trousers. "Anyway, I've been thinking—"

"So, have I," said Eleanor. "After last night's events, we've no idea who we can trust."

"We can't trust Winters," said Steve.

"But we don't know for certain," said Eleanor. "That car could have been programmed from the Haven offices. Or whoever killed Rex could be controlling Winters."

"Or Winters could have sent us to our death all by himself," said Hartley.

"Do you think so?" she said. "I suppose it's possible. I just don't know anymore, so I've come to a decision."

"Can I help?" said Blessing.

"No, dear," said Eleanor. "I need to find Steve's parents. If this device that Abel left with you was intended for your father, he must know what it is."

"I think you're on to something there," said Hartley.

"Can I come with you?" said Steve. "To find Mum and Dad." He wanted to say that he missed them, that he wouldn't feel safe until he was with them again, but that seemed too childish to put into words so instead he just said, "Please?"

"Steve, can I be honest with you?" she said.

"Yes," said Steve quietly. *This sounds like a no,* he thought.

"I'm not used to children. You're a lovely boy, but if I'm to find your parents, I really need to concentrate on that and not looking after you."

"I wouldn't be a bother," he said. "Hartley, have I been a

bother?"

"Well…" Hartley began.

"I want to keep you safe," she interrupted. "I don't know if I'm going to be safe where I'm going. I don't even know where I'm going. At least, if you're here, with Hartley and Blessing, I know you'll be protected."

"I get it," said Steve, feeling that he really didn't.

"Hartley, can you help me with your door magic?" she said. "To find the Havens?"

"I'm afraid that I have no idea where they might be," he said. "I can travel you to the train station though, or the airport."

"That's no good without my passport, and money. If only I could go home."

"I wish I could get you there," said Hartley. "Unfortunately, I can't travel to a place I haven't already visited. I can take you into the city."

"And what if her apartment is being watched?" said Steve. "That's too dangerous."

"But I need to get in there." Eleanor slammed down her mug on the table, spilling a dollop of the coffee grains. "Sorry, sorry." She put her face in her hands.

"No worries." Blessing retrieved a cloth from a drawer. "I'll get it."

"Thank you." Eleanor dropped into a chair and clasped her hands on the table. "I'm so used to knowing exactly what to do."

"Sometimes, dear lady, you just have to wing it." Hartley patted her shoulder.

"What if…?" Blessing began. "Hang on, let me think about this."

"Think about what?" said Steve.

"I'm still figuring this all out." Blessing closed her eyes and screwed up her face.

"Is she doing magic?" said Steve.

"Looks like constipation to me," said Hartley.

"I'm trying to think," said Blessing. "When I heal, I have to make a connection with the person I'm healing. I have to connect with the person they were before they were injured or became ill."

"Like telepathy?" said Steve.

"Kind of," she said. "So, here's the thing. Hartley, you can only travel somewhere you know. Right?"

"Indeed," said Hartley.

"So, to travel to Eleanor's home, you need to know that place. What if I could connect with Eleanor and then, somehow, add you to that connection?" She opened her eyes. "Would that work?"

"It might," said Hartley.

"Can I help?" said Steve.

"You can be my fuse," said Blessing.

"Right," said Steve, looking at Hartley. "Will that hurt?"

Chapter Twenty-Six

"You know how a fuse works in an electrical circuit, don't you?" Hartley stood with his hand on the back door in his kitchen.

"Of course," said Steve.

"That's good." Hartley held out his hand to Blessing. "Because it's a mystery to me."

"Stop worrying him." Blessing took Hartley's hand. "Steve, I just need you to watch out for me. Just in case. I haven't done this before."

"I can do that," said Steve.

"If it looks like things are going wrong, I need you to stop me. Don't worry." She grinned at his worried expression. "Just tell me to stop, or shake me."

"Or separate our hands," said Hartley. "That should do it."

"Is this safe?" said Eleanor. "I don't want to hurt anyone."

"It should be," said Blessing. "I just want to connect with your 'knowing' about your home and pass it to Hartley."

"That doesn't sound too bad." Eleanor took Blessing's free hand and closed her eyes. "I'm ready."

"Okay then," said Blessing." Here we go."

*

Eleanor's apartment was as smart and co-ordinated as its owner had been when Steve first met her. The open-plan area, from its walls to the closed metallic blinds to the sleek kitchen cabinets, were all coloured in a palette of lilacs. The room wasn't immense, but the high ceilings made it feel spacious.

"It worked!" Hartley did a little jump and punched the air with his fist. "I knew it would," he said as the others frowned at him. "I'll just…" He pointed to the door and pushed it shut.

"I'll pack some things. Make yourselves at home," Eleanor said as she opened a door. "Hartley?"

"Yes, dear lady?"

"Try not to touch anything."

"Wouldn't dream of it," he said as she closed the door behind her. "As if."

"I love this place." Blessing stood in the middle of the room, eyes wide and hands grasped before her. "Is this what your home is like, Steve?"

"A bit," said Steve. "I mean, we live in an apartment; nothing as luxurious as this, though. I suppose working for the biggest technology manufacturer in the world has its benefits."

"This is swish." Hartley lowered himself onto a sofa and bounced slightly. "It's all a bit match-y though."

"Not like your place then," said Steve. "You prefer clash-y."

"It's so pretty." Blessing touched a throw that was neatly folded over the back of a chair. "And soft."

"I'll grant you that," said Hartley.

"Come here." Steve beckoned Blessing over to a panel on the wall. "Touch it."

"I don't know if I should," she said. "What does it do?"

"Touch it and find out."

"Okay." Blessing carefully tapped on the screen. There was a tiny *'blip'* sound as the screen sprang into life, revealing a rotating palette of colours.

"Choose one," he said.

"Any colour?"

"Whatever you like."

"I think… this." She tapped on a deep-sea turquoise circle. "Now what?"

"Look." Steve turned her around. "What do you think?"

Everything in the room—the sofa that Hartley sat on, the walls, the throw, the carpet, even the ceiling—all gradually changed from tones of lilac to a range of turquoise shades.

"That is impressive," said Hartley, checking his hands for turquoise as he snatched them from the sofa and stood up. "Do it again."

"No, don't," said Eleanor. "It isn't a toy."

Dressed in her own clothes, Eleanor looked more like herself. She rummaged in a small handbag as she walked into the room, a coat folded over her arm. Behind her, a small robot lugged an oversized travel bag across the floor.

"I didn't touch anything," said Hartley. "It was them."

"Tell-tale," said Blessing.

"Shall I call a taxi, Eleanor?" said the robot. An orange light blipped on the robot's central cylindrical body part when it spoke. "I see that you have your passport with you. Are you going on holiday?"

"Thank you, Hetty, but that won't be necessary."

"You gave it a name?" said Steve.

"It felt like the polite thing to do," said Eleanor. "Calling her by her model number just seemed odd."

"Her?" said Hartley, walking around the room. "Do robots have a gender?"

"Legally, no," said Eleanor. "But she seems like a 'her' to me."

"Will that be all?" Hetty crouched beside the travel bag at the front door.

There was a clatter and a smash, and Hartley dodged back from the kitchen counter.

"Sorry, sorry." A broken teacup lay at his feet.

"I did say…" Eleanor began.

"I'll sort that." Hetty the robot crossed quickly to Hartley. "Excuse me, please," she said, looking up at him.

"Of course, of course," he blustered, retreating.

"Thank you." Hetty picked up the broken pieces with two appendages, while a third converted into a narrow tube and sucked away the smaller remnants.

"Fascinating." Hartley knelt down beside the robot. "Do you cook?" he said.

"What would you like me to cook?" said the robot.

"Nothing, Hetty," said Eleanor. "Disregard."

"Very well, Eleanor." The robot sped to the other side of the kitchen counter, where a door flipped open to reveal a bin.

"That is a very well-mannered robot," said Hartley.

"It's part of the bonding process," said Steve. "The robot's behaviour protocol is aligned with the personality of the owner."

"I see," said Hartley, frowning. "I'll pretend I understood what you just said."

"Right, first things first." Eleanor pulled on her coat and closed her handbag. "I need to get to the airport. A friend of mine, who doesn't work for Haven Corp, keeps a private jet there. It's probably best if I avoid the commercial airlines just in case someone is watching."

"Oh, I can do the airport," said Hartley. "I've travelled there before."

"Secondly, I've instructed Hetty to allow you access to the apartment. Just in case you ever needed to come here. I know it's not ideal—"

"It's ideal to me," said Blessing.

"Thank you." Eleanor looked around the apartment. She wore the same sad smile that Steve had seen on his mum's face when she had dropped him off back at school. "I suppose we'd better go."

"Will you be out for long?" said Hetty. "I hear the weather is likely to improve."

"I'll be gone for a few days," said Eleanor, looking down at the robot who crouched at her feet. "I think."

"Have a nice few days, Eleanor."

"Ready?" Steve picked up the travel bag.

"As ready as I'll ever be," said Eleanor. "Hartley, if you can do the honours."

Steve looked back as Hartley opened the doorway to the airport. Hetty the robot crouched in the middle of the room, watching them. He knew she was just a robot, but he felt that she looked sad, and a little abandoned. He waved at her, then stepped through the door and it closed behind him.

Chapter Twenty-Seven

"It feels odd not having Eleanor around." Steve and Hartley sat at the kitchen table. The place was beginning to feel like home to Steve.

"It does seem rather quiet without her," said Hartley.

"Do you think she'll find my parents?"

"I'm sure she'll do her best," said Hartley. "I doubt she fails at much, when she sets her mind to something."

"What do we do now? I can't go back to school; I'd be in so much trouble if I did, and those men might turn up again." *And I don't want to go back there,* he thought.

"True, true," said Hartley. "Our next course of action, I suppose, should be to find Abel, which unfortunately means tracking down Braeden Kendra. "

"Is that a problem?"

"All I know of Braeden Kendra's whereabouts is that he occupies a section of abandoned underground stations somewhere in the city. Which ones, I have no idea. It could take weeks to find him. What we need is someone in-the-know.

Someone who frequents the city."

"What about James and Michael?" said Steve. "They live in the city. James knew about Braden Kendra looking for Abel."

"It's possible," said Hartley. "More than possible. Good man, Steve."

"So what do we do?"

"I pay the boys a visit," said Hartley, standing up and going to the hat stand. "I've been there before. I can use the back door—"

"*We* pay them a visit." Blessing stood at the bottom of the stairs. "You're not going without me."

"And me," said Steve. "It was my idea after all."

"I see." Hartley looked from Steve, to Blessing, to Steve again, then he shrugged. "It seems I'm outnumbered. But no detours: straight there and straight back. Agreed?"

"Agreed," Blessing and Steve said together.

"And no magic out there either," said Hartley. "You never know who might be watching."

*

"I don't think I'll ever get used to that." Steve stared back through the doorway he had just stepped from. He could still smell the burnt porridge in Hartley's kitchen.

"It still surprises me sometimes." Blessing grabbed the door handle. "Best shut it in case someone on this side finds it."

"No, leave it open," said Hartley. "Just in case."

"Just in case of what?" said Steve.

"Just in case we need to make a quick exit." Hartley sniffed the air. "On the off-chance."

"Are we likely to need to make a quick exit?"

"Anything is possible," said Blessing. She shrugged and followed Hartley into a pool of light that fell from a circular window behind them. Their shoes slapped on the ceramic floor tiles, chequered black and white and veiled with dust.

"What is this place?" whispered Steve as he trotted after them.

"The Deepening Theatre," said Hartley. "No need to whisper. It's been abandoned for years."

"James and Michael live here?" said Steve. "In this dump?"

"They sleep here sometimes," said Blessing.

"Out of the rain," said Hartley, "and away from the eyes of the workaday police."

"Makes sense." Steve's eyes slowly became accustomed to the shadows of the theatre foyer as he looked around. A wide staircase swept up from the tiled floor. Five chandeliers hung above their heads, the light from the window playing dully on their glass droplets.

"Through here, I think." Hartley charged towards a pair of tall doors, Blessing close behind him.

"Wait for me," said Steve, hurrying after them.

Beyond the doors, the theatre auditorium sat in dusty darkness. Steve could feel the dust in his nostrils when he breathed in.

"Light orb?" he said.

"Too risky," said Hartley. "We can't use magic in the city."

"Why not?" said Steve.

"Didn't I mention it?" said Hartley. "Theoretically, we're not allowed to do magic outside protected areas like Darkacre."

"Theoretically?"

"Well, it's not as black-and-white as that. It's more a case of not being obvious, or not getting caught. Hang on."

Steve heard Hartley muttering under his breath, then there was a click. Hartley swung a torch around the room, the yellow light flitting across chair backs and wooden panelled walls.

"Do you think they're here?" Steve followed Hartley along an aisle between the seats.

"James," Blessing called. "Michael?"

"James?" Hartley called out as the torchlight fell upon a crumpled form on the stage.

The teenager moved his head to look at them, his lips moving silently.

Hartley bounded up the steps onto the stage, with the others close behind. "Here." He shoved the torch into Steve's hand. "James, my boy." He knelt down and touched the teenager's face. "Who did this?"

"Kendra," James whispered. "We put up a good fight though. You should have seen his thugs' faces when I dropped a chandelier on them."

"Steve, shine the light on him," said Hartley. "We need to see the extent of his injuries."

"Okay." The torchlight revealed the teenager's body, clothes disarrayed and a spreading patch of blood on his sweatshirt.

"Blessing," said Hartley. "I think this is your area of expertise."

"I'm here." She knelt on the other side of James and took his hand. "Look at me, James."

"Please." James turned to her, gripping her fingers. "Michael zapped Kendra, so they took him. You have to get him back."

"I need to concentrate," she said, "to find out how bad the injury is." She closed her eyes and touched her free hand to his side.

"Can we move him, Blessing?"

"No," she said, opening her eyes. "The wound is too deep. I have to heal him here. At least stop the bleeding."

"Steve, keep the light steady," said Hartley. "James?" The teenager slowly moved his head towards Hartley. His eyelids drooped. "James, Blessing is going to stop the bleeding, but you have to stay awake. Can you do that?"

James's eyes closed.

"James!"

"Your breath smells." James opened his eyes with a pained smile.

"Good boy." Hartley patted his hand.

"Will it hurt?" said Steve.

"It hurts now," said James.

"Good point," said Steve. "Is this safe? Using magic in the city? You said not to."

"Healing is a natural process," said Hartley. "All that Blessing is doing is encouraging and accelerating that process. It'll be fine."

"That's good," said Steve.

"James, are you ready?" said Hartley.

"As ready as I'll ever be."

"Good enough," said Hartley. "Blessing?"

"If you want to cry, that's fine." Blessing touched a hand to the wound in James' side. "Don't worry."

178

"Thanks," said James. "I'm sure I can cope."

"I'm sorry," she said.

"What for?"

"This." She pushed her hand down on the wound.

*

"Not too fast." James staggered with one arm around Steve's shoulders, the other hand clamped to his injured side.

"Not far now." Hartley walked beside them, the torch in his hand. "Once we're home, I'll get you some food and we can have a sit down."

"There's no time for that." James grunted with the effort of each step. "Michael needs me."

"You'll be no good to him if you don't rest," said Blessing. She stood on the Darkacre side of the open doorway, the light of Hartley's kitchen casting her shadow into the foyer.

"Hartley?" Steve looked across at the shopkeeper. "Doesn't your door magic show up if you use it outside of Darkacre?"

"Not really," said Hartley. "It's over and done with so quickly that it's hardly a blip, magically-speaking."

"But if you left the door open?" said Steve. "What then?"

"If I did that—" Hartley frowned at the open doorway. "I see what you mean. Come on, James." Hartley slapped James' free arm around his shoulders and took the teenager's weight. "No dawdling."

"I'm going as fast as I can," James moaned as Hartley dragged him along.

Steve fell back to let them through the door. Warm air drifted through from the lit stove in the kitchen beyond.

"Shut the door, Steve," barked Hartley from the kitchen. "Quick."

A sound like a vacuum seal releasing echoed in the foyer. Steve looked back at a lone, masked figure who stood in the circle of light cast in the foyer by the window above. He or she was dressed in grey from the hood on their head to the boots on their feet. Their hands were sheathed in heavy gloves edged with metal and their face was covered by a mirrored mask. As the figure turned to regard him, Steve realised that he could see his own face reflected back at him.

There was a second sound like the first, and a third, as two identically dressed individuals appeared. They raised their left hands in unison and charged towards the open door.

"Close it, Steve." Hartley struggled to support James as the teenager turned around to see what was happening. "Quickly."

Steve retreated to the open door with quick, jagged steps. His heel slammed into the bottom rail of the door frame and he hurtled backwards into Hartley's kitchen.

"The door!" Hartley shouted.

The three masked figures were almost at the threshold. They squeezed their outheld hands into fists. A mist sprayed from their gloves, scattering through the doorway. One by one, Steve's friends collapsed to the floor like abandoned ragdolls.

Steve stumbled to his knees, dragging himself up by the door handle.

The three, grey figures reached the door and as the first lifted their foot to step through, Steve slammed the door shut.

Chapter Twenty-Eight

"Blessing!" Steve patted her face, but she didn't respond.

"Hartley." Steve crawled over and checked the pulse in the shopkeeper's wrist. He found one but he had no idea whether it was a good pulse or a weak pulse, or what to do at that exact moment.

"Steve." James lifted his head, then grunted at the pain in his wounded side. "Was it the Hidden?"

"Do the Hidden wear mirrored masks?"

"That's them."

"Then, yes, it was the Hidden," said Steve, going to his side. "I don't think you should move."

"In total agreement with you there, mate." James lay his head back down. "I'm also bleeding. The fall must have opened the wound up again."

"What do I do?"

"Get Frobisher. He'll help."

"But he doesn't know about Hartley's back door."

"Needs must," said James in a sleepy voice. "Excuse me, Steve. I'm just going to pass out."

*

Steve hammered on the door of one of the terrace houses attached to the archway. He hoped he had the right house. This was going to be awkward to explain to a stranger.

"What you want?"

The door swung open suddenly to reveal Frobisher frowning down at him. A polka-dot oven glove dangled from his grasp.

"I need your help."

"The gate is shut." Frobisher began to close the door.

"Not the gate." Steve stamped his foot inside the doorway, blocking it from shutting. "Hartley needs your help at his shop."

"Why? What's he done?"

"He…" Steve stopped. Just how much could he tell the gatekeeper without getting Hartley into trouble? "He's hurt. Blessing too. And James. I don't know who else to ask."

Frobisher looked him up and down, sniffed, then stepped back. "You'd better come in."

"But we don't have time," said Steve as the gatekeeper disappeared inside. "Frobisher, wait."

Frobisher's home, as Steve found when he followed the old man inside, was comfortably furnished with mismatched furniture that had seen better days. Floral plates and glass paperweights sat on a shelf that ran around the wall close to the ceiling. The green-tiled fireplace seemed too generous for a room so small.

"I need details," said Frobisher. "How were they hurt?"

"Well, we went into the city, to the Deepening Theatre to find James."

"Not through my gate, you didn't." Frobisher looked up from the dresser drawer he was rooting through.

"Err, no," said Steve. "Hartley can explain that. I think."

"Hmm." Frobisher grunted and returned to his search. "Go on."

"So, we found James and he'd been in a fight, and we were leaving, and then the Hidden turned up."

"What?" Frobisher's reaction was so violent that the drawer was wrenched out of the dresser, spilling its contents onto the floor.

"And then they kind of used this spray?" Steve could feel his voice getting squeaky. "And I closed the door, and everyone is lying on the floor in Hartley's kitchen," he finished.

"I see," said Frobisher. "Well, it was a good thing you were there." Frobisher grabbed a tin that had fallen out of the drawer. "Lead on."

*

"Stop fussing. I'm not a child." Hartley batted Frobisher's hand away. He sat at the kitchen table, a bandage held to a cut on his forehead.

"Stop acting like one, then." Frobisher left him alone and turned to James.

"Don't start on me," said James. "I'm fine. Blessing healed me."

"I only stopped the bleeding," she said. "I can heal you proper now we're back."

"You'll do no such thing," said Frobisher. "I've no idea how the sleep haze might affect your magic. You could make his wound worse. Fools, the lot of you. Bringing the Hidden down on yourselves like that. Hartley, you should be ashamed."

"I thought you were all dead." Steve stood beside the back door, a mug of Hartley's pungent coffee in his hands. "The way you all went down like that."

"That's the sleep haze," said Frobisher. "The Hidden use it to subdue magicals. Sometimes workadays too. I'm surprised you didn't feel the effects yourself."

"Good thing, he didn't," said James, "otherwise we wouldn't be sitting here. Once the Hidden get their hands on you, that's it. No chance to escape." He rubbed a hand across the top of his nose. "Leaves a stinking headache."

"They had mirrors for faces," said Steve, remembering his own reflection staring back at him. "What are they?"

"Police, of a sort," said Frobisher. "The powers-that-be decided that magicals should live under a number of rules. They didn't want the workadays knowing that magic was real, see, especially after a certain contingent almost messed that up for us all. So the decision was made to form the Hidden Army to police any interaction between us and the workaday world."

"I fear I may be to blame for our current dilemma. I should have known better than to leave my door open for so long," said Hartley. "The Hidden must have picked up on it."

"Or my magic during the fight," said James.

"You used magic in the city?" said Frobisher.

"They had Michael. What did you expect me to do?"

"Idiots, the both of you," said Frobisher. "You see, Steve, we can practice magic out there, outside Darkacre, as long as it's in secret and subtle." He tutted and rolled his eyes. "And these two are about as subtle as a brick wall."

"So what would have happened if they'd caught us?" said Steve.

"Best not to think about it," said Frobisher, shuddering.

"Why not?"

"People disappear. That's all I'm saying. Sometimes, they come back. Sometimes, they don't. That's why it's important to obey the rules."

"We're perfectly safe now, Steve," said Hartley. "You don't have to stand guard." He patted the table. "Sit down. We need to take stock before we three head out again."

"Four," said James. "I'm coming too. I know where Braeden Kendra's at. I heard one of his yobs say they were heading back to Barrowdown Station."

"Three," said Hartley. "You're in no state to come with us. You need to rest. You can go home with Frobisher."

"But—"

"He's right." Blessing reached across and touched his arm. "Michael needs you to be well."

"I should stop you," said Frobisher. "Illegal travelling. Illegal magic use. It's not right; it's not safe."

"It's not your decision to make," said James.

"There are rules," said Frobisher. "There are rules for a reason. To keep us all safe from those who would take advantage of us. Those who would harm us."

"Like Braeden Kendra?" said Steve. "He's a magical and he doesn't obey any rules. He just takes what he wants and, at the moment, he has our friends. What use are rules if they don't keep everyone safe?" He crossed his arms, surprised at himself for speaking out, but also a little impressed.

"You can't use this back door," said Frobisher.

"It's Hartley's door," said Steve. "That's up to him."

"No, I mean you can't use this back door because the Hidden will be trying to locate it," said Frobisher. "Soon as you open the door, they'll find you."

"That's unfortunate," said Hartley. "Of course, you're right, so there's really no other option." He raised his eyebrows at Frobisher.

"What do you mean?" said the gatekeeper. "You want to travel through my gate? You expect me to let you out after what you've done? I should be handing you all into the authorities."

"But you won't, will you?" said Blessing. "Michael needs us. Abel too."

"Please, Frobisher," said James, trying to stand. "He's my little bruv. I can't leave him there."

"Sit down." Frobisher pushed James back into his seat. "You'll open the wound."

"Please, Frobisher," said Steve. "Then, once we have them back here safe, we'll hand ourselves in to the authorities, won't we, Hartley?"

"Well, I'm not sure…" Hartley spluttered.

"Hartley!" Blessing snapped.

"We'll hand ourselves in, yes," said Hartley. "If it's necessary," he added.

"Well, when you put it like that." Frobisher looked at each of them in turn, his frown looming over his generous nose. "On your own heads be it."

"Thank you, Frobisher," said Steve. "You won't regret it."

"I'm already regretting it," said Frobisher. "What's new?"

Chapter Twenty-Nine

"I can't believe it brought us out here." Steve slowly turned around to stare at the archway. "It stands out a bit, doesn't it?"

The archway, by comparison to the straight lines and clean surfaces of the City Centre Plaza around it, was constructed of weathered, grey stone brick. Above the archway, and just off centre, sat an equally grey stone gargoyle.

"Where did you think it would bring us out?" said Hartley.

"I don't know. Some unmarked back alleyway? It's so busy and public here. How come I've never noticed this archway before?" Steve stared up at the gargoyle. "That is the spitting image of Frobisher."

"It's Frobisher's eye on this side of the gate, plus it marks the archway for mag—" He paused. "For people like me. It's odd that you can see it."

"Because I'm not like you?" said Steve. "Hartley, not many people are like you."

"You know what I mean. We." Hartley silently mouthed

'magicals'. "We can see the archway. It's how we find our way into Darkacre, but workadays, non-you-know-whats, generally don't see it."

"Maybe I'm soaking up the—" Steve silently mouthed the word 'magic', then snorted a laugh.

Hartley's lips trembled into a smile, then he too began to laugh in booming chuckles.

"If you two have stopped messing around, which way do we go?" Blessing crossed her arms and scowled at them. "What?" she said, as Steve and Hartley continued to laugh. "What?"

*

"Barrowdown Station." Hartley brushed his hand across the grimy surface of the station sign. "See?"

"I've never heard of this place." Steve peered through the wire mesh that encased the two sides of the station.

"You wouldn't have." Hartley tugged on the fence. "They closed it decades ago." A section of the mesh broke away. "Excellent."

"So we're going in there?" *Obviously,* he thought, feeling a definite tug towards flight rather than fight.

"As I recall, you insisted on coming."

"Don't worry, Steve." Blessing took his arm. "I'll protect you."

"But who's going to protect me?" Hartley rolled back the wire mesh until there was a comfortable gap to squeeze through. "Shall we?" he said.

"Is it dark in there?" Steve peered in through the space. "It looks dark in there."

"Only one way to find out." Hartley pushed him inside. "Onwards."

What had looked to Steve like a dark cave from the street opened out into a dimly lit, red-tiled room with a concrete floor. Half-collapsed posters of theatre shows and holiday destinations plastered the walls. Footmarks trod twisting routes in the floor dust. A shuttered window, bearing the word *'Tickets'* sat in the light of two flickering, wall-mounted electric lights.

"Look at this." Steve ran a hand over a glass panel that covered a map of the underground network. A red arrow and the words *'You are here'* pointed to their current location.

"Barrowdown." Hartley tapped his finger on the station name. "Over there is the city centre." He gestured to the central portion of the map. "So where is Braeden Kendra's fortress?"

"Fortress?" said Steve. "Like a castle?"

"In his eyes." Hartley scanned the map. "Arrogant as ever."

"There's a big unmarked area over here." Steve followed the tunnel line from Barrowdown to a black, blank square.

"That could be it," said Hartley. "We'll know it when we see it. Now then." He turned on his heel and marched to the ticket window. "Here we go." Hartley raised a hand to knock, then stopped. "Let me do the talking," he said.

"Fine by me," said Steve.

Hartley knocked on the shutter. There was a snort, a creak, a prolonged sigh, and then the shutter slammed open.

"What do you want?" snapped the woman inside, a coil of smoke furling out from her open mouth. She was elderly and pale, skin stretched tight across the bones in her heavily painted face. In one hand, she held a stubby, lit cigarette.

"We require passage, dear lady," said Hartley.

"I ain't no lady." She tapped a scratched badge that was pinned to her chest. "What's my name?"

"We require passage, Mrs C," said Hartley, squinting to read the writing on the badge. "Please," he finished with a grin.

The woman leaned out of the window, like a turtle extending its head from its shell. "Do you have goods?" She pointed at Steve with her cigarette. "The boy?"

"No," squeaked Steve.

"No," said Hartley. "But I do have coin."

"Let's have it then."

Hartley reached into the sleeve of his jacket. "Can't be too careful." He removed a rolled-up scrap of velvet. "Will this suffice?"

Mrs C snatched it from his hand, licking her lips as she unrolled the velvet. The candlelight glinted on a silver coin. "Nice." She polished the coin on her blouse front, raised it to her mouth and bit on it. "It'll do."

The shutters slammed shut and a moment later, a door to their right opened.

"Hurry in," snapped Mrs C with a dripping candle in her hand. "Step in." She beckoned to them. "Be quick."

Steve felt Blessing take his hand as they followed Hartley, and then Mrs C yanked the door shut behind them.

"Is this the way in?" said Steve as he stared down into a darkened stairwell.

"*Is this the way in?*" sneered Mrs C. "Does it look like a way in?"

"Yes?" said Steve, secretly hoping the answer was no.

"There you are then." Mrs C shuffled back to her office, muttering under her breath.

"Mind your step," said Hartley. "I'll go first."

The staircase travelled down in a stone-stepped spiral. Rough holes pocked the walls, holding remnants of candles, some lit, others expired.

Steve placed his hand on the bannister and peered down the centre of the well. All he saw was more darkness.

"Best not to lean on the bannister," said Hartley.

"Why not?" Steve snatched back his hand. "Is it broken?"

"Possibly," said Hartley. "But you never know who or what's been touching it before us."

*

One-hundred-and-eighty-nine. One-hundred-and-ninety. Steve counted the steps as they descended. Hartley walked ahead of him, whistling, while Blessing walked behind them both.

"Stop!" barked Hartley.

Steve froze with one foot outstretched. "What's wrong?"

"We appear to have run out of staircase." Hartley knelt down and stared into a gaping hole. "No way around, I'm afraid."

"Do we go back?"

"We could go down," said Blessing.

"Hang on." Hartley patted his hands around the edge of the hole. "There's a ladder."

"Is it safe?"

Hartley swung himself over the edge of the hole.

"Hartley," Steve gasped as his friend disappeared.

"Still here." The shopkeeper's head popped back into view. "It's secure enough. Just a little rickety. Come on."

"Do you want to go next?" Blessing asked from just behind him. "I don't mind going last."

"No, it's okay." He watched her climb down, then realised that maybe it wasn't such a good idea to be last. What if someone was following them? He brushed the thought away after taking one last quick glance up the stairwell, and then followed the others down.

The ladder finally dropped them down onto an underground rail line where the only faint light came from the stairwell above.

Steve found himself shivering in the chill of the tunnel. He could smell smoke, old smoke that hung to the walls, and oil.

Hartley stared down the tunnel. "Now then, which way?" He turned around and looked in the opposite direction. "Blessing, can you raise a light orb, please?"

"Okay." She breathed across her open palm. An orb popped into existence, bigger and brighter than the one she had created at the Gathering.

"You're getting better at that," said Hartley.

"You keep giving me practice." She flicked her wrist and the orb floated to his side.

"That way, I think." Hartley pointed down the track.

The light of the orb revealed dusty brick walls, rusting train tracks and rotting pipes. For some reason, Steve had expected there to be signs saying 'This Way', or copies of the underground tunnel maps, but there was nothing to indicate their location.

"I think it's this way." Steve pointed in the opposite direction to the one Hartley had chosen. "Now I've got my bearings."

Hartley shook his head. "This way. Definitely this way." He started down the tunnel. "I can feel it in my bones," he called back as he picked his way along the train track with Blessing at his side.

"But the map…" Steve looked in the direction he was sure they should be heading in, then back at his friends who were rapidly disappearing into the dim tunnel. "Wait," he called as he trotted after them. "Wait for me."

*

"Hartley," said Steve, after a while. "Is it safe to walk along the train tracks?"

"Perfectly safe." Hartley and Blessing walked with their eyes on the ground, finding a route through the rubble.

"So they don't run trains down here anymore?"

"Not for years."

"Right," said Steve, coming to a halt. "So what's that?"

"What's what?"

"That."

Ahead of them and travelling in their direction, two circular lights carved their way through the darkness.

"Hartley!" Blessing screamed.

Steve half-fell and half-jumped as he dragged Blessing aside. The three friends tumbled into a gap in the wall as the train scuttled by on six long legs, hissing and rattling as it went.

Two figures ran behind it, yelling and waving their arms. The first was short with pointed ears and nose, shouting and waving a stick around. The second lumbered a few steps behind his companion. His head brushed the roof and his shoulders pressed against the walls.

"Bad beetle," screeched the first. "Come back."

"Beetle." The second figure spoke in a deep, dull voice. "Here, beetle-beetle."

Steve sat perfectly still until the voices of the chasers and the sound of their footsteps had dimmed to a muffled echo.

"Did they say 'beetle'?" he whispered.

"They did." Hartley offered him a hand. "Looked like a scarab to me."

Steve took Hartley's hand and clambered to his feet. "As in what are normally this size?" He held his thumb and finger a couple of inches apart.

"'Normal' is such a relative term." Hartley slapped Steve on the back. "All right? No broken bones?"

"I don't think so."

"Good, good. Blessing?"

"I'm fine." She brushed herself down. "That was exciting."

"Sounds like the coast is clear." Hartley blew the orb back into the tunnel and peered out. "Yes, they're gone."

"What were those things that were chasing it?" said Steve.

"A goblin and a troll." Hartley stepped out onto the track. "Odd mix, I'll give you that. They don't usually get along." He looked up and down the tunnel. "So the question is: do we follow them or not?"

"They were heading in the opposite direction to us." Steve stepped out onto the train tracks.

"Exactly," said Hartley. "Best continue the way we were going."

"Or not." Steve ran a couple of strides in the direction of the scarab and its chasers, then stopped. "Are you coming?" he called back.

"But the troll and the goblin are in that direction," said Hartley.

"I know. They're hardly the normal kind of person you meet in an underground railway tunnel. I bet they're connected with Braeden Kendra."

"He's right," said Blessing.

"We could walk around these tunnels for ages and not find anything. This is a 'thing'," said Steve. "We should follow them."

"Well, when you put it like that, how can I argue?" Hartley slapped Steve on the shoulder and sped off at a pace in the right direction this time, after the troll and the goblin. "Come on," he called. "Onwards."

Chapter Thirty

"This must be it." Hartley trotted up a set of steps that led from the track to a platform.

"How can you tell?" Steve placed a foot on the bottom step.

"Well, for a start, this one is lit. None of the other platforms that we passed were lit." Alongside the two archways that led from the platform, four glowing jars hung from rusty nails. "Plus, there's the trail."

"What trail?"

"Look at your feet."

Steve looked down. Along the track and up the stairs, a thin line of fluid faintly glowed green.

"What's that?" He dabbed a finger in it and rubbed it against his thumb.

"It's produced by the scarab we saw. The people down here use it as a light source. See?" Hartley pointed to the jars.

"This one is injured," said Blessing. "That's why there's a trail."

"Is this blood?" Steve held out his hand. "You could have told me before I stuck my finger in it." He rubbed his still-glowing finger and thumb on his trousers.

"Which way, which way?" Hartley pointed to one of the archways, picking one seemingly at random. "You'll do."

The chamber beyond was immense. It was no mere underground walkway between platforms, but instead a long, arched room that reached up high above them. Jars of the glowing beetle blood ran along a row of hooks and nails on each of the tiled walls. The far end of the room halted at a curtain of wire mesh.

Steve covered his nose. "What is that smell?"

Revealed in the light of the jars, cages piled upon more cages leant at haphazard angles, resting on the walls and each other. Cats, bats and foxes cowered within their prisons. Hares and dogs blinked from their cages. A wolf, its grey fur hackled, snarled and snapped his jaws at them.

"This is awful." Blessing clung to Hartley's arm. "We have to help them."

"Please," said a voice. In one of the cages, a child reached out his hand. "I can't breathe in here."

"Hang on." Steve went to the cage and pulled at the padlock. "We'll have you out of there in a minute, okay?"

The boy nodded. He was wrapped in a cloak that covered his head and enveloped his body.

"Hartley, this one's a kid." He pulled at the padlock again. "Do you know where the keys are?"

"The goblin has them," said the boy.

"No need to worry. I have just the thing." Hartley patted his pockets, then drew a bunch of gnarled, rusty keys from inside his jacket. "One of these is sure to fit."

"They don't look like they'll fit," said Steve.

"Looks can be deceiving." Hartley licked his thumb and forefinger, then slid them along the length of a small, thin key. The rust crumbled away from its surface to reveal a shiny, silver edge. "See?" He fitted it into the padlock and turned it. There was a click and the padlock fell open.

"So not just door magic then?" said Steve as he opened the cage door. "Keys too?"

"It's a knack." Hartley winked at him. "Out you come."

"Thank you," said the boy as he crawled out of the cage. "Thank you, sir." He stretched his body, arms outreached, and face upheld. The cloak dropped to the ground.

"You're not…" said Steve.

The boy's hair framed his face like a crown of soft leaves. Two long, furred ears sprouted from the top of his head. His chest was bare, but his legs were covered in tangled fur.

"Hooves." Steve clamped his hand over his mouth. "Sorry," he said from behind his fingers.

"How wonderful. He's a faun," said Hartley. "That's rare. There aren't many forest-folk left in this world anymore."

The faun leapt and galloped in a circle in the centre of the room. His feet skidded on the tiled floor and he tossed himself back into a roll.

"What's your name?" Hartley asked when the faun finally paused for a moment.

"Boyce," said the faun. "Boyce, Boyce, Boyce." He bounced with each mention of his name.

"Be still, goat." A ragged female voice stopped the faun's dance.

Boyce crouched behind Hartley's legs. "You can't eat me while you're in that cage. The humans won't let you out. You won't let her out, will you?" he asked Hartley.

In the largest cage in the room, half-covered with a dirty sheet, sat a bird with its face to the wall. Its size was difficult to gauge in the confines of its imprisonment.

"Leave me alone," said the bird. "You are free now. Go. Let me sleep."

"What's that?" said Steve.

"I am not a 'that'." The bird ruffled its feathers.

"Of course not," said Blessing, elbowing Steve. "I'm Blessing and this is Steve. My other friend is Hartley. What's your name?"

"Why should I tell you?"

"Introductions are in order." Hartley held out his keys. "If I am to free you."

"Free me?"

"For the price of a name and your promise that you will not harm us. Any of us."

"My name." The bird began to turn around. "Nobody has asked for my name in a very long time."

"There you are," said Hartley as she completed her turn. "Beautiful."

Her body was that of an enormous bird of prey with strong wings and taloned feet, but her black feathers stopped at the top of her head to frame a human woman's face. The harpy blinked, looked at them all one by one, and then she ruffled her feathers.

"My name is Oraswift."

"I am honoured." Hartley bowed. "May I?" He nodded to the lock.

"You may," she said, retreating a shuffled step. Her lips trembled into a smile. "I have dreamed of stretching my wings once more."

"Don't let her out," bleated Boyce, running to Steve. "She'll eat me. You too."

"I have given my promise, foolish goat," said Oraswift. "Besides, you are a bag of bones. Not even a snack."

Hartley repeated the process on a second key and opened the cage door. "There. You are free, dear lady."

Oraswift took a step, then stopped. "Is it safe?"

"Probably not," he said, "but you have a better chance out of the cage than in."

"Your point is well made." She shuffled out and shook herself as she straightened to her full height, towering over the elderly shopkeeper. "Why are you here?"

"To rescue a friend."

"That is as good a reason as any. Stand back, Hartley"

"I told you she'd eat us." Boyce cowered behind Steve, his hands pressed to his ears.

"Silly goat," said Oraswift. "I merely wish to stretch my wings. Imprisonment has been unkind to my feathers."

*

"That's the last one." Blessing helped a hare from its cage.

The room was filled with freed animals: natural hunters and prey all pressed together.

"How will they get out?" said Steve. A cat pushed its body against his leg.

201

"The same way we got in," said Hartley. "Or through some other exit, once they recover their bravery and decide to leave."

"What about the scarab?" Oraswift preened her feathers. "Will you free him?"

"Where is he?" said Blessing.

"In the chamber beyond," said the harpy. "After his last attempt at escape, they have chained him up in there."

"Is he guarded?" said Hartley.

"Sometimes," said the harpy. "A troll."

"We need to find Abel," said Steve. "We've spent too long here already."

"Please," said Oraswift. "He is an old and trusted friend." She stumbled over the last word as if it was new to her.

"In for a penny, in for a pound." Hartley rubbed his hands together and grinned. "Lead the way, dear lady. Lead the way."

*

The scarab lay chained on the floor in a puddle of his own glimmering blood, which seeped from a wound in his side. In the resulting light, his body revealed its jewel shades: gold, emerald and sapphire blue.

Above him, three large cages hung from the ceiling, all secured by an arrangement of ropes and pullies.

"Poor thing," Oraswift cooed as she ran a wing over the scarab's back.

The scarab lifted his head and exhaled a faint, rattling sound.

"What have they done to you?" Blessing laid a hand on his back and stroked him. "We have to help."

"We will." Hartley jiggled a key in the lock on the chain. "Not long now."

"What if the troll comes back," said Steve. "What do we do?"

"There we go," said Hartley as the lock fell open. "Free, my fine fellow. Give me a hand, Steve."

Together, they unwound the chain from the scarab's body. One leg at a time, the creature raised himself up until his back stood taller than Steve's shoulder.

"He does understand that we helped him, right?" said Steve, looking at the scarab's massive jaws.

"He is very grateful," said Oraswift. "As am I."

"That's reassuring." Steve patted a hand on the beetle's side as it trundled past. The scarab tensed, hissed and wheeled around, knocking Steve off his feet.

Steve clambered up. "I don't think he likes me."

"Not you." Blessing pulled him to the beetle's side. "That."

The troll stood in one of the archways, hunched over as it squeezed itself through the entrance. Its bloated skin was pale like a maggot, its bulbous features pushed in on two black button eyes. It reached for Hartley.

"Look out." Steve lunged at Hartley, but the scarab knocked him out of the way as it charged at the troll.

Hartley dodged the troll, and then the attacking scarab, stumbling to his knees. "Get back," he yelled at Steve.

"Bad beetle." The troll swiped a hand at the scarab. "No run away this time."

"We must help," said Blessing.

"No." Oraswift swooped in front of her. "This is a matter of honour."

"But he's old and injured."

"He deserves the chance to avenge himself."

"The troll might kill him."

"Then his will have been a warrior's death. If he dies, I will kill the troll," said Oraswift. "I will take pleasure in doing that."

"Bad," grunted the troll. "Beat you," it growled.

In the enclosed space, Steve found himself backed against the wall, separated from the others by the scarab and the troll.

"What can we do?" he called to anyone who could hear him.

"Nothing," snapped Oraswift. "Leave this alone."

The scarab began to back across the room, still hissing and shaking, as the troll plodded after it, arms outheld.

Steve looked over at the others: Hartley a few feet away on his left, Oraswift restraining Blessing on his right. There had to be something they could do to help, even if it was against the harpy's orders.

Then the scarab did something that Steve would never have thought possible for such a large, heavy creature. It somersaulted—well, more of a back flip—twisting as it went until it was facing in completely the opposite direction. Steve found himself nose-to-mandible with the scarab.

"Beetle, come 'ere." The troll stumbled after the scarab. "Bad beet—"

Steve dodged out of the way as the scarab snapped its mandibles together on a rope tied to a hook on the wall. The rope dropped, as did the cages it had been holding up, sending them clanging down onto the troll below.

"Is it over?" asked Blessing, struggling to push the harpy out of the way.

"I think so." Steve leant over the troll's unconscious form. "Scarab one, troll nil," he said.

"You did well, old friend." Oraswift bowed to the scarab. "Very clever."

"No, no, no, no, no!" A goblin leapt through the archway where the troll had entered, a wooden stick in its hand. "Kill you!" It pointed the stick at the still-turning scarab.

"No." Steve rushed at the goblin before he had a chance to think. "Get away."

The stick, which Steve realised too late was a wand, sparked as a ball of fire shot towards the scarab, plunging into the creature's head. The scarab dropped to the floor.

"Kill you." The goblin pointed its wand at Steve. "Tasty little boy. Eat, eat, eat."

"Stop it!" Blessing barrelled into the goblin, pushing it off-balance. "Leave him alone."

"Eat you too." The goblin poked its wand at her. "Kill you."

"No. No more." She threw her arms wide as if she was going to hug the goblin. "No more killing."

The air around the goblin began to shine. It scuttled back on its hands and knees, its wand clacking on the floor.

"Leave be!" The goblin stabbed at the air with its wand. "Get it off."

The light that surrounded the goblin dimmed, thickened and set into a sphere. The imprisoned creature screamed, stabbing at the walls of its prison, but the sphere did not break. The goblin dropped its wand and used its fists. The sphere still held.

"Kill it," screamed Oraswift.

"No. Blessing is right." Steve stepped between the harpy and Blessing. "No more killing."

The imprisoning sphere, with the goblin still struggling inside, floated up to rest at the roughly-hewn ceiling. Below, the scarab gasped a last hiss, and was still.

Oraswift was silent for a long moment, her eyes so intent on Steve that he wondered if she might eat him. Finally though, she sighed, ruffled her feathers and eventually wept.

Chapter Thirty-One

"Are you sure this is the right place?" Steve brushed away the cobwebs that tangled on his clothes from the walls of the corridor they were walking along. Blessing trailed behind him, her eyes on the floor.

"When they first caught me, they imprisoned me here." Oraswift's taloned feet tapped on the concrete floor and her shoulders brushed the walls of the narrow corridor as she walked. "If they have your friend, this is where he'll be."

Tattered timber doors lined one wall of the corridor. From behind each, Steve heard voices groaning, growling, weeping. Hartley pressed his ear to every door they came to, shook his head, and moved on to the next.

"We're running out of doors," said Blessing. "Where is he?"

"If he's not here, he must be dead," said Oraswift.

"Don't say that," Blessing snapped. "We'll find him. We have to."

"Well, this is it." Hartley stopped at the final door. He leant against it and listened. He shook his head. "I don't hear anything."

"He must be here." Blessing pushed Hartley aside and turned the handle. The door opened an inch.

"Wait." Hartley pulled her back. "It should have been locked like the others." He peered through the gap.

"What can you see?" said Steve. "Is he in there?"

"Now I understand." Hartley pushed the door open. It slammed back on its hinges. "That's why it wasn't locked."

The cell was lit by a single candle which stood on a small, crooked wooden table. Within its light, Abel sat with his hands wrapped around his head. At the edge of the light stood a figure.

"What is it?" said Steve.

"A revenant," said Oraswift. "Captured souls that are used as guards and torturers."

The revenant leant over the cowering man, its hands outheld over his skull. Its head jutted forward as if too heavy for its long neck, mouth open, jaw loose. Short, bent legs carried a broad, top heavy body.

"It doesn't appear to be aware of us, yet." Hartley examined the door frame. "I suspect an alarm has been cast on the doorway, should anyone pass through it."

"So we can't go in?" said Steve.

"Not unnoticed, no."

"We have to," said Blessing.

"Can you make another of those bubbles?" asked Steve. "To trap it?"

"I'm not sure," she said, rubbing her eyes. "I'm so tired."

"Blessing has done enough," said Hartley. "She's exhausted from imprisoning the goblin."

"I'm fine," she said. "Don't fuss."

"Your magic would not work on a revenant," said Oraswift. "They are creatures of air and shadow. They have no solid form. The only thing that can contain them is the location to which they are tied."

"This room?" said Steve. Oraswift nodded. "So if we can get Abel out of there, it can't follow us?"

Oraswift tilted her head and blinked. "You have something in mind?"

"Maybe," he said, peering into the cell but careful to keep himself on the corridor side of the door. "Hartley, how quick are you on your feet?"

"How quick do you need me to be?"

"Very?"

"I'll try anything once," said Hartley, pushing up his sleeves.

"Oraswift, how powerful are your wings?" said Steve.

"As powerful as I need them to be," she said. "Why?"

"I've got this idea. It's just a thought," he said. "But it might work."

*

"How long do you think we'll have?" said Hartley.

"No idea," said Steve. "It depends how long Oraswift can keep that thing busy."

"Once I step into the room, the revenant will become aware of my presence," said the harpy. "Then it will be up to you to rescue your friend."

"Have you ever gone up against a revenant?" Steve watched

the harpy preen her feathers.

"No," she said. "I enjoy a challenge."

"I've never heard of a revenant being defeated before," said Hartley. "This may be the first time ever."

"If not, it will be a glorious death." She took a deep breath, stretched her neck so that she stood her full height above them all, and then stepped into the cell.

The revenant withdrew its hands from Abel and swept its eyes to the harpy, glaring at her dully. It raised its arms and released a deep, guttural snarl.

"I do not know whether you experience fear, revenant," said Oraswift as she spread her wings. "But my hopes are that you do."

The revenant growled and lurched towards her. Oraswift beat her wings once, raising an eddy of dust in the cell, then again, clashing the tips of her wings against each other and the grimy walls. The revenant gasped as it was blown back, floundering to keep its balance.

"It's working," said Blessing.

The revenant bent into the force of the wind that drove it back, reaching for the harpy.

Oraswift raised her wings higher, touching the ceiling of the cell. The eddy of dust was now a storm, clawing its way around the room.

The revenant reached for her with trembling arms. It slid one foot forward, staggered back as the wind pushed it off-balance, then bent into it again.

"I think this is as good as it's going to get," said Steve, grabbing Hartley by the arm. "Come on." He dropped to his knees to dodge under the harpy's wings and crawled into the cell.

"I wouldn't call this 'good', exactly," said Hartley as he knelt down and followed.

The revenant squeezed its hands into fists and forced itself forward a step. It reached for Oraswift again but, as its hand touched her wing, a fragment of the revenant's substance tore away. It watched the fragment fly past its head then it raised a hand to its face. With each beat of the harpy's wings another fragment, and another, unfurled from the revenant's body.

"Here, Hartley, help me." Steve grabbed Abel's arm. "Come on. We've got you."

Abel recoiled at the touch, drawing his arms tighter around his head.

"He doesn't want to come," said Steve.

"Don't be silly, Abel." Hartley grabbed the old man's arm. "We don't have time for this nonsense."

"No, no, no." Abel squirmed away from Hartley, slapping at the air.

"This is useless," said Steve.

"I'm afraid there's only one thing for it." Hartley reached into his pocket.

"What are you doing?" said Steve.

"Improvising." Hartley pulled himself to his feet, yanked Abel's arm away, and blew a handful of blue dust into the man's face. Abel collapsed back off his chair and onto the floor. "Sorry, old friend."

"What did you do?"

"Sleep elixir. I always carry a little, just in case. It was the only way. He wouldn't have come of his own accord." Hartley hooked his hands under Abel's arms. "Grab his feet."

Behind them, Oraswift opened her mouth and began to sing: high, soaring notes that matched the beat of her wings.

"What's she doing?" shouted Steve as he grasped Abel's legs.

"Victory anthem," Hartley shouted back as they retreated to the door with Abel's body. "She's enjoying herself."

"Is that normal?"

"It is for a harpy. Just don't get too close when she's finished."

"Why?"

"Victory gives harpies an appetite."

With a final lunge, they dragged Abel through the door.

"It's done," Steve shouted into the room. "Oraswift, you can stop now."

By now, the revenant was a spiralling eddy of scraps of its substance, imprisoned by the force of the harpy's wings.

"Oraswift," he shouted. "It's done."

Her song rose to a long high note, then she closed her mouth and was silent. Her wing beats slowed as she backed out of the room, humming to herself. The revenant reclaimed its form, piece by piece, coming to rest on the floor like a discarded cloak.

"You're sure it won't follow us?" he said.

"I don't think so," said Hartley. "But best to be certain." He slammed the door shut, then wrapped his hands around the handle. A cobweb line of smoke trailed into the air from the gaps between his fingers. "There." Hartley slowly released the handle. "Now nobody will open that door again." He wiped his hands on his trousers, leaving charcoal smears on them.

Chapter Thirty-Two

"Must you leave us, Oraswift?" said Blessing.

She and Hartley stood with the harpy while Steve helped Abel onto a bench which sat at the solid end of the platform they had gathered on, the other end having collapsed into dust and rubble at some time in the distant past. They were illuminated by two glowing jars mounted on the wall behind the bench.

"I must assist the others in their escape from the tunnels," she said. "That silly goat has no sense of direction."

"You will take care of them, won't you?" said Blessing. "Keep them safe?"

"Do not worry," said Oraswift. "I shall not eat them, although I cannot say the same for any goblins we may encounter on the way."

"We are indebted to you, dear lady," said Hartley.

"No, the debt is repaid," she said. "A freedom for a freedom."

"Thank you, Oraswift."

"You may not be so grateful the next time we meet. I now owe you nothing."

"Just as it should be," he said. "Should we meet again, dear lady, I'd like to think that you would help me because you wanted to, not out of obligation."

The harpy tilted her head at the old man and blinked. "You are odd, Hartley Keg," she said.

"So people tell me."

Oraswift stalked to an archway, took one last look at them and then stalked into the passageway beyond.

"Are you feeling any better, Abel?" Blessing slumped into a sitting position beside the bench, faint shadows under her eyes.

"A bit." He leant back and rested his head on the wall. "My mind is my own again." He wiped a hand across his eyes. "My head hurts."

"You were reluctant to leave the cell," said Hartley. "We had to persuade you."

"He used sleep powder on you," said Steve.

"Out of concern for your well-being," blustered Hartley, "and possibly self-defence."

"Abel, what was that thing doing to you?" said Steve.

"Not now," said Hartley. "Let the man recover."

"It's a fair question." Abel took a deep breath and blew it out through pursed lips. "A revenant replays a person's fears over and over again. If you hadn't rescued me when you did, I think I might have gone mad." He fell silent, shaking his head.

"What happened, Abel?" asked Hartley. "Eleanor told us you were taken."

"You found her? Is she all right?"

"She's fine," said Steve. "You know Eleanor; she's decisive. She's gone looking for my parents."

"Just like Eleanor," Abel nodded. "She likes to be useful."

"What happened to my uncle?" Steve hadn't known how important that question was until then. His throat tightened around the words, making it difficult to talk. "Who killed him?"

"I don't know," said Abel, "but I have my suspicions. What is happening at the Haven Corporation?"

"Winters is in charge, until Dad takes over."

"You've spoken to Winters?"

"We tried to," said Steve. "We went to his apartment. He seemed to be on our side, but it didn't end well."

"You think he turned on you?"

"It looks that way." Steve shrugged. "But I don't know. I don't know anything. That's the problem. Until all of this happened, I had nothing to do with Rex or his world. The nearest thing I had to a villain in my life was the headmaster's secretary and the school bullies."

"This is not your fight," said Abel.

"It is now," said Steve. "I can't go back to school. Winters is, at best, unreliable. And I can't talk to Mum and Dad because I don't know where they are. You guys," he said, looking around at them all, "you're all I've got."

"I assume Eleanor told you what I told her?"

"About the laboratory in the basement, and taking part of the machine away with you, and then Rex?" said Steve. "She told us all that."

"There was more," said Abel. "Details I kept back. I didn't want to overload her. She had enough trouble getting her head around the existence of magic."

215

I know how that feels, Steve thought. "The disc you left at school for me," he asked. "What is it?"

"The Reactor," said Abel. "Magical, but also what its name implies. A power source."

"So why was it in the lab? I mean, Rex didn't use magic, did he?"

"A story for another day," said Abel, glancing at Hartley. "I have never been subject to hunches. Either a thing is, or it is not. This situation, however, nagged at me. I found a laboratory in the basement. The door was open. Inside, the Reactor was powering a process to drain the essence of a darkling."

"What's a darkling?" said Steve.

"Workadays call it a fairy." Blessing slowly climbed to her feet. Steve could see that it was a struggle for her.

"Fairies exist?" he said. *Of course, they do,* he thought. *Why am I surprised?*

"The darkling was in a glass globe. Terrible thing to see," said Abel, shaking his head. "There was barely anything left of it."

"But why?" said Blessing. "That's horrible."

"And how would they catch a darkling in the first place?" said Hartley.

"There have been stories of darklings being hunted down in the city," said Abel, "but I didn't believe them."

"Not that I know what draining a darkling's essence is," said Steve, "but why would anyone do that? What good would it do?"

"The drained essence was wired up to a robot power cell. An unnecessary act. The robot power cells work perfectly well. I have no idea how darkling essence would affect them. I took the Reactor and the process stopped."

"And the darkling?" said Blessing.

"There was nothing I could do for him. He faded away."

"And now Braeden Kendra has the Reactor," said Hartley. "Gods know what he'll do with it."

"No, he doesn't," said Abel. "I sent it away."

"Sent it where?" said Hartley. "I hope you were careful, my friend."

"Of course, I used a safe seal spell. I posted it to Miss Farspringer."

"Oh no, not her."

"It was the safest place I could think of."

"Well of course it'll be safe," said Hartley, striding around the platform. "It's her, isn't it? She never lets anything go."

"I have an idea for that," said Abel. "If we hurry…"

"We can't leave," said Steve. "We have to find Michael."

"Michael?" Abel looked at Hartley. "The street urchin?"

"Braden Kendra has him," said Steve. "We can't leave him here."

"But the Reactor—"

"Is safe where it is. Miss Farspringer will see to that," said Hartley. "Michael, however, is not."

"Kendra uses homeless children to run his errands. If he's taken Michael, he'll have him in the Keep," said Abel.

"What's the Keep?" said Steve.

"The central, most heavily guarded part of Kendra's Fortress. It's where he keeps his most valued items. There's only one way in and one way out."

"I thought that might be the case," said Hartley. "I'm sure we can manage. We've got this far after all."

"One day, your optimism will get you killed, Hartley Keg," said Abel.

"Not today though, eh?" Hartley pulled his friend to his feet. "Shall we?"

*

A featureless iron door blocked the entrance to the Keep. On either side stood two guards: one human, the other shrouded in a cloak that reached to the ground and concealed the guard's form.

"Well." Hartley peered at the door from the safety of a shadowed corridor. "As I see it, we have two options. We fight our way in—"

"What's the other option?" said Steve.

"We pretend that I'm a slave trader and you are my offerings to Kendra."

"I can't say I'm big on that one either," said Steve. "Can't you just magic us in there?"

"No, I've never been inside the Keep."

"I don't like our chances against the guards," said Abel.

"We could just announce ourselves," said Hartley.

"Or you could follow me," a lilting voice whispered in Steve's ear. Something yanked at his hair. He flapped at it with his hand, knocking a tiny body somersaulting to the ground.

"What did you do that for?" The creature sat sprawled on the ground, rubbing its head. "I was only teasing."

It was no taller than the length of Steve's hand and was

dressed in close fitting, green clothes with bare feet. A swathe of short, red hair framed the creature's angular face.

"What is it?" said Steve.

"Not it: she," snapped the creature.

"A pixie," Blessing whispered in Steve's ear. "Be careful."

"That's right." The pixie jumped to her feet and brandished her fists. "Be very careful. I'll get you, I will."

"No need for that, little one." Hartley crouched down in front of the tiny figure. "We mean you no harm."

"That's good for you, then." She dropped her fists and planted her hands on her hips. "I was going to help, but that," she squeaked, pointing at Steve, "that oaf hit me."

"You took him by surprise."

"Not my fault he's ignorant." She stuck out her tongue at Steve.

"Sorry," he said. "I thought you were a bat or something."

"A bat?" She stamped her foot. "Do I smell like a bat?"

"I don't know what a bat smells like," he said.

"See? Ignorant," she said. "I am a helpful pixie, a good pixie, a pretty pixie."

"You are that," said Hartley.

"I heard you," she said. "I heard you talk about the big house."

"The Keep?"

"You want in."

"We do."

"I know a way in. A secret way. I could show you."

"That would be very kind."

"I could show you for a pretty."

"A pretty?" said Steve. *A pretty what?*

"Or a sparkly."

"A pretty or a sparkly." Hartley reached into the pockets of his jacket. "Would this do?" He drew out a loop of red ribbon. "Pretty?"

"Shiny and pretty." The pixie clapped her hands and snatched the ribbon. "So pretty." She rubbed her cheek against it then wrapped it around her waist and shoulders. "Pretty pixie." She spun in a dance, hugging the ribbon to her.

"Pretty indeed," said Hartley. "Now, can you show us the way?"

"Of course, I can." She stopped dancing. "But you'll have to be quick." She scampered back down the corridor. "Keep up, if you can."

Chapter Thirty-Three

"Sorry." Steve bent over with his hand pressed to his waist. "Stitch. I'll be all right in a minute."

"Take a moment." Abel collapsed onto a large chunk of concrete which sat beneath a matching hole in the ceiling above. "I am."

Blessing sat on the floor, knees drawn up to her chin. "Pixies run fast," she gasped.

Hartley was balanced halfway up a collapsed section of bricks and tiles while the pixie scampered around his feet, pointing and chattering.

"Can we trust her?" said Steve.

"I think so," said Abel. "Hartley has a way with the fair ones, plus we gave her a gift."

"A pretty," said Blessing, smiling.

"A shiny and pretty," said Steve, smiling back.

"Good news." Hartley trotted down the rubble. "We can get through this way."

"Where does it bring us out?" asked Steve.

"An abandoned corner of the Keep," said Hartley. "Our friend tells me that they've sectioned it off as too dangerous to use. She treats it as her own back door so she can find her pretties and sparklies."

"And food." The pixie brushed dust from her clothes. "Moths and worms are juicy but so boring. In the big house, they have sweets and treats." She rubbed her stomach. "Yummy cake."

"Is it safe?" said Steve.

"I am careful," she said. "They never see me."

"That's good, but I meant is the entrance safe for people of our size?"

"It's as safe as it's going to get," said Hartley. "We either give this a try or we take our chances with the guards."

"This way it is, then," said Steve. "I'll go first."

"No, no, no," said the pixie. "I must be first." She turned on her heel and ran up the pile of rubble. She stopped at the top and waved at them. "Come on then, big people." She giggled and disappeared into a gash in the wall.

"That's us told," said Steve, wondering if all pixies were this annoying.

"Apparently so," said Hartley with a grin. "I suppose this could be a trap. Pixies can rarely be trusted."

"Only one way to find out," said Steve.

"Careful," said Blessing. "You're starting to sound like Hartley."

One by one, the four friends squeezed themselves through the ragged hole. After the corridor's green illumination, the abandoned interior of the Keep was too dark to see a hand in front of their face.

"Can you make one of your light orbs, Blessing?" said Steve.

"I'm too tired." Her voice was quiet. "Sorry."

"I'll do it," said Abel. Steve heard a hoarse breath, then light flooded the room. The orb was white and the size of a man's head, whereas Blessing's orbs had a warm, golden tint to them.

"That's better," said Hartley, nudging the orb ahead of them.

"Pretty." The pixie stared up at the orb with her little mouth open.

"My dear," Hartley knelt down beside her. "We have one more favour to ask."

"What will you give me?" Her eyes remained on the floating light.

"Let me see." Hartley reached into his jacket. "I have a shiny pebble." He drew out a polished, chunk of granite.

"No." She shook her head. "Don't like stupid rock."

"Hang on." He dropped the pebble back into his pocket and reached into the other. "I have this," he said, holding out a coin.

"No." She pointed to the orb. "I want that."

"I can't give that to you, little one."

"Want it." She stamped her foot. "Now."

"Let me." Abel blew into his cupped hand and balled it into a fist. "Here." He bent down and offered his hand to the pixie.

"What is it?" she asked.

"Have a look." He opened his fingers.

"Ooh." The pixie climbed onto his hand and picked up a tiny, shining orb. "My own," she whispered.

"Just your size," said Abel.

"Now, you have a gift," said Hartley, "may I ask you the

223

second favour?"

"I suppose." She jumped off Abel's hand and nodded her head once.

"We need to know where Braeden Kendra is keeping our friend. A boy called Michael."

"Sparky?" She waggled her fingers. "The little man with the lightning in his hands."

"That's him," said Steve.

"Bad man took him." She screwed her face up into a scowl. "Locked Sparky away."

"Where, my dear?" said Hartley.

"In the dust room." She shivered. "I don't go there. Bad man steals us away and keeps us in a jar." She pressed the orb to her cheek. "Keeps our pretties."

"A gift deserves a favour," said Hartley.

"No!" She scuttled away to the other side of the room. "Mine now."

"You know the rules."

"Rules." She stuck out her tongue. "Stupid rules."

"Well, of course, if you're too scared to show us," said Hartley, "I suppose we'll just have to take the orb back and find our own way there."

"No." She hugged the orb to her. "Don't take my orb."

"Then show us the way, dear one."

"Maybe." She tucked the orb under the ribbon that she had tied around her torso, turning herself into a glowing bundle. "If you're quick."

"Not too quick," said Steve.

"Oaf," she said. "Shall I go slow for the big, stupid, oaf?"

"Oi," said Steve. "Less of, well, any of that."

*

"Here." The pixie stopped and crossed her arms as she reached a point where one corridor met another. "Second door to the right. Mousehole at the bottom."

Steve peered out into the corridor. "I see it. No guards."

"No need for guards." The pixie shivered. "Bad man knows when you go in there."

"Does he now?" said Hartley.

"Yes." The pixie nodded her head. "Even through the mousehole. Me try."

"Thank you, little one." Hartley knelt down and offered his hand to the pixie. "You have been very helpful."

The pixie considered his hand, which would have easily fitted around her waist, then touched his thumb. "Don't let him get you," she whispered. "Bad man, bad room. He'll make you into dust if he catches you." She tightened the ribbon, which still held the glowing orb, and sped off out of sight.

"What do you think she meant?" asked Steve. "That he knows when you go in there?"

"Probably an alarm cast on the threshold," said Hartley. "Come on."

"But what are we going to do?" said Steve as he followed the others to the door. "What's the plan?"

"I don't think we have much choice," said Hartley. "We'll just have to go in there and hope for the best."

It was a weird sensation, even for a darkling. She dwelled—that was the most fitting word she could think of to describe her condition—part shadow, part dust; imprisoned in a jar on one of the shelves in Kendra's room.

Etched into the inside of the jar were a million or more enchantment runes which kept her in. Her shadow-self couldn't pass through the glass of the jar, and neither could she take solid form and break the glass. She was stuck.

She heard voices outside the door to the corridor. Had Kendra returned with the boy? She cursed at her helplessness.

The door edged open a fraction, then slammed wide.

*

"Nothing." Hartley poked his foot across the threshold, balancing on the other foot as he looked around him. "Either the door isn't alarmed at the moment or it's a silent alarm. Ah well." He stepped inside.

"Hartley!" Steve remained in the corridor, eyes wide.

"What, dear boy?"

"The door might have been booby-trapped." Pictures of slashing blades and flying arrows sped through Steve's mind. "You could have been killed."

"No," said Hartley, patting his torso. "I appear to be alive and proverbially kicking." He grinned. "Now, stop worrying and get in here. All of you."

The room within was long and narrow with a door at the far end. Polished, wooden cabinets lined each wall, laddered with labelled drawers and shelves which were filled with bottles and jars. Hanging from the ceiling, a hundred storm lamps held flickering candles.

In the middle of the room a long, dark wooden table with ornately carved legs sat on an equally long rich red rug. Scattered across the polished tabletop, a handful of tattered books lay open, their pages in various stages of age and decay. A tall-backed, leather-clad chair sat at the top of the table.

"So this is the dust room?" Steve followed Abel and Blessing through the open door. *No Braeden Kendra at least,* he thought, relaxing a little. *For now.*

"I wonder." Hartley took a pair of small, unarmed spectacles from his pocket and balanced them on his nose. "Let's see what he has here." He bent down to examine the bottles and jars, each and every one labelled in an ornate handwritten script.

"Shouldn't we look for Michael?" Blessing leaned on the table, her breathing shallow. "That's what we came here for."

"We need an advantage before we face Kendra," said Hartley. "If we have to face him, that is. Now then."

"Desiccated Pixie." Abel picked up a bottle from a shelf. "That's what our guide meant."

"Harpy dust." Hartley ran his hand along the shelf. "Fire imp. Sphinx dust. Soul dust." He picked up two test tubes of this last one. "This is how he's making revenants."

"Put it back. We can't fight a revenant without Oraswift." Blessing closed her eyes and fell backwards.

"Blessing." Steve caught her and lowered her to sit on the ground. "What's wrong?"

Hartley dropped the test tubes into his pocket and knelt beside Blessing. He touched her face. "She has a fever."

"Is she sick?" said Steve.

"She's exhausted, poor thing. Magic takes its toll. The orb she imprisoned the goblin in is draining her. First time spells are always the most tiring to cast."

"You mean she hasn't done that kind of thing before?" said Steve.

"Not that specific spell, no." Hartley patted her hand. "It's my fault, I'm afraid. I shouldn't have brought her with us."

"I'm okay," she whispered.

"No, you're not," said Hartley. "But you will be once you go to sleep and the orb fades away. I tell you what," he said, standing up, "why don't you rest on the chair while we have a look around. It's got to be more comfortable than the bare floor."

"Come on." Steve helped Blessing to her feet, wrapping his arm around her waist. "I've got you."

"Here we are." Hartley pulled out the chair. "What's that?" He picked up a notebook that had been hidden from view on the tucked-in chair. "This looks interesting."

"What is it?" said Abel. "Anything we can use?"

"Kendra's notes on, well, all of this." Hartley nodded his head to one of the cabinets. "Instructions on how to use the vials. Related spells." He flicked through the book to the end, then tucked it inside his jacket. "A definite advantage for us."

"What do you think of this?" Abel tapped on a large, heavy jar that sat on one of the cabinets alongside a pair of mirror-lens sunglasses. "I can't tell if the contents are liquid or smoke."

"How peculiar." Hartley joined him and peered into the jar. "I do believe something's moving in there."

The door at the end of the room shook a little as Steve heard a key turn in its lock. He pulled Blessing behind him and wondered exactly how good a shield he would make.

"If you want to have a comfortable life here, Michael, then all you have to do is follow my rules."

The man who walked through the door was dressed in a dark, sleek suit. Steve couldn't judge his age. With the lines around his eyes and mouth, he could have been in his fifties but something in the way he hunched his shoulders suggested that he was older.

"Yes, Mr Kendra." Michael walked a step behind him, the grime on his face smeared with wiped-away tears. His bottom lip was swollen and bloody.

"What the demons!" Kendra stopped as he saw first Steve, and then the others. "How did you get in here?"

"The door was open." Hartley's voice sounded its normal, jovial tone to Steve, but the expression on the shopkeeper's face was cold and watchful. "You should be more careful, Braeden. You never know who's about."

"We just want Michael back." Blessing stepped out from behind Steve. Her voice was steady but quiet. "We don't want any trouble."

"Trouble?" sneered Kendra. "You have no idea."

"Braeden." Abel stepped forward. "We can make a trade."

"I thought I left you in a cell to rot. How did you get out?"

"I'll tell you." Abel edged closer to him. "In exchange for our freedom, all of us, including Michael."

"You're in no position to make deals, old man. You know how easy it would be for me to end you all." He clicked his fingers. Steve saw Abel flinch at the gesture.

"You've got a lot of nice things here." Hartley ran his hand along the shelf at his side. "It'd be a shame for any of them to get broken."

"They can be replaced," said Kendra, his smug grin dropping for a second.

"Really? I mean, how many times do you come across sphinxes these days? Ooh, this is a rare one." He tapped on one of the jars. "Boggart. I haven't seen a boggart since we left the old world."

"Get away from there!"

"And what about this?" Hartley picked up the large heavy jar that he had peered into a matter of minutes before. "Why doesn't this one have a label?"

"Put that down." Kendra pointed a finger at him. "I'm warning you."

"It's not very heavy but the glass is rather slippery." Hartley feigned dropping it. "Whoops."

"Careful!" snapped Kendra, his eyes widening.

"Oh, did you want this?" said Hartley. "Here you go then."

Abel dodged out of the way as Hartley threw the jar at Kendra. Steve pulled Blessing down to the floor, wrapping his arms around her. He didn't know whether he was more afraid of Kendra at that moment or the release of whatever was imprisoned in the jar.

"No, no, no!" Kendra leapt for the jar, arms flailing, mouth wide.

Steve waited for the sound of smashing glass. It didn't come.

"Ah, good catch." Hartley backed away a couple of steps. "Well done."

"You stupid old man." Kendra hugged the jar to his body. "You'll be the first to die."

"Now, now." Hartley raised his hands. "You wouldn't hurt an unarmed man."

"Oh yes, I would." Kendra's grin returned. "As soon as I—"

His words turned into a prolonged gurgle and his body began to shake as Michael, taking advantage of his captor's distraction, thrust his hands, dancing with electricity, into Kendra's side. The jar, inch by inch, slipped from Kendra's grasp.

What's in the jar? was the first thought that dashed through Steve's mind as he watched, closely followed by, *And is it friendly?*

The jar smashed at the feet of the convulsing man, releasing its contents into a rising swirl of darkness.

"What's that?" Steve heard Michael shout the question as the boy backed away, bringing Kendra's electrocution to an end. A final spark darted from Michael's finger.

The darkness stretched, taking weight as it formed itself into a recognisable shape. All at once, the darkness snapped into the form of a teenage girl with short dark hair, dressed in everyday casual clothes. Only her large indigo eyes betrayed the fact that she wasn't human.

Kendra, released from his torment, collapsed to the ground with a monotone moan. His muscles jerked for a second longer and then he closed his eyes and was still.

"Is he...?" Steve slowly stood up. "Is he dead?"

"Unconscious." The teenager tilted her head to look at the unconscious man. "He'll live."

"Who are you?" said Abel.

No, the question is definitely 'What are you?' thought Steve, looking from the girl to the glass shards of the jars that only seconds before had held her.

"She's a darkling," said Hartley, stepping forward. "Aren't

you?"

"I know you," said Michael. "From the shelter."

"Hello," she said, turning to him. "It is good to see you again."

"When Blessing said a darkling was a fairy, I thought—" Steve stopped. *I don't actually know what I thought, but it definitely wasn't trainers and a hoody.*

"Perhaps twinkly lights and a pretty dress?" said the darkling, smirking. She knelt beside Steve and Blessing. "The girl needs to sleep. You are her protector?" she asked him.

"I suppose so." He hadn't thought of it that way round.

"Good." The darkling stroked a hand across Blessing's cheek. "She burns bright, but she will need you."

Blessing's eyes flickered open and the swiftest of smiles crossed her lips.

"Rest," said the darkling. Blessing's eyes closed again.

"I can help you escape this place," said the darkling. "But first I must discover the whereabouts of an item."

"We don't need help escaping," said Steve. "We just came to rescue Michael."

"If you'll excuse my curiosity," said Hartley, "what exactly are you looking for?"

"Something you would not understand."

"Try me."

"No," said the darkling.

"Let me guess then," said Hartley.

"I don't have time for games."

"Just one guess, and then I'm done," he said. "And if I get it right, you come with us."

"My quest is my own," she said. "I travel with no one." *Anymore*, she thought.

"That's the thing," said Hartley. "I've known darklings all my life and there are two things you can always say about them. They love company. It's quite a thing attending a darkling moot," he said, turning to Steve. "Wonderful parties, they are."

"What's the other thing?" said Steve.

"They are the most self-centred, whimsical and unreliable beings I have met: unless bound by a boon, of course, but they hate being in someone's debt—"

"What's your point?" said the darkling.

"I've only ever heard of one darkling who was different, who committed herself to an oath. Her name was—"

"That's enough!" said the darkling.

"You're looking for the Reactor," said Hartley. "Just like we are."

"And we know where it is," Steve added. "What?" he said as Hartley turned to him with a raised eyebrow. "I'm just saying."

"Take me to it." The darkling advanced on Hartley.

"Just as you wish," he said, going to the door. "Once we've dropped in at home for a few things first."

Chapter Thirty-Four

"Take me to the Reactor, now." The darkling scowled at Hartley as he stirred sugar into a mug of coffee. "It isn't yours to keep."

"It isn't yours either," he said, turning his back on her.

"Let us talk this through." Abel stepped in between them. "Find a way to work together."

"There's nothing to talk about," snapped the darkling. "I must have the Reactor."

"Why?" Steve had stood silent since their return to Hartley's shop. "Tell us why it's so important to you."

"I don't have to explain myself." Up close, the boy's aura, or lack of it, was even more disconcerting to the darkling. She could never trust someone so unnatural.

"Stop it." Blessing sat slumped at the kitchen table. "This is getting us nowhere."

Even in her exhausted state, the darkling could see that the girl's aura was immense and powerful, containing all the colours the darkling had ever seen, including some that only her own kind could perceive.

"I'll zap her." Michael stood at Steve's side. "Just say the word."

"Please," said Abel. "Let us settle this without violence, or zapping."

"Enough damage has already been caused by the Reactor being in human hands." The darkling stalked back-and-forth. She was so close to completing her mission.

"So a darkling could do a better job?" said Steve. "Is that what you're saying?"

"Do you know how many darklings have died because of that device? Do you?" she snapped, lunging towards him and stopping herself inches short of his face.

"No," said Steve, holding his ground and placing a protective arm in front of Michael. "But that doesn't mean I'm going to just hand it over to you."

"How do we know you're not working for the villains who are after the Reactor?" jibed Michael. "How much are they paying you?"

"I would never—" The darkling stepped back, eyes wide and distraught. "You don't know how long I've searched for the Reactor."

"Then tell us," said Steve. "Let us in on the secret. We can't trust you if you don't tell us anything."

The darkling looked at each of them in turn: Hartley, leant on the kitchen sink with his mug rested on his chest; Abel, nervously pacing; Steve, hands tense as he stared her down; Michael, tendrils of electricity leaping between his splayed fingers; and Blessing who sat at the table with her head in her hands.

It had been a long time since the darkling had spoken of her mission to anyone, let alone a group of humans who were strangers to her. Had she been so focused on her target for all these years that she had veered off course in her isolation? Was companionship and a common goal a better way to live?

"The Reactor is but one element of a larger device," she eventually said. "Built *by* human hands *for* human hands."

"But it's magical, isn't it?" said Steve.

"It's compatible with magic," said Abel. "I'm not sure that is the same thing as *being* magical."

"The inventor saw the device as an entirely scientific endeavour," said the darkling. Now that she had begun to explain, the words flowed easily. "The magic came later."

"What did the device do?" said Steve.

"That doesn't matter now," said the darkling. "What you need to know, what you all need to understand, is that it became necessary—crucial even—to break the device down into its component parts."

"And keep those components far away from each other," said Hartley, nodding. "I know the story." His eyes darted to Steve, then back to the darkling. "And I know who you are," he said to her.

"Then you understand why the Reactor can't be in the hands of mankind."

"*I* don't," said Steve, crossing his arms. "And after all the trouble the Reactor has got me into, I think I deserve an explanation."

"I suppose you do." The darkling sighed. "Very well. The Reactor may only be a component, but it is incredibly powerful in its own right. It drastically strengthens the powers of any magical who possesses it. They would be almost invincible."

"What about you?" said Steve. "What would you do with it?"

"I would keep it safe. I have searched for the Reactor ever since its guardian was destroyed," she said. "I tracked it down to your city's museum. It was part of a display about a catastrophe that happened here: an explosion involving a bank robbery."

"I've seen that display," said Steve. "Are you saying the guardian was killed in the explosion?"

"Killed is not technically correct. A golem can only be destroyed."

"A golem?"

"A golem is— " Abel began.

"I know what a golem is," said Steve. "Well, what it's supposed to be. I just didn't think golems really existed. Next you'll be telling me ghosts and angels are real."

"Don't be silly," said Michael. "There's no such thing as angels."

"Really?" said Steve, then, "Whatever. So why didn't you take the Reactor from the museum?"

"The display held a replica of the Reactor. The original had been purchased by a 'TW' on behalf of the Haven Corporation."

"TW," said Abel. "But that's—"

"Helpful," said Hartley. "At least now we know for sure where Winters's loyalties lie."

"I say the Reactor stays where it is," said Abel. "It's safe there."

"But can we be sure of that?" said Hartley. "Wouldn't it be better to—? "

"I must have it!" the darkling snapped.

Everyone in the kitchen stared at her. Even Blessing raised

her face from her hands.

"Miss Darkling," Hartley began.

"This is too important," she said in a quieter voice. "I made a promise to safeguard the Reactor."

"My dear, I understand." Hartley stepped closer to her, the mug now abandoned in the sink, his hands outheld. "Really, I do, completely and abso—"

"What are you doing?" growled the darkling as the shopkeeper clamped a hand around her wrist. She was too shocked to begin the return to shadow.

"I claim a boon," he said. "For freeing you from that jar. As a darkling and a fae, you are bound to grant my boon. Say it."

"I…" Her human form trembled. She didn't know whether it was from anger or the discomfort the boon placed on her. "I grant your boon," she growled.

"You'll help us to retrieve the Reactor and deal with it as we see fit."

"Yes," she muttered. "I'll help you."

"All of us." He looked around at the others. "Not just me."

"All of you," she agreed.

"Good." Hartley released her and smiled. "I'm glad that's settled." He walked across the kitchen and took down a plate from a shelf. "I'm starving. Anyone else?"

"You'll regret this," she snapped. "All of you." She released a rasping breath and melted back into the comfort of shadow.

*

"Where did she go?" said Steve. He'd all but forgotten that the darkling was anything other than a teenage girl. Watching her change into a shadow again had been an unsettling experience.

"Dunno," said Michael, still streaming lightning between his hands.

"I do." Blessing pulled herself to her feet. "I can see her shadow trail. Come on."

"That's a new one," said Hartley.

"I'll come with you," said Steve.

"Is that wise?" Abel barred their way. "Blessing, you're exhausted, and the darkling may be dangerous. Hartley and I will find her."

"I'm all right," said Blessing. "And you'll never find her without me. I'm the only one who can track her."

"With the Reactor at stake, the darkling won't have gone far." Hartley peered into two covered pans on the stove. "And she's under the rules of a boon. She has to do what we say. She isn't allowed to harm her boon-claimers."

"You and I should go, Hartley," said Abel. "It would be the sensible thing to do."

"My belly disagrees with you." Hartley opened a cupboard and pulled out half a loaf of bread. "The children will do fine without us. And you're hardly in the best of health yourself after your ordeal."

"I suppose not." Abel shrugged and moved away from the doorway.

"The three of you can go," said Hartley. "On one condition. Michael?"

"What?"

"No zapping the darkling."

"All right then," he muttered, releasing a dramatic sigh. "If you say so."

"Blessing, be careful." Abel paced the floor with increasing speed. "Don't anger her."

"I think she's already angry," said Steve.

"Good point," said Abel. "In that case, don't put yourselves at risk. We have the upper hand at the moment. She doesn't know where the Reactor is, and she's restrained by a boon."

"She's a friend," said Blessing, heading for the door. "She won't hurt us."

"She *can't* hurt us," said Steve. "Because of the boon. Right?" he asked as he followed Blessing. "Right?" he said a second time as nobody answered.

"That's what I'm here for," said Michael. "I'm the muscle."

Now I'm really worried, Steve thought as he followed the other boy.

*

The darkling heard the children before she saw them: their footfalls and the sparks of Michael's lightning, but mostly their voices.

"She went this way." That was the girl, Blessing.

"Do you think she'll still be angry?" That was the boy called Steve.

"I can always zap her."

"No, Michael. Hartley said no zapping." Blessing again.

"All right. You don't have to nag."

She wasn't surprised the girl could track her. Blessing had so much untapped power pulsing through her young body. It was inevitable that new talents would present themselves over time.

"I know you're there." Blessing stopped a couple of feet away, staring at the darkling's hiding place in a doorway. "Don't hide anymore. We just want to talk. Michael, stop that."

"Okay," he moaned. The electricity at his fingertips disappeared with a sizzling pop. "Happy now?"

"We set you free," said Steve. "The least you can do is talk to us."

"My freedom is largely down to accident," she said as she returned to her solid form. "There was no good intention involved."

"It had the same result though," he said. "That's got to count for something."

"Perhaps," said the darkling.

"We need you." Blessing staggered back a step, collapsing onto Steve. "Sorry, I'm so tired."

"Here, let me." The darkling picked Blessing up as if she were a small child. "The girl needs to rest."

"Try telling *her* that," said Steve.

"I'm fine." Blessing closed her eyes and rested her head on the darkling's shoulder. "I just need to rest my eyes." She yawned. "Then I'll be good as new."

"She's asleep," said the darkling.

"And somewhere a goblin is free," said Steve.

"What?"

"Never mind," he said. "It's a long story."

*

"Her bedroom is upstairs." Steve held the door open as the darkling carried Blessing through. "The stairs are in the kitchen."

"She needs to sleep back her strength." The darkling marched through the shop as if Blessing weighed nothing more than a feather. "She won't wake for a few hours."

"Hang on." Michael stumbled through the doorway onto his hands and knees. "What's going on?"

"You all right?" Steve closed the door and offered a hand to the boy.

"I don't feel so good."

"Maybe you need to eat," said Steve. "I don't know what Hartley has in, but—"

"Something is wrong." The darkling slowly turned around. "Can't you feel it?"

"Workaday, remember?"

"It's like something's soaking up my magic." Michael took Steve's hand and struggled to his feet.

"Or someone," said the darkling.

"What's this?" Steve picked up a charred bundle of ribbons from the floor. It smelt of herbs and soot.

"Looks like a charm," said Michael. "It's been used up. That's why it's all burned."

"Hartley?" Steve dodged past the others into the kitchen at the back of the shop. "Hartley?" he called again. The room was empty.

"What's happened?" Michael stumbled in. "Where are they?"

Two of the kitchen chairs lay on the floor. A puddle of milk swam around a spilled pan a few inches away.

242

"Look." The darkling, still carrying Blessing, stood at the kitchen table.

Carved into the tabletop in jagged letters, were the words, *'I have them. Bring it to me. TW'*.

Chapter Thirty-Five

"Sorry, I'm not used to making tea." Steve handed the mug to Blessing. "And there was no milk or sugar."

He sat down beside her on the doorstep of the shop. It was early morning. He had no idea what the exact hour was because all of the clocks in Hartley's shop said different times, but he reckoned it was maybe six o'clock.

"It's fine." Blessing took a sip, then rested the mug on her knees. Her eyes were red from crying but the shadows under them had gone. "Thanks."

"I added honey though," he said, wondering why it was suddenly awkward to be alone with her. "How do you feel?"

"My head hurts," she said, keeping her eyes on the mug. "That's all."

Steve looked up at the sky. It was the palest blue, and the rooftops across from him were still silhouetted with a swathe of pink from the sunrise. Except of course there wasn't a sun there in Darkacre.

"Don't you find it strange that there's no sun or moon or

stars here?"

"It's just the way it is."

"So you were born here then?"

"No, but I came here hours after I was born." She said that last word strangely, but Steve dismissed it. Everything was strange now. "Are they still arguing?"

"Just a bit."

"My fault," she said.

"I don't think Frobisher and the darkling were ever going to see eye-to-eye."

"No, I mean last night. If I hadn't gone after the darkling, we'd have been here to fight Winters."

"The darkling says it wouldn't have made a difference." He shrugged. "And Winters might have taken us, too: or worse."

"What good am I if I can't help the people I love?" she said, wiping a hand across her eyes.

There was a shout from inside the shop, Frobisher calling out their names, and then the sound of a slamming door.

"Looks like we're needed." Steve stood up and offered his hand to Blessing. "Coming?"

She shook her head. "I don't want to see the table."

"It's covered up now. Promise."

"Okay." She let him pull her to her feet but clung onto his hand. "Will you stay with me?"

"Always," he said. "We're in this together."

*

"We've come to an agreement," said the darkling. "About the way forward."

"I'm not happy about it." Frobisher stomped around the kitchen with his hands dug into his trouser pockets. "But something has to be done."

"So what next?" said Steve.

"Next, you tell me where the Reactor is," said the darkling. "Then, we make a plan about how to obtain it."

"But how do I know you won't just shadow out of here and go get it without us?"

"That's what I said." Frobisher crossed his arms, with a sniffy look on his face. "Can we trust her?"

"I don't know," said Steve. "Without Hartley..."

"I trust her." Blessing had kept to the edge of the kitchen, as far from the covered table as she could get, but now she stepped forward. "She's good. I know she is. I feel it. If she says she'll help us, then I believe her."

"You can't decide these things on feelings," said Frobisher.

"I think that's all we've got." Steve shrugged. "If Blessing says she can be trusted..."

"I'm still here, you know," said the darkling. "Can you stop talking about me?"

"Sorry," said Steve. "I suppose you could have gone, left Darkacre by now, or tortured the truth out of me."

"She wouldn't do that," said Blessing.

"Not unless I had to," said the darkling with the subtlest of smiles.

"What I don't get is how this Thomas Winters managed to get into Darkacre. It's fair got my hackles up." Frobisher pulled out a chair and slumped down onto it. "Even if he used some sort of charm, anyone entering Darkacre through my gateway who isn't authorised or a local will set off an alarm. There was no alarm."

"And you know about everyone that's authorised?" said Steve.

"Of course."

"Then Thomas Winters must be a local," said the darkling. "With magic."

"You don't always need magic to use a charm," said Frobisher.

"He has magic," said the darkling. "My kind, we can see the auras of both workadays and magicals. He is what you would call a devourer."

"He can't be," said Frobisher.

"What's a devourer?" said Steve. *And do I really want to know the answer?* he thought.

"It's not good," said Frobisher. "A devourer can drain magic. From people, from non-people," he said, nodding to the darkling, "sometimes even from a place heavy with magic. But that doesn't make sense. The only family with that birth-magic were Nanon and her boy. Nanon's been dead a long time now and her boy…" He shook his head. "No, can't be him. He was a weak strip of a brat. He wouldn't survive out there without help."

"It would explain how he overpowered two experienced magicals," said the darkling.

"Well, I'll be." Frobisher huffed out a sigh. "Who'd have thought it?"

"Back on point," said the darkling. "Where is the Reactor?"

"With Miss Farspringer," said Steve, before turning to Blessing to ask, "Who is Miss Farspringer?"

"The worst," said Frobisher. "Which makes her the perfect guard-dog for a precious item."

"This complicates matters," said the darkling.

"Just a bit," said Frobisher, scratching his head. "I need to gather a few things for you to take with you. I'll meet you at the gate."

"Weapons?" said Steve, imagining a shield and sword.

"You've watched too many movies," said Frobisher. "You'll need your wits about you for this adventure. No weapon will help with that."

*

"Why can't I come too?" sulked Michael. "I can fight."

"I'm not looking after your brother on my own," said Frobisher. "I'm a very busy man, I'll have you know."

They stood at the gateway between Darkacre and the city. Steve and Blessing wore outdoor coats, which Steve was glad of in the morning chill. The darkling waited a step away, her hood pulled up.

"But—"

"Off you go inside. I need to speak to these three in private."

"Whatever." Michael tutted and rolled his eyes, but he did what he was told, stomping off into Frobisher's house.

"Right, first things first," he said. "Miss Farspringer can be a bit difficult to deal with."

"A diplomatic way of putting it," said the darkling. "She is dangerous, and cunning."

"I know," said Frobisher, frowning. "I just didn't want to

worry the children."

"We're not children," said Steve. "We can handle the truth."

"You haven't met Miss Farspringer yet," said Frobisher. "Right, when you get to the Ministry of Yesterday, stupid name if you ask me, but when you get there, don't speak to them big, floaty, black obelisk malarkeys. Whatever you do, don't. Go to the Special Enquiries Desk instead. It's not difficult to find. The lady there will give you something for Miss Farspringer. Don't open it, whatever kind of sound it makes. It's to appease Miss Farspringer and keep her calm. Believe me, you don't want to offend her."

Okay, thought Steve. *That's not at all worrying.*

"You'll have to reason with her," said Frobisher. "Not an easy thing to do. She'll want something in return for the Reactor."

"Like what?"

"I'm coming to that. Here." Frobisher picked up a small parcel from his deckchair and handed it to Steve. "She'll ask for three gifts. They're all in there."

"That will help," said the darkling, "to an extent."

"Keep your wits about you," said Frobisher. "Don't agree to anything, don't let Miss Farspringer touch you, and don't turn your back on her."

"Right," said Steve. *What have I got myself into now?*

"I'll keep them safe," said the darkling.

"You'd better," said Frobisher. "One last thing."

What now? thought Steve.

"I don't do this for everyone." He went to the archway and patted the bricks as if it were a favourite pet. "The Ministry is way over the other side of the city. You need to save your strength, so I'll move the gateway. Just this once, mind."

"Thank you, Frobisher." Blessing took his hand. "For everything."

"Get away with you now." He pulled his hand free and nodded to the archway. "There's no time for sentiment."

"Thanks." Steve nodded to the gatekeeper as Blessing and the darkling stepped through the archway. "See you soon."

I hope, he thought, as he followed the others.

Chapter Thirty-Six

The Ministry of Yesterday was a thirteen-storey box, clad in bands of synthetic timber and dull metal. Unlike the towers that made up the city skyline, the Ministry had a pitched roof, tiled with more of the dull, dark metal, which only added to its intimidating appearance.

"What is this place?" Blessing stood in the shadow of the Ministry, with Steve and the darkling on either side of her.

"You know the Tree of Remembrance in Darkacre?" said Steve.

"Yes," she said. "Are there trees inside there?"

"No, nothing like that," said Steve, "but the Ministry does a similar job. It holds a record of everyone who has died in Caercester city and the surrounding area. It stores all kind of records: a person's will, every image ever created of them, their purchase history, their DNA, everything."

"All of that information in there?" she said. "For hundreds of people?"

"Thousands, maybe even millions. Most of it's held digitally.

There's a library too. My Dad took me there a couple of times when he was doing some family history research into the Havens."

"Why?" said the darkling.

"He was looking for information on a twentieth century ancestor. Did you know the Havens have lived in Caercester for more than seven generations?"

"No, I mean why is it necessary to keep so much information? Do people not pass down stories of their ancestors? And why lock down every detail of a person's life? Isn't it best to just remember the valuable and happy parts?"

"I've never thought of it like that," said Steve.

"Shall we go in?" Blessing stepped a little closer to the Ministry, wide-eyed.

"That's the plan," said Steve. "Come on."

*

"Special enquiries… Special enquiries…" Steve muttered under his breath. He couldn't see any kind of reception desk, just twenty or more tall, black obelisks that moved between a crowd of visitors.

"Can I help you?" said a polite voice.

Don't be an obelisk, please don't be an obelisk, Steve thought as he slowly turned around. It was an obelisk, floating a few inches above the floor. At Steve's head height, a cartoon emoji smiled at him from the obelisk's black stone.

"Don't talk to it," Blessing whispered to Steve. "Frobisher said—"

"Can I help you?" The emoji swivelled round to face Blessing. "What would you like to do today?"

"Well." Steve looked at the darkling who just shrugged in response. "I, err, well..."

"I'll deal with this. Return to your station, attendant." A small, white haired woman dressed in an alarming shade of pink shooed the obelisk away. "Special enquiries?" she asked Steve, adjusting a pair of thick, equally pink glasses. A name tag on her blouse read 'Cassie Moran'.

"That's right. How did you...?"

"This way," she said, beckoning them all after her as she started off away from the obelisks and the visitors. "I haven't got all day."

"We were told to ask for—" Steve began as they hurried after her.

"Yes, yes, hold your horses," she called back. "Let's do this properly."

"Is this what Frobisher meant?" Blessing whispered to him.

"I hope so," said Steve. "Only one way to find out."

Cassie led them to a sectioned-off area beside the entrance to the Ministry of Yesterday. A pink-cushioned chair sat behind a chunky, mirrored desk. Cassie pressed a finger to her lips as she pulled out the chair and reached under the desktop. There was a sudden sound, or rather a non-sound, a reverse sound, as the chatter of the visitors and the shuffling of their footsteps stopped.

"That's better." Cassie sat down at the desk and smiled at them. "Don't worry. It's Council-approved magic," she said as Steve peered over the surrounding half-height partitions at the bustling, but now silent, visitors. "They can't see or hear us."

"I thought the Council didn't like magic being done in the city." Steve wished he had a better word than 'done'. Cast? Committed? After all that had happened, he still had no idea how this all really worked.

"You're a workaday, aren't you? New to magic? I thought so." She didn't stop to let him answer either of her questions. "The Council aren't completely unreasonable. There are a number of official safe points in every city where a magical, or a workaday in-the-know, can seek advice."

"I suppose that makes sense," he said, "How did you know we needed your help?"

"You have a darkling with you," said Cassie. "It goes without saying that you'd want my expertise. Don't worry," she said to the frowning darkling. "Your disguise is perfectly sound. I've just learnt to recognise the signs over the years."

"That is reassuring," said the darkling.

"So, how can I help you today?" said Cassie, tapping on the screen of a tablet that seemed to have appeared from nowhere.

"We need to speak to Miss Farspringer," said Steve.

"Are you sure?"

"Yes," said Steve. "We were given her name as—"

"Hang on." Cassie slipped off her chair and dipped down behind the desk.

"Hello?" he said. "Are you all right?"

"Here we are." She popped up into view again with a small box in her hand. "Give this to her." She pushed the box across the desk. "To sweeten her mood. She only likes the live ones. Whatever you do, don't open it. We don't want an infestation."

"Okay." Steve pocketed the box. "And where will we find her?"

"The stairs over there." She nodded to a series of steps leading down from behind them. Steve was sure they hadn't been there before. "You can't miss it. There's only one door."

"Thanks," he said, backing towards the stairs.

"Good luck," Cassie called after them. "I'll see you again soon. Hopefully."

"What do you think's in the box?" said Steve as they started down the stairs.

"Probably crickets," said the darkling. "Or cockroaches. Or mealworms."

"Really? Does Miss Farspringer have a pet?" he said as they reached a closed, tall, panelled door. "Do you think?"

"You're about to find out," said the darkling as she grasped the door handle with the tiniest of smiles.

*

The door opened onto a dimly lit room. On all sides, floor to ceiling bookcases divided the space into a number of narrow corridors. Desks and bare wooden chairs sat at uniformly spaced distances amongst it all, each desk overseen by a table light.

"Miss Farspringer?" called the darkling.

From the depths of the room, somewhere unseen, came a dry rattle and the swish of fabric on floorboards.

"Miss Farspringer?" said Steve. "The lady upstairs sent us down. She gave us a box for you."

"Are they still alive?" said a deep, dry voice.

"I think so," said Steve.

They heard slow, measured footfalls and then a tall, willowy woman glided out from behind one of the bookcases. Jutting cheekbones daubed with rouge sat below large, black sunglasses that hid her eyes completely. Above the sunglasses, jet black, unnaturally arched eyebrows had been drawn on her painted skin. To frame it all, her head was wrapped in a deep emerald turban.

"Are you Miss Farspringer?" said Steve.

"I am she." As she walked towards them, her long, black dress trailed out behind her and, when she stopped before them, Steve noticed that a jewelled snake brooch hung down from the turban onto her forehead. "May I have the box?" She stretched a gloved hand towards them. "Please."

"Sure." Steve pulled it from his pocket. "Here you go."

"At last." She snatched the box and pressed it to her face, inhaling deeply. "Fresh," she said, with a lick of her tongue. "What do you want, boy?"

"A friend gave us your name," said Steve.

"Friend?" she snapped. "I do not have friends."

"A mutual acquaintance," said the darkling, stepping forward. "He recently posted an item to you."

"Oh, that." She turned her back on them. "I added it to the collection."

"But we want it back," said Blessing.

"I beg your pardon?" Miss Farspringer slowly turned around to face them. "Once a donation is made to the collection, it cannot be withdrawn."

"There's been a mistake. It wasn't a donation," said Steve. "He only meant to leave it here for a bit."

"I do not make mistakes," said Miss Farspringer.

"Everyone makes mistakes," said Blessing.

"How dare you!" It seemed to Steve that Miss Farspringer grew in height as she spat the words, her head swaying from side to side. "You insult me."

"She didn't mean to," said Steve. "We're sorry, aren't we?"

"Yes." Blessing nodded. "Very sorry."

"Is it not bad enough that you bring this shadow spy into my midst?" snarled Miss Farspringer. "And now, you tell me that I have made a mistake?"

"The children do not understand the system," said the darkling. "Of course, the item was a donation. We simply wish to make a withdrawal."

"That's it," said Steve. "A withdrawal."

"A withdrawal?" Miss Farspringer turned her head quickly to look at each of them in turn. "Why didn't you say so? That's altogether different. What will you pay? I require three gifts."

"I have this." Steve pulled the package that Frobisher had given to him from his coat pocket. "Will it do?" he said, offering it to her.

"Open it," she said. "I must make sure that this is not a trick."

"All right." He went to the nearest table and opened the package with Blessing and the darkling at his back. Inside the messily tied brown paper were three items wrapped in tissue paper.

"What is it? said Miss Farspringer. "Tell me."

"There's this." Steve unfurled the tissue paper of the first and held up a large, conch shell: yellow cream on the outside, fleshy pink on the inside. "To hear the sea?" he suggested, hoping that was the right thing to say.

"Oh, the sea, the sea." She held the shell to her ear. "I have missed the sea. What else?"

"Sweets." He peered inside a white paper bag of amber-coloured candies.

"Let me have one." She snatched the bag from him, plunging one of the sweets into her mouth. "Barley sugar. I love barley sugar. They're so good for my throat."

"Right," said Steve, watching her as she closed her eyes with glee. "And this," he said, unwrapping the final tissue-parcel. "A gem?" Golden flecks within the orange, many-faceted jewel caught the dim light of the lamps.

"A sunstone," said the darkling. "To bring you the rays of the sun."

"Are these enough?" Steve handed over the sunstone, and then retreated from the table and from what he hoped was the reach of Miss Farspringer. "Will these pay for a withdrawal?"

"Well." Miss Farspringer turned the gem in the light to make it glisten.

"Yes?" said Blessing.

"Almost," said Miss Farspringer, still admiring the sunstone.

"What else do you want?" said Steve. *I've nothing more to give*, he thought.

"I get so bored here," she said.

"With all these books?" said Blessing. "How could you ever get bored?"

"After a century has passed, reading becomes tedious." Miss Farspringer left her treasures on the table and slowly moved towards them, her head swaying slightly from side to side. "I need a distraction."

Does she mean us? thought Steve. *Are we the distraction?* He reached for Blessing's hand, ready to run.

"What would you suggest, Miss Farspringer?" said the

darkling.

"Well." Miss Farspringer's lips drew back into a smile that reminded Steve of old-time movie vampires. "Leave me with a little magic," she said.

"Magic?" said Steve. *Not our blood or beating hearts?*

"Make me a light orb." Miss Farspringer clapped her hands. "I adore light orbs."

"I can do that." Blessing sounded as relieved as Steve felt.

"And then we can make the withdrawal?" said Steve. "And you'll let us leave?"

"Of course," said Miss Farspringer. "What do you take me for? A monster?"

Chapter Thirty-Seven

When they arrived at Saint Mungo's Sanctuary, the place bustled with the clanking of cutlery on serving trays and the chit-chat of the city's homeless as lunch was served.

"What are we doing here?" Blessing stopped just inside the doorway, her hands clutched together. "This isn't helping Hartley or Abel."

"We can't just charge in there," said the darkling, keeping her voice quiet. "We need to be prepared; we need a plan. Come on." She led them to an empty table, pulling out a chair for Blessing. "I'll get some food."

"I'm not hungry," said Steve as she left them. His stomach disagreed, rumbling noisily; he tried to remember when he'd last eaten anything.

"What do we do now?" Blessing slumped onto the chair. "Do you think Hartley's okay?"

"Hartley's always okay." Steve took the seat beside her. "Yeah?"

"Yeah." She nodded but didn't look convinced.

"Here." The darkling dropped onto the table two or three protein bars and a bottle of water. "It's all I can get without queuing up."

"It'll do." Steve tore the wrapper off one of the bars and bit into it. He was so hungry that even the synthetic texture of the bar felt good in his mouth. "Do you come here a lot?"

"It is a useful place to rest." The darkling sat and opened one of the bars.

"You eat?" said Steve as the darkling took a small bite.

"This form requires a little sustenance." The darkling took another bite and then offered the bar to Blessing, who shook her head. "You need to keep your strength up."

"What if Winters has hurt them? What if we can't beat him?"

"You should have more faith in yourself." The darkling took another bite of the bar. "And as far as Winters is concerned, it's in his best interests to keep your friends alive."

"Should we be talking about this here?" Steve looked around at the increasing number of diners, old and young, all crammed into the hall. "Someone might hear."

"This is as safe a place as any," said the darkling. "These people look after each other, keep their secrets."

"I didn't think places like this existed anymore." He finished the protein bar, screwing up the wrapper. "I didn't think there was a need for them."

"Caercester, like most cities, is very good at hiding its underbelly," said the darkling. "Including those who are in need."

"I suppose." He stuffed the wrapper in his coat pocket. His knuckles knocked on something hard and smooth. "What's this?"

"Soul dust," said Blessing as Steve pulled the test tube from his pocket and held it up. "From Braeden Kendra's dust room."

"To make—" He mouthed the word 'revenants', then frowned as he realised that nobody in the Sanctuary would know what that was.

"Useful," said the darkling. "Your friend, Hartley must have put it in your coat pocket before he was taken."

"Maybe while he was being taken," said Blessing. "Hartley is very good at sleight of hand."

"Do you want it?" Steve held it out to her. "I don't know what to do with it."

"And I do?" She tilted her head to consider the test tube. "No, you keep it. You never know when it might come in useful. Where's the Reactor?"

"Here." Steve patted his other pocket.

The darkling ate the last piece of protein bar and licked her fingers. To Steve, she looked like a normal teenage girl: a little messy and dirty, but definitely not a magical warrior on a quest.

"What?" she said as she caught him watching her.

"So… Next steps," he said, looking away. "Are we really going to hand the Reactor over?"

"Of course, we are," said Blessing. "How else are we going to rescue Hartley and Abel?"

"That doesn't sit well with me." The darkling clenched her hands before her, nails digging into the skin. "It's a terrible idea."

"It's a shame we can't trick Winters in some way," said Steve. "Make him think he has the Reactor, when he actually doesn't. Of course, I don't know how…" He stopped.

"What?" said Blessing.

"I've got an idea," he said. "At least, I think I've got an idea. Maybe. How long would it take to get to the City Museum?"

"On foot, an hour," said the darkling.

"Come on then." He stood up, grabbing the water bottle. "Best hurry. I'll tell you on the way."

*

It was the middle of the afternoon by the time they arrived at the museum. Steve tried to remember what day it was, eventually arriving at the conclusion that it was a Tuesday. Three days since the attack at his school. Five days since the whole crazy adventure had begun. *Five days,* he thought. It felt like a lifetime. Still, Tuesday was a good day to be visiting the museum. There'd be no weekend tourists. He hoped that would make it easier to slip in and out unnoticed.

"So this replica is convincing, then?" said Steve as he and Blessing followed the darkling into the museum.

"It fooled me," she said. "For a little while."

"Fingers crossed it'll fool Winters too."

Blessing stayed close to Steve as they passed through the reception into the first room of the museum. He wondered if he should take her hand. He wanted to.

"Have you been to this display before?" asked the darkling.

"Years ago," he said. "I don't remember seeing the Reactor, but then I wasn't looking for it."

"This shouldn't take long," said the darkling. "If we wait for our moment, I can easily take it."

"Hold up there." The door to the next chamber, the one

they wanted, was cordoned off by a holographic banner which streamed the words, *'Closed to the public'*. Next to the door stood a security guard, staring at the three of them. "You can't go in there. Not today."

"Why?" the darkling demanded.

"School trip." The security guard crossed his arms. "They'll be here any minute, so off you go. You'll have to come back tomorrow."

"But we can't," said Blessing. "It has to be today."

"Not my problem," said the security guard.

"Thank you." Steve linked arms with Blessing and the darkling and pulled them away. "We'll come back another time."

"What are you doing?" The darkling pulled her arm from his grasp as they walked away.

"We don't want to make a fuss, and he's not going to let us in. We'll find another way."

"What do you suggest?" said the darkling. "Wait until the museum closes?"

"I suppose we could do that," he said. "Or we could join them." He nodded across the room to a group of children following a bored-looking woman towards them. "Look like a school trip to you?"

"Your point being?" said the darkling.

"Isn't it obvious?" he said, heading for the children. "We're children. They're children. Really?" he said as both Blessing and the darkling looked at him with no expression on their faces. "Am I the only person seeing the possibilities here? They're even dressed casually. We could easily pass as one of them."

"She couldn't," said Blessing.

"She is a shadow." By the time, Blessing and Steve looked in her direction, the darkling had gone.

*

"Do you think anyone will notice?" Blessing whispered to Steve as they stood amongst the schoolchildren gathered around the curator in the Central Plaza Bank bombing display chamber.

"We're the same age as them," he whispered back. "Let's just keep our heads down."

"Now, does anyone know when the bombing took place?" The curator stood by a slowly rotating holographic display of the bank as it had been before the explosion.

Unlike the buildings that filled the current Central Plaza, the bank had been constructed from limestone, with ornate arched windows, faux pillars set into the walls, and a carved stone sign on the roof above the main entrance, stating the words 'Savings Bank' in gold capitals.

"Anyone?" said the curator when nobody answered. "That's a shame." He sighed. "The Central Plaza bank was destroyed forty-eight years ago in 2062 during a bank heist. The assailants were never identified because the power of the explosion destroyed the bank and everything in it. Unfortunately, this also meant that it was nigh-on impossible to identify any customers or passers-by who were caught up in the explosion."

"Eww," said one of the children, screwing up her nose and setting off a ripple of giggles and chat.

The holographic display changed to an image of the interior of the bank. It had been busy that day. Each holographic bank teller was engaged with a customer, with more people waiting to take their turn.

"This is the last image we have before the robbers blocked the camera feed," the curator continued. "It is still unknown whether the robbers were targeting the money held at the bank or the customers themselves. The Central Plaza bank only dealt with online transactions and as such had no need to store any actual money. It is known that the majority of customers were businesspeople, tourists, or the representatives of the wealthy."

"Do you see that?" Steve whispered to Blessing. "At the back of the bank."

In the holographic image, a tall, wide man dressed in a suit that looked too small for him, stood with his hands folded in front of him. Beside him stood a teenage girl, maybe sixteen or seventeen years old, dressed in a pretty blue dress. Her hair was short and dark and, even though they were indoors, she wore sunglasses that hid her eyes.

"The few remnants we have from the explosion were all found outside the bank and are likely to have been from people walking on the street. The one exception to this, well, I say one. There were two, actually. The first was a metal disc, which is thought to have been a pendant. How it survived when everything else was obliterated is still unclear. The other item was a statue. Again, we have no idea how the statue survived the blast, and the bank have always denied that there was a statue on-site. A mystery." He smiled at the children, pausing for effect. When he got none, the smile dropped from his face and he sighed.

Steve looked around as the curator continued with his presentation. He wondered where the darkling had got to.

"A number of display cabinets have been opened especially for your visit," said the curator. "I would ask that you do not touch the items in the cabinets but do feel free to take photographs."

"Off you go then," said the teacher.

While she stood talking to the curator, the schoolchildren broke up into groups and pairs to sullenly drift around the chamber.

"Time to go," said a familiar voice from behind Steve.

"There you are," he said, turning to find the darkling waiting for him. "Won't it look suspicious if we leave before the others?"

"Not as suspicious as when they find that the replica is missing and we're not part of this class."

"Good point," he said.

"Quick. I think the teacher's seen us," said Blessing.

"Right you are," said Steve, taking her hand. "Hartley would have come in handy right around now."

Chapter Thirty-Eight

"This is it," said the darkling.

The sun had set on their walk across the city and now, in the early evening, the three of them stood in the light that radiated through the glass walls of the Haven Robotics Corporation building.

"You're not coming with us, are you?" said Blessing.

"I can't. This building has been designed to keep magical creatures out." She paused. "Or in. Magical humans, however, should be fine."

"But we can't do this without you," said Steve. The darkling had forgotten how young he actually was. The boy who had faced her down in Hartley's kitchen now looked small and unsure.

"There is one advantage to the way this building has been warded," she said. "The Hidden will not be able to trace the use of magic within. You don't have to worry about bringing them down on you. Use whatever magic you need to get the job done."

"That's one thing, I suppose," said Steve, "but we're just kids. We need, well…" He looked at Blessing, frightened and wrapped up in an ill-fitting coat, then his own messy reflection in the glass wall. "We need…"

"An adult?" said the darkling. "You're not just kids, as you put it. You are a team. You will protect each other. Blessing has her magical skills, and you, Steve Haven, have a keen intellect, a brave heart, and a relentlessly annoying but nevertheless effective curiosity."

"Thanks," said Steve. "I think."

"Why not leave the real Reactor with me?" The darkling held out her hand. "That way you can't mix them up, and there is no chance that it will fall into the hands of Winters."

"No," said Steve. "If I hang onto the real one then you'll have to help us. You can't just run off with it when we go in there."

"Very well," she sighed. "Then all I can do is wish you both good luck."

"You'll stay here, won't you?"

"I will be here," she said. "Waiting for your return."

With that, the darkling released her form to shadow, watching the two children stare up at the heights of the Haven Corporation building. They were scared—she could see that in them—and yet they did not run away. She watched them join hands, exchange a look, and then silently step towards their fate.

*

Steve and Blessing walked into the Haven Corporation building, hand-in-hand and with the same startled rabbit look on their faces.

Blessing stumbled over the threshold, frowning down at the engraved Haven Robotics Corporation plate.

"All right?" said Steve, taking her arm.

"I just came over dizzy," she said. "Fine now."

"Good evening, Master Haven," said the robot who sat at the glass reception desk. "Mr Winters is expecting you." The robot extended a limb towards a pair of lift doors at the rear of the lobby, which silently opened. "Mr Winters left instructions for you to go up to the penthouse office suite."

"Right," said Steve. "Shall we?" he said to Blessing.

"Might as well," she said, trying to smile.

"Come on." Steve drew her with him as he walked towards the open lift doors. *Keep to the plan,* he thought. *That's all we have to do. Just keep to the plan.*

"Steve," she said as the doors closed behind them. "I just wanted to say—"

"Shush." Steve placed a finger to his lips and nodded to the camera that pointed down at them.

"Top floor," said an identical voice to that of the receptionist robot.

Steve took a deep breath, then noticed that Blessing was doing the same thing. He smiled at her and she smiled back.

Ready? she mouthed silently.

Before he could answer, the doors opened.

*

In comparison to Winters's home penthouse apartment, the office suite which was located on the topmost floor of the

Haven Robotics Corporation building was a picture of old-world charm: from the dark wood floor to the leather armchairs and the wall-mounted portraits. A fire, which Steve assumed to be holographic, roared and flickered in a stone hearth on one side of the room.

"Your uncle always had good taste." Winters sat in the furthest most chair, leaning back with one leg across the other and a drink in his hand. "That's one of the things I admired about him."

"Where are Hartley and Abel?" said Steve as he and Blessing stepped out of the lift.

"Locked up, where they can't get up to any mischief."

"I want to see them." Steve could feel the heaviness in his pockets from the items contained there. He let go of Blessing's hand. "This is a trade. The Reactor for them."

"I don't take orders from you," Winters snapped. "I'll decide when and if I free the hostages." He drained his glass and set it down on a small side-table. "Hand it over."

"I have it here." Steve reached into his coat pocket.

"And don't think of trying anything," said Winters. "Or I'll hurt the girl. You know I can."

"Sure," said Steve, pulling the replica from his pocket. "No tricks." He went to a cabinet that was halfway between them and left the replica there. "There you go."

"Bring it here." Winters held out his hand. "Don't be obtuse."

"Where are they?" Steve clenched his hands, which were shaky and damp with sweat. "I want to see them."

"Bring. It. Here," Winters growled.

"Okay." Steve picked up the replica and slowly walked the remaining space between them. "Here."

271

Winters snatched it from Steve's hand and held it up to look at. "I honestly didn't think you'd be brave enough to bring this to me. Or stupid enough."

"Did you kill my uncle?" Steve hadn't meant to ask, but the words had formed themselves.

"What was that?" Winters held the replica up to the light. "Oh, it wasn't part of my plan. I couldn't tell him what I was doing."

"And what were you doing?" said Steve, returning his hand to his coat pocket as he backed away.

"Building a bright future for the Corporation, and for me. I developed a new kind of robot that would guarantee that."

"And Rex didn't like the idea?" Steve continued to back away towards Blessing. They had to be near the lift doors. "He tried to stop you, didn't he?"

"Your uncle was a good man." Winters said the word 'good' as if it was an insult. "He couldn't see the merits of what I was doing. Draining a handful of inconsequential darklings to create a new kind of robot power cell was an easy trade for me; but for him?"

"Why darklings, though?" said Steve. "It's not like you can use magic to power robots."

"It's that kind of narrow thinking that has kept communities like Darkacre under the thumb of the Council for centuries. Of course, magic can power robots. What I created is more than that though. Self-perpetuating power cells: imbued with a mixture of magic. That's what darklings are after all: pure magic. With the added ability to drain magic—my own personal talent— there'd be no stopping them. There's enough magic in the air to keep them running for years and, if needed, there are people like her." He looked at Blessing. "Easy, unsuspecting pickings."

"You're a monster," said Blessing.

"There are plenty of monsters in this world," said Winters. "I'm just a good businessman. I saw the opportunity and I seized it. I already have interested parties." He weighed the Reactor in his hand, lips spreading into a smug grin. "I never realised quite how useful this device was until I had to face Rex. The Reactor gave me the power to get rid of him, you see: to drain his life force. Just like I'm going to do to you, and her, and the others." Winters pressed his finger and thumb to the indentations on the sides of the replica, tensing his body. Nothing happened. He frowned and then tried again, shaking the metal disc. "What's wrong with it? The bars should slide out. Why isn't it working?"

"Steve?" said Blessing. "I think now—"

"What have you done? This isn't it!" Winters threw the replica to the floor. "Where's the real Reactor?"

"Steve?" said Blessing, a little more loudly, as Winters advanced on them.

"Got it." Steve pulled the test tube of soul dust from his pocket. "Please do what you're supposed to," he whispered to it, then pulled back his arm and threw it with as much force as he could.

"What is this?" cried Winters as the test tube smashed at his feet.

"Justice," said Steve, as the scattered dust began to spin around Winters's legs. "For Rex."

"No!" Winters lunged towards them as the rising dust gained substance, weighing him down. "I'll get you."

"Come on." Blessing dragged Steve to the closed lift doors. "Steve."

"Stupid boy! One revenant can't stop me." Winters tried to break free as the revenant furled its arms around him. "I'm too powerful."

Blessing jammed her thumb on the lift button. "Come on, come on."

"Why isn't it working?" Steve knocked Blessing's hand aside and pummelled the lift button with the side of his fist.

"You can't beat me!" The substance of the revenant waned and formed as Winters fought to drain it.

Finally, the lift doors opened and Steve and Blessing tumbled inside. Steve jabbed at the button for the basement.

"No!" Winters lunged at the lift, blocking the doors with his hands. "You're not getting away."

"Come on." Steve kept his thumb on the basement button. "Work. Please, work."

Winters reached for them as the revenant grasped a hand to his head, twisting long fingers through its captive's hair. Winters scrabbled for a hold on the doors, then fell back into the room, kicking and screaming.

The doors closed. Steve slid to the floor as the lift began its descent.

*

Steve rubbed his arms as they walked through the empty, concrete corridors and rooms of the basement. He was trembling but he wasn't sure if it was because of the chill temperature or the after-rush of adrenaline. Maybe he was just plain scared.

"Is it odd that I feel bad for Winters?" Blessing walked with her head down.

"We had no choice."

"That doesn't make me feel any better."

"I wish the darkling was here," said Steve.

"You like her, don't you?" said Blessing. "I get it. She's dangerous and brave."

"Yes," said Steve. "But not like that. I just—" He stopped talking before he said the wrong thing.

"I hope Hartley and Abel are all right."

"Hang on." Steve stopped at the next entrance, holding Blessing back with a protective arm. "I think someone's in there," he whispered.

"They're not moving," Blessing whispered back.

"We need a closer look."

"Okay." She moved his arm aside and disappeared into the room.

"Blessing, wait."

"It's clear," she called back. "Come on."

Lined up on either side of the room stood human figures, all dressed in trousers and what looked like hospital smocks, all male with different faces and hair colours. Several of them had torsos that had been stripped back to metal, some of them had fist-sized holes in their chests that dripped with a creamy fluid.

"This is what Winters was talking about," said Steve. "A new kind of robot."

"They look like real people," said Blessing.

"No wonder he kept them a secret." Steve poked the face of one of them. It felt like living skin: tendon and muscle. "It's against the law for robots to look human. They can't stand on two legs or have five-fingered hands. They definitely can't have faces."

"They're like big dolls."

"Or puppets," said Steve.

"What's the gooey stuff coming out of them?"

"It looks like the fluid in robot power cells," he said. "We examined one in a science lesson once."

"I don't like them," said Blessing, wrinkling her nose. "They scare me a little."

"A self-powering robot that could pass for a living human being," said Steve. "Imagine what Winters could do with that."

"But I thought robots did everything in your world already. Hartley said they walk dogs, and serve in shops, and drive cars. Eleanor's robot could cook."

"That's true," said Steve. "Even the military use robots now: no wages or medical bills to pay. So why would you need a robot that could pass for a human?" He looked around at the humanoid robots, turning it all over in his head. "Winters said he had 'interested parties'. That's how he worded it."

"So?"

"This is illegal," he said. "Anyone interested in buying these things is either a criminal, or someone with a lot of power who wants to keep things quiet."

"Someone like that could build an army," said Blessing.

"Winters could build his own army," said Steve. "And there's something else. If he could change how they look, if he could make them look like someone in power—" He stopped, realising the full weight of what he was about to say. "Winters could replace them with a lookalike robot, one that *he* controlled. He could take over the world without anyone knowing."

"Can we go?" Blessing backed away to the next doorway, keeping an eye on the robots as she walked. "Now?"

"Sure." Steve took one last look at Winters's failed experiments. Just like Hetty, the robots looked sad and abandoned. *But they're dangerous, too,* he thought. *Too dangerous to be allowed out into the world of humans.*

Chapter Thirty-Nine

"Is this it?" Blessing stood in front of a white door which blocked the entrance to the next room. The door was completely smooth, with no distinguishable handle or lock, and reached all the way to the low ceiling.

"Big scary white door in the basement," said Steve, looking around the room they were stood in. "I think it's a good bet that Winters's lab is behind it."

Blessing ran her hand across the door. "Whatever the door is made of, it's—" She pulled her hand away, hugging it to her. "It absorbs magic."

"Like Winters."

"I can't do anything with this," she said.

"If Hartley was here…"

"I don't think he could travel through this. What do we do now?"

"Hello?" Steve knocked lightly on the door, then with more force. "Abel? Hartley?"

"Can you hear anything?" she said.

"Nothing. Maybe there's—"

"Get away from there!"

Winters stood at the other end of the room, barring any chance they might have had of escape. His suit was dusty and torn, his usually polished hair unkempt. He reached a clawed hand towards them.

"How?" said Steve. "The revenant should have stopped you."

"One measly revenant?" Winters clicked his neck. "You'll have to do better than that. It's only ash bound together by magic. Hardly a challenge to deal with. Now, where is the real Reactor?"

"You have it," said Steve. "We gave it to you."

"Don't lie," snarled Winters. He pointed at Blessing then curled his fingers into a claw. Blessing staggered back a step, falling against the wall.

"Stop it," said Steve. "I've got it here. Leave her alone."

"Steve, you can't," Blessing whispered, her face growing paler by the second.

"I have to." He pulled the Reactor from his pocket. "It's the only way."

"Bring it here," said Winters. "And no tricks this time."

"Okay." Steve took a deep breath and walked slowly towards Winters. The Reactor sat on his open palm. "Just stop hurting her."

"Finally." Winters snatched the device from him with his free hand, the other still holding Blessing firm in the draining spell. "You want to see your friends? Open the door."

Steve straightened his back and glared at him. "Do it

yourself."

Blessing let out a groan as Winters clenched his fist even more. "If you value your friend's life, you'll do as I say."

Steve frowned but he couldn't see any other option. "I don't know what to do."

"There's a panel on the right-hand section of the door. You can't see it. You can only feel it. Open it."

"Okay." Steve felt around the door until his fingers found the panel and flipped it open. "Now what?"

"Back off."

Steve did as he was told. He could see Blessing out of the corner of his eye, leant against the wall, legs shaking as her magic was drained. *I've got to do something,* he thought as Winters went to the door. *Anything. Think.*

Winters pressed his finger to an identifier on the panel and breathed into the hole that appeared in the door.

"Don't move," said Winters, turning to Steve. "Now I have the Reactor, I'm more powerful than ever. Nobody in their right mind would dare challenge me."

As the laboratory door slid across, a hand whipped out from the room beyond and grabbed Winters by the collar, pulling him off-balance.

"Steve, help me!" Hartley, beaten and bruised, grappled with Winters, his arm around Winter's throat. "The Reactor. Grab it!"

Released from Winters's draining of her magic, Blessing leapt at the same time as Steve. She grabbed Winters's free hand, pinning it to his side as Steve went for the Reactor.

Close up, Steve watched Winters's face redden, veins throbbing at his temples and lips drawn back in a snarl. Steve peeled the man's fingers open, tugging at the device.

Winters roared as he ripped his hand from Blessing's grasp and slapped her away. "Get off me!" He punched out at Steve, who fell to the floor, his hand clenched to his nose. Nothing had ever hurt as much, not the backstreet attack or any of the beatings by Curtis. Pain radiated out from his nose to the rest of his face in a burning wave. For a second, everything he could see went double.

"No!" Hartley lost his grip on Winters, tumbling out of the laboratory to land on the floor.

"That was a mistake." Winters clicked his neck and squared his shoulders. "I don't need any of you alive. I just need this." He raised the hand that the held the Reactor. "And then…" His hand jerked as a blue spark crackled its way around his wrist with a hiss. "What?" He opened his fingers. Flat on his palm, the device began to rattle.

"Where's Abel? We've got to go." Steve grabbed Blessing's hand, pulling her upright. "I might have done a bad thing."

"Here." Abel crawled out of the laboratory.

"Come on, old friend." Hartley pulled him to his feet. "Abel's in a bad way," he said to Steve and Blessing.

"Steve, what have you done?" said Abel, leaning heavily on Hartley. "Don't tell me you…"

Steve held up the metal bars that he had removed from the top section of the Reactor. "It was something Winters said upstairs, about needing the bars to make the Reactor work. I thought if I could remove them, he wouldn't be able to use it."

Winters roared as he did his best to fling the sparking Reactor away, but it held fast to his hand. A network of lightning pulses meshed around his fingers and wrist. "No, no," he moaned as the muscles in his hand and arm began to convulse.

"But without the bars to stabilise it, the Reactor will go into meltdown," said Abel.

Winters's body jerked as fingers of electricity ran up his arm and reached around his waist. He cried out, batting his hand at the lightning that entwined his body.

"I thought it would stop him," said Steve, with a growing grip of panic in his stomach.

"If the Reactor explodes, it will take out most of the city," said Abel. "We have to get out of here."

"We can't go. We have to stop it," said Blessing.

"*Can* it be stopped?" said Steve.

Abel shook his head. "Not once the bars have been removed. If we can contain it in some way—"

"Like with the goblin?"

"I can do that," said Blessing. "At least I think I can."

"No, that's far too dangerous," said Hartley. "If we can find a door, I'll travel us back to Darkacre. We'll be safe there."

"Hartley?" Steve knew what he had to do. It was stupid, reckless even, and if he thought too long about it, he realised he might chicken out. "The door," he said. "It drains magic, right? What about the rest of the lab?"

"The same. Winters set it up to make sure the darklings couldn't fight back when he was draining their essence. Oh, I see what you mean," said Hartley, eyes widening. "But that wouldn't be enough."

"We have to try."

Steve braced himself, then barrelled into the bent-over Winters. Arcs of lightning sparked onto Steve's skin, furling around his wrist. *This has to work,* he thought; then, with all the strength he could gather from his beaten muscles, he shoved

Winters backwards into the laboratory.

"You're a genius," said Hartley. "Almost. How do we close the door?"

"I don't know," said Steve. "Winters used his fingerprint and his breath. How do we get round that?"

Inside the laboratory, Steve could see Winters trembling on the floor in the clutches of the now-incandescent Reactor. The lightning mesh had engulfed the man's entire body, clawing up the legs of the workbenches and leaping between light fittings which blinked on and off in response. Glass containers exploded and smashed, giving off a smell of hot metal and ozone. Above everything was the sound of Winters's scream.

"What do we do?" said Blessing.

"Hartley's right." Steve jumped a little as the door frame cracked and the surrounding walls shook. "We need to get out of here."

"Good idea," said Hartley, shooing them in front of him. "Go on, go on."

"Hartley, you said it was going to explode, take out most of the city." Blessing stared into the lightning filled laboratory. "We can't let that happen."

"There's nothing we can do, sweet girl." Hartley took her hand. "Nothing."

"I can do it," said Blessing. "I'll contain the blast."

"It's too much," said Hartley. "Even for someone like you."

"What choice do we have?" She released Hartley's hand. "We're the good ones, remember? We help people."

"She's right." Steve staggered a couple of steps as the floor shook. "We caused this. Well, I did. I didn't mean to, but…" He shrugged. "It's down to us to put it right."

"You two young people put me to shame." Hartley took a deep breath. "Very well."

Blessing turned to face the misshapen laboratory door frame and flung her arms wide, just as Steve had seen her do in the underground tunnels. "Steve, will you be my fuse again?" She stumbled a step as the floor shook. "Please?"

"Absolutely." He wanted to wrap his arms around her, but he wasn't sure if that would help or just get in the way. Instead he took his place at her shoulder. "I'm here."

She took a deep, deep breath and brought her cupped hands closer together, leaning into them as if she was willing something into being. The air around the open door shimmered and darkened. A curved wall, slowly ripping its way into existence, ran across the room, cutting through wall, ceiling and floor alike. A twitch of lightning arced between the encompassing sphere and the laboratory within.

"It's working," said Steve, hoping she could hear him.

Tremors growled from all around, shaking chunks of concrete from the walls. The ground rumbled. A force within the laboratory coughed out dust and sparks. Steve winced, but the sphere held, containing the bulging walls and the lightning that lashed out from within.

Steve saw Hartley and Abel tumble to the ground as another eruption thundered through the lab. The two men crawled towards them, Hartley with a hand sheltering his head.

"Steve?" Blessing's whole body was twitching now. Her hair floated around her shoulders and face as if she was underwater.

"Still here," he shouted. The noise of the electrical arcs and the complaining building was deafening.

"I don't think I can hold this much longer." Her voice sounded very young, and very weary. A tear rolled down her cheek.

The ground shook again, almost throwing her off her feet. Steve caught her, holding her as the tremors continued.

Lightning tapped on the inside of the now glass-like sphere, speeding up until the taps merged into a single, high pitched note that hurt Steve's ears. There was a sound like the ting of a glass bell; a small circular crack broke through the surface of the sphere. The crack sprinted out into a network of lines. Fingers of light reached out into the dusty air, illuminating the disintegrating room.

"Steve, I can't mend it," said Blessing. "I can only— "

The sphere shattered and the lessened force of the exploding Reactor engulfed the room. With a roar, the walls and the ceiling were torn apart.

*

The darkling waited in the deepening night, paralysed by her inability to help. She felt as useless as she had when imprisoned in the jar in Kendra's Fortress. All she could do was watch and hope that she had prepared the children well enough.

She felt the barest of tremors in the ground, so tiny that any workaday passer-by wouldn't notice. She hunkered down to the pavement, listening to the agitation beneath.

Then came the smell: the scent of burning dust and charred steel. She cast around for the source. The ground shook again, stronger this time, and the smell was joined by a sound: the sizzling lick of lightning.

Within the blink of an eye, what had been an empty pavement outside the Haven Corporation building was suddenly filled with a smoking, shattering, black orb. Another blink and the orb had gone.

In its place, within a circle of glass shards, four blackened figures clung to each other.

The larger of them opened his eyes and lifted his head. For a second, he looked around. He coughed, just the once, and then he began to laugh.

Chapter Forty

"This is it then," said Steve. Dressed again in his pyjamas and slippers, he stood in the square of morning light cast from the window in the ceiling of Hartley's kitchen. "It's all over."

"That sounds very final," said Hartley, his hand resting on Steve's shoulder. "It's not like we'll never see you again."

"It isn't?"

"Of course not." Blessing perched on the edge of the table. "You're not that lucky."

"That is a matter of opinion," said the darkling. Steve wondered if darklings did sarcasm.

Steve sighed. "I have to go back to school, don't I?" he said, glancing round at the others in the hope that someone would disagree and offer him a way out. Unfortunately, none of them did.

"It's where your parents will expect to find you when they return," said Abel. Even with the benefit of Blessing's healing, he looked pale and tired.

"And if Braeden Kendra's men turn up again? What then?"

"They won't," said Abel. "With the Reactor gone, you aren't important to Kendra. You can get back to normal."

Not important, thought Steve. *This really is 'back to normal'.*

"Abel's absolutely right," said Hartley. "The danger has passed. Wonderful news."

"Except for the danger of Miss Scritch's temper," Steve joked. Although it didn't feel very funny, now he thought about it.

"I almost forgot. You know what this is." Hartley pulled a piece of purple chalk from his pocket. "Only to be used in case of emergency, mind. Here."

"Thanks." Steve took the chalk and looked around the shabby kitchen. He'd got used to the place: the smells of the cooking, the ticking of the cooling stove, even the cold stone floors. "Will I remember? I want to remember. I deserve to remember."

"If that's what you want," said Hartley. "You'll remember it all. Even the terrible bits."

"What do I tell my parents when they get back?"

"Everything," said Abel, raising a hand as Steve opened his mouth to protest. "Your father will understand."

"Like he would have understood about the Reactor?" said Steve. "That's why you wanted him to have it, isn't it?"

"Just like that," said Abel.

"Right," said Steve. "I'll talk to Dad when he comes home." He turned to the darkling. "What about you? What will you do now the Reactor's destroyed?"

"I'm not sure it's as simple as that," said the darkling. "The Reactor has survived one explosion already. I must confirm its fate."

"Yes, well, I'm sure everything is in order. Nothing for you to worry about, Steve," said Hartley quickly.

"Come here, you." Blessing wrapped her arms around him. "I'm going to miss you."

"Thanks. Me too." He hugged her back, gently. She had used her powers to heal all their injuries, but she was still bruised and battered herself from the excitement of the last few days.

"Are you ready?" said Hartley once Blessing had released Steve, and he had gone round the room saying awkward goodbyes to everyone.

"Not really sure," said Steve. "There'll be a lot of explaining to do when I get back to school. How long have I been gone?"

"You've only been away for a few days." Hartley took Steve's arm and led him to the door. "Blessing, would you mind? If you can connect Steve and myself like you did with Eleanor, I should be able to travel him back to whence he came."

"You make it sound so simple," she said, going to stand between them. "I've only done this once, you know."

"And you did it marvellously." Hartley took her hand. "Steve?"

"Okay?" said Blessing as she took Steve's hand.

"As long as you don't fry my brains," he joked.

"No promises," she said, with a lop-sided smile.

She closed her eyes for what seemed like only a second, her slim fingers cool in Steve's grasp, then she nodded. "That should do it."

"Let's give this a go, shall we?" Hartley ran his hands over the door frame, knocking at seemingly random intervals. "Yes? Yes? Ah, there we are."

"Did it work?" said Steve as Hartley opened the door.

"See for yourself."

Steve peered through the doorway into the headmaster's office, the room where he had left Abel and Eleanor a few days before. It was empty and lit only by the early morning light that outlined the window blind. Normality was just a stride away.

"Sometimes the place you least want to go," said the darkling, "is the place where you are most needed to be."

"I still don't know your name," he said.

She glanced at Hartley, then shrugged. "Names are not always necessary. You *know* me: that is enough."

"Quick now. Time to go," said Hartley. "Best not to be caught in the headmaster's office."

"Right," said Steve, nodding. "Right." He turned around to face the open door. "Here we go."

"Bye, Steve," he heard Blessing say as he stepped through the door. "Take care of yourself."

"You too," he said, turning to wave goodbye.

The door closed behind him and he stared at it for a second. He wanted to fling it open, but he knew that all he would see would be the headmaster's stationery supply.

"Come on! In here! Quick: while it's empty!"

Steve heard the door to the corridor open, hurried footsteps and a familiar laugh. The laugh of a boy up to no good.

"Hello Curtis." Steve stood with his hands behind his back, the chalk concealed in his grasp.

"Haven?" Curtis's companions knocked into him as he stopped at the sight of Steve. "What are *you* doing in here?"

"Maybe he's in trouble," said one of the others.

"Of course he's in trouble." Curtis nodded at them to close

the door. "*I'm* here."

"Careful, Curtis." Steve smiled a wide, confident grin that he didn't altogether feel.

"Why's that then?" Curtis took a step closer. "Are you going to hurt me? I'm *so* scared." He looked at the others and smirked.

"Things have changed," said Steve. "You can't hurt me, or my friends, anymore."

"I can do whatever I like," said Curtis.

"I think your father would disagree."

"What are you on about?"

"My dad owns the Haven Robotics Corporation now." Steve paused, waiting for the realisation to sink in. "You don't get it, do you?" he said when Curtis's expression didn't change. "Your father's company depends on the Haven Corp for its entire business."

"He's right," said one of the others.

"Shut up." Curtis's face gradually turned red.

"We should go," said the other boy.

"I'd listen to him if I were you," said Steve.

"Why's that then?"

"Because I'm not scared of you." Steve took a step closer. "I've met people a lot worse than you could ever be, people who would give you nightmares."

"What did you just say to me?" Curtis's face slowly returned to its normal colour.

"Come on," said one of the boys, dragging on Curtis's arm while the other boy opened the door and peered outside. "The headmaster could come back any minute."

"This isn't over, Haven," said Curtis as he retreated to the door.

"You think?" Steve lunged towards them. Curtis flinched and stumbled back, slamming the door shut behind him.

Steve let out a long breath, running a hand through his hair. *I can't believe that worked,* he thought, then he smiled. *Wait until I tell Jon.*

The door to the headmaster's room opened again as Miss Scritch strolled into the room, a plate of biscuits in one hand and a teapot in the other.

"Haven!" she screeched, coming to such an abrupt halt that the biscuits slid off the plate and tea splashed from the teapot's spout.

"Hi," said Steve, his feelings of triumph fading away. "I'm back."

"Detention. So many detentions. No, I'm going to turn you over to the police. I'll see that the headmaster expels you for this!"

"This is most irregular." Steve heard the headmaster's voice accompanied by the tap-tapping of high heels in the corridor outside.

"Apologies for the early hour." Eleanor Palmer, resplendent in sapphire blue, followed the headmaster into the room. "But when I heard—" She stopped as she saw Steve, a warm smile spreading across her face. "Steve, here you are."

"I found him," Miss Scritch began, bristling with rage.

"How clever of you. You found him exactly where he was supposed to be." Eleanor went to Steve, gave him a swift kiss on the cheek and whispered, "Just go with it."

"This is a serious transgression, Mr Hendrickson," seethed Miss Scritch. "I've told him that he'll be expelled."

"He most certainly will not," said Eleanor.

"It isn't up to you!" snapped Miss Scritch.

"Miss Scritch, it isn't up to you either," said Mr Hendrickson.

"Of course not, Headmaster." Miss Scritch pressed her lips into a smile. "I just thought, what with Haven running away from school—"

"I didn't run away," said Steve. "I was—"

"Kidnapped," said Eleanor, patting his arm.

"What?" Miss Scritch's mouth fell open.

"The first period of time away from school was a failed kidnap attempt. Steve did try to explain but you," Eleanor looked directly at Miss Scritch, "refused to believe him. Headmaster, why you didn't call the police when Steve went missing the second time is beyond me. I'd go so far as to call it neglect of duty."

"Well, I... Well..." blustered the headmaster. "Miss Scritch, why didn't you call the police?"

"Me?" said Miss Scritch. "But you said—"

"When did the police return you to school, Steve?" Eleanor raised her eyebrows at him. "This morning?"

"Yes," he said. "Just now. They couldn't find the headmaster, so they left me here."

"I suppose they might still be on the school grounds," said Eleanor. "Maybe Miss Scritch could locate them. I'm sure they'll want to know why they weren't informed of the kidnap of the son of the owner of the Haven Robotics Corporation."

"Miss Scritch." The headmaster jerked his head towards the door.

"But he..." Miss Scritch looked at Steve. "I don't think he—"

"Miss Scritch, now," said the headmaster.

"Yes, Mr Hendrickson." Miss Scritch left the room without her usual speed and malice, still carrying the empty plate and the teapot.

"Well, it's nice to have you back, Haven." The headmaster clasped his hands behind his back and attempted a smile. "I… err… I do hope you are recovered."

"I wasn't ill," said Steve. *I wasn't kidnapped either*, he thought. *Well, not really.*

"No, of course not," mumbled the headmaster.

"I think it might be best if Steve was allowed to rest," said Eleanor. "Perhaps for the whole day?"

"I am very tired," said Steve, feigning a yawn.

"Of course, of course." Mr Hendrickson began to nod his head rapidly up and down. "Whatever you say, Miss Palmer. I'll escort Haven back to his room."

"No need," she said. "I'm sure you're very busy, Headmaster."

"Well, yes, I am," said the headmaster. "But—"

"I'll take him," said Eleanor. "Just to make sure he gets back safely."

"As you wish, Miss Palmer." The headmaster started towards his desk like a nervous swimmer heading for dry land.

"And then we can talk about the repercussions of the school's actions," said Eleanor.

"Repercussions?" spluttered the headmaster as Eleanor and Steve stepped out into the corridor. "I really don't think—"

Steve pulled the door shut behind them and rested his head on it. His knees felt shaky and his hands were clammy with sweat.

"I'm so glad you're safe." Eleanor gave him a brief hug, then held his shoulders as she stared into his face. "Are you all right?"

"I think so. Are you?"

"Never better," she said, drawing him along the corridor. "I have so much to tell you. You won't believe the things I've seen. I thought Hartley and his shop were a revelation but—"

"Eleanor." He stopped, pulling his arm out of her grasp. "Did you find Mum and Dad?"

"Unfortunately not," she said. "I was prevented from leaving the country."

"Who by?"

"Well." She looked around before continuing in a quiet voice. "I believe they're called The Council. They're like Hartley."

"Nobody's like Hartley."

"You know what I mean," she said. "It turns out they knew what had happened at the Haven Corporation, Rex's murder, Winters's involvement. All of it."

"But why didn't they stop him?" said Steve.

"They did. That's why you're back, isn't it? You're safe now. Anyway." She started off down the corridor, Steve following in her wake. "Apparently, they're taking over the Haven Corporation until your parents come home. Just in a caretaker role. They're even going to help locate your parents. Everything is solved. You can get back to normal now."

The wake-up alarm, telling school that the canteen was open, sang out along the corridor. A cleaning robot sped around the corner, polishing the floor as it travelled. Steve heard footsteps on the staircase at the end of the corridor: the teachers heading down for breakfast.

Normal, he thought. *I don't think I know what that is anymore.*

What did Hartley say?

"Normal' is such a relative term," he whispered.

"What?" said Eleanor.

"It doesn't matter. Normal, it is then." He looked at the piece of travelling chalk that Hartley had given to him.

My kind of normal, he thought. *Wherever it takes me.*

THE END…

…For Now…

Did You Enjoy This Book?

If so, you can make a HUGE difference.

For any author, the single most important way we have of getting our books noticed is a really simple one—and one which you can help with.

Yes, you.

Us indie authors and publishers don't have the financial muscle of the big guys to take out full-page ads in the newspaper or put posters on the subway.

But we do have something much more powerful and effective than that, and it's something that those big publishers would kill to get their hands on.

A committed and loyal bunch of readers.

Honest reviews of our books help bring them to the attention of other readers.

If you've enjoyed this book, I would be really grateful if you could spend just a couple of minutes leaving a review (it can be as short as you like) on this book's page on your favourite store and website.

https://books2read.com/u/3RaKLY

Thank you so much—you're awesome, each and every one of you!

Warm regards

Fi

Acknowledgements

There are so many people I would like to thank who have helped me along my bumpy ride to published author. Where do I begin?

Well of course, I begin with home and those folks who put up with my writerly ways,

- my husband for our brainstorming sessions and for putting up with me when I frequently get a story idea in the middle of the night,

- my daughter for the fabulous artwork on my website, my son for providing a valuable insight into young folk, and both of them for always being enthusiastic about my writing,

- and my dog for making sure that I don't stay locked to my keyboard 24 hours a day.

Thank you to my parents for raising me in a house of books and encouraging me to read.

Who next? My publishers – the wonderful people at Burning Chair – for believing in me and Haven Wakes, and for helping me to see my book with fresh eyes.

Thank you to my beta readers—Ami Agner, Alison Belding, Heather Blanchard, Andreas Rausch, Suzanna Williams and Lisa Wright—for taking the time to read my book and help shape it into its current form.

Thank you to the friends who have kept me going through life's cloudy days. Some of you are writers. Some of you aren't. All of you are absolute stars.

And thank you to you, dear reader, for joining Steve on his journey into magic. Don't go away. The journey hasn't ended.

About the Author

For many years Fi Phillips worked in an office environment until the arrival of her two children robbed her of her short-term memory and sent her hurtling down a new, bumpy, creative path. She finds that getting the words down on paper is the best way to keep the creative muse out of her shower.

Fi lives in the wilds of North Wales with her family, earning a living as a copywriter, playwright and fantasy novelist. Writing about magical possibilities is her passion.

You can follow her on Twitter - @FisWritingHaven

Or at fiphillipswriter.com - where you can also sign up for an exclusive short story from the universe of Haven Wakes, absolutely free!

About Burning Chair

Burning Chair is an independent publishing company based in the UK but covering readers and authors around the globe. We are passionate about both writing and reading books and, at our core, we just want to get great books out to the world.

Our aim is to offer something exciting; something innovative; something that puts the author and their book first. From first class editing to cutting edge marketing and promotion, we provide the care and attention that makes sure that every book fulfils its potential.

We are:

- Different
- Passionate
- Nimble and cutting edge
- Invested in our authors' success

If you're an **author** and would like to know more, visit

www.burningchairpublishing.com

for our submissions requirements and our free guide to book publishing.

If you're a **reader** and are interested in becoming a beta reader for us, helping us to create yet more awesome books (and getting to read them for free in the process!), please visit

www.burningchairpublishing.com/beta-readers.

Other Books by Burning Chair Publishing

The Infernal Aether Series, by Peter Oxley:

>The Infernal Aether

>A Christmas Aether

>The Demon Inside

>Beyond the Aether

Beyond, by Georgia Springate

Going Dark, by Neil Lancaster

Burning: An Anthology of Thriller Shorts, edited by Simon Finnie and Peter Oxley

The Wedding Speech Manual: The Complete Guide to Preparing, Writing and Performing Your Wedding Speech, by Peter Oxley

Printed in Great Britain
by Amazon